DETROIT PUBLIC LIBRARY

3 5674 04872496 8

Satisfy Me Tonight

D0834977

KNAPP BRANCH LIBRARY
13330 CONANT
DETROIT, MI 48212
852-4283

KN FEB 0 9

Other books by Fiona Zedde

Bliss

A Taste of Sin

Every Dark Desire

Hungry for It

Satisfy Me
(with Renee Alexis and Sydney Molare)

Satisfy Me Again
(with Renee Luke and Sydney Molare)

DETROIT, MI 48212

Published by Kensington Publishing Corporation

Satisfy Me Tonight

Fiona Zedde
Sydney Molare
Kimberly Kaye Terry

APHRODISIA

KENSINGTON BOOKS
http://www.kensingtonbooks.com

All characters, companies, and products in this book have no existence outside of the imagination of the author. Events depicted are purely fictional and are not inspired by any person living or dead.

APHRODISIA BOOKS are published by

Kensington Publishing Corp.
850 Third Avenue
New York, NY 10022

"Sexual Attraction" copyright © 2009 by Fiona Zedde
"Driving My Man Wild" copyright © 2009 by Sydney Molare
"Captive" copyright © 2009 by Kimberly Kaye Terry

All rights reserved. No part of this book may be reproduced in any form or by any means without the prior written consent of the Publisher, excepting brief quotes used in reviews.

All Kensington Titles, Imprints, and Distributed Lines are available at special quantity discounts for bulk purchases for sales promotions, premiums, fund-raising, and educational or institutional use.

Special book excerpts or customized printings can also be created to fit specific needs. For details, write or phone the office of the Kensington special sales manager: Kensington Publishing Corp., 850 Third Avenue, New York, NY 10022, attn: Special Sales Department, Phone: 1-800-221-2647.

Aphrodisia and the A logo Reg. U.S. Pat & TM Off.

ISBN-13: 978-0-7582-2904-5
ISBN-10: 0-7582-2904-6

First Kensington Trade Paperback Printing: March 2009

10 9 8 7 6 5 4 3 2 1

Printed in the United States of America

Contents

Sexual Attraction

Fiona Zedde

1

Antwerp, Belgium: Winter.
Friday night

It was Benoît's last night on top of the world. And that world was spread out for him in tempting shades of cream, cocoa, and caramel, dancing to the beats he spun from the DJ booth, gyrating in their short shorts, miniskirts, and teasing wisps of cloth that barely qualified as clothing. Some of these girls danced for him, he knew. In the chaotic swirl of multicolored lights, Benoît felt their eyes on him. Adoring. Lustful.

"DJ Dionysus!"

One of them leapt, catlike, up to the DJ booth raised three feet above the rest of the room. Brown corkscrew curls exploded around her café au lait skin. She gripped the edge of the booth, fingers curling over the chipped black wood. With an inviting grin, she threw her head back, giving him a glimpse of breasts swelling above her neckline. Benoît tipped the headphones away from his ear. "What?"

"Play 'Sex Machine,' " the catgirl demanded. Her eyes

sparkled like mints in a candy dish. She'd slipped him her number earlier in the evening, but she wasn't anything he wanted a piece of.

Benoît nodded at her, grinned.

She stepped back and dropped down, the crowd swallowing her again, and Benoît lost himself in the music once more, in the symphony of flesh and flirtation on the dance floor below him.

It was the last time. Although it didn't feel like it. Tonight felt like any other night at Orgy. The girls. The feverish high. Music vibrating the walls of the building, which like every other one in Antwerp, was ancient but sturdy. He thought he would feel something different tonight. Regret at leaving it all behind. An unbearable sense of nostalgia.

But he felt neither of those things. He was moving toward something that he wanted more. Another life. Another career. Something other than the dead end he would butt his head against in this country. Benoît bobbed his head to the music. Threw his fist in the air. He felt its pulsing beat in his bones, but his mind felt locked in the "after." After the gig ended. After he packed up his things. After he got on that plane. What would—?

A flick of a hip jolted his attention. A playful gaze turned over a bare shoulder. But the strobe lights flashed and the image that caught his eye flickered away under the bright beams.

"This music is *tight!*" someone shouted nearby. "Go DJ D!"

Benoît grinned and rained more bass on the crowd.

"Yes!"

He scratched through the intro of a song and cued the next mix on the iBook glowing white near his hand. Michael Jackson flowed seamlessly into Kanye West. The crowd screamed. Girls flung their hair, shook their sweat-covered breasts at him. Benoît threw his head back and laughed. This he would definitely miss. He felt the sweat beading down his hairless scalp, heat from hundreds of bodies that danced for him.

The pretty shoulder emerged from the crowd again and Benoît paused, taking more than a second look when the girl, dancing with a taller and paler girl who only served as a foil to her curvaceous darkness, caught his eyes and held them. She was gorgeous. Nothing like he was used to seeing here at the club and maybe that was cause enough for his body to react to her strongly. He licked his lips. Yeah, she was hot. A good distraction and maybe incentive for him to stay and dance after his set was over.

This was a moment Benoît was more than familiar with. When the music and his looks—muscled chest and arms under the thin shirts, smirking red lips—worked together to bring him what he wanted. He waited for her to come. Benoît felt the warmth percolate in his belly as he waited. But instead of approaching, the girl dipped to the music, twitched her backside, and looked away. He felt the unpleasant slap of surprise. This never happened. Through the galloping beat of the music, his hands flying automatically over the turntable, cuing the next mix, ramping up the sound effects, he stared at the girl.

The pale yellow tank top. Hair a thick halo around her round face. Those ass-hugging jeans. His heart pounded faster. Before he could check himself, Benoît jumped down from the DJ booth and swam through the crowd toward her.

"Hey."

Up close, her amazing doll's eyes, large and brown with thick and curling lashes, nearly brought him to his knees. A cascade of silver stars sparkled on a silver chain around her neck. "What did you say?"

Her English jarred him. An American. That explained her amazing ass.

The bodies, jerking and flowing to a techno remix of "Thriller," bumped him on repeat as he drifted into the girl's orbit. Her body was hypnotic. Breasts lifting as she raised her arms to the ceiling, ass shaking, that glitter-bright smile. A boy moved close to her now. He was slim and feminine enough to let Benoît know that he wouldn't have any objections to someone making a play for the girl's attentions.

"I thought you were coming over to say hello," he said in English.

She laughed. A husky gurgle that he leaned closer to hear above the music.

"Not a chance, pretty boy." She spun away from him, shaking her ass to the music, watching him with her laughing gaze over one shoulder. "I'm here to look, not touch." The sweat clung like silk to her bare shoulders.

"I don't mind if you touch." He had to shout near her head to be heard. "We're all here to have a good time, right?"

"I thought you were here to work." She flung her head toward the empty DJ booth.

"I *am* working," Benoît said, moving his body suggestively closer. Matching her rhythm for rhythm. Thrust for thrust. Holding her hips in the cradle of his hips as she let him. When she let him. With a teasing smile, she shoved him away.

"Shouldn't you be spinning music tonight, deejay, not bullshit?"

He laughed. "You're a hard one."

"Not really. Not when you get to know me." She pressed her soft ass into his crotch as if to make her point.

Her friend, dancing hard in his sweat-soaked T-shirt and tight jeans, didn't back off. If anything he moved even closer while Benoît tried to talk to the girl. But the boy's look wasn't antagonistic. Merely curious.

So was she interested or not? There were certain women he found hard to read, and she was one of them. This one definitely put out the mixed signals. Come. Stop. Go. No farther. The thick smell of her—a combination of hair dressing, sweat, and her perfume—already had him half hard. But he couldn't stay and play with her for long. His six-minute set was almost over. There was only about forty seconds left until the Michael Jackson and Justin Timberlake mix spun out. Benoît turned to go back to the DJ booth. A hand snared his shirt.

"Come back down and talk with me later. When you have time." Her juicy lips poured the words into his ear. "Either make time for me or don't bother wasting mine." Thirty seconds.

Her breath huffed against his face, clean and empty as if she'd been drinking water for hours. She leaned in and he felt her mouth against his, quick and sloppy. How much time did he have left? Nineteen seconds? With one last look at the girl, Benoît headed back to work. He pushed his way through the overheated bodies, fighting against hands that plucked his clothes, slapped at his back, squeezed his arms and ass.

With five seconds to spare, he swung back into the booth and recaptured the music.

"How are you feeling tonight?!" He howled the question in Flemish above the music. Whistles rose up in response. Shouts. Screams. "Nice!" Under the flashing strobe lights, the crowd dipped and rocked. "This next one goes out to the American girl." He continued in English. "You know who you are."

The screams rose up again, fewer this time, but just as loud. He dropped into the opening beats of Lil Wayne's "Lollipop."

A bright image of the girl wrapping her mouth around him pushed the blood, like a shot of nitro, through his veins. Benoît's heart throbbed with anticipation of what was to come. He had another two hours to spin before the next DJ came on. Two hours to rev the crowd even higher and keep them sweaty and pumped enough so that he could feel *their* heartbeats in his chest. Benoît wanted an imprint of tonight, a guarantee that he would never forget it. The girl already guaranteed that tonight was going to be good. She was hot, and he looked forward to getting burned.

Nearly an hour and a half later, his replacement, Sergio, came, grinning with his shirt already off. He lifted his old-fashioned records in a crate, carrying it low enough to flex his biceps and earning him more than a passing glance from the women in the club.

"Nice grooves, Benny. The girls are just lapping it up." Sergio grinned, flashing his white teeth as he moved past Benoît to drop the crate.

"Oh yeah," Benoît nodded, imaging the American girl lapping *him* up. He hadn't been able to keep his mind off her all night.

Not that she would let him if he had the inclination to. His American dream appeared out of the crowd at regular intervals, teasing him with glimpses of her thick ass and bare shoulders. Her tongue flicked out toward him as she danced.

At his side, Sergio laughed when he spotted the girl. "I can take over early for you if you'd like."

"No, no. I'm good." But his eyes didn't stray far from her.

The last fifteen minutes of every set, Benoît played reggae. He warmed up with some oldies—Murder She Wrote, Ting-a-Ling, Bad Boys—then eased into the latest Sean Paul. Most of the guys made way for the girls, who suddenly became wild sex goddesses, winding their hips, bouncing their asses and breasts to the drumming rhythm of the music. Although the crowd didn't part especially for her, Benoît's gaze easily found his girl. She had turned her ass for him. Its roundness was almost unbearably juicy in the low-rider jeans that dropped even lower the more she dropped that ass to the floor. He swore he could see the sweat drip down the small of her back and between twitching ass cheeks. That beautiful ass shook as she dipped low to the ground and made her slow, then fast, way back up. Benoît swallowed.

He had no control over the liquid lust that pooled in his groin, thickened him. This girl was—he couldn't even describe what she was. All Benoît knew in that movement was craving.

Lust. Heat. He licked his lips. Switched over to the iPod mix, a seamless transition, and jumped down from the DJ booth to the soundtrack of Sergio's laughter.

He fought his way through the crowd and came up behind the girl. "You look good like that." His voice a low growl. From her dancing squat, she slowly wound her way back up to her full height. She pressed her ass into him. His hands settled on her hips, pulled her more firmly against his straining dick for her to feel what she was doing to him. She turned, dancing slower now.

"Yeah?" The breath brushed his lips.

His fingers sank into her hips. "I have time for you now," he gasped into her neck.

She looked at the DJ booth, then back at him. Benoît cupped her ass, pulled her into him. He felt nearly sick with lust. His dick throbbed. The pulse hammered at his throat.

"But can you handle it, Mr. DJ?"

He took her hand and pressed it against his aching cock. "Can *you*?"

She squeezed and just then he knew for sure she was the right one for him tonight.

"What's your name?" she rasped.

"Benoît." He could barely speak with the delicious torture of her hand slowly stroking him through his jeans.

The girl laughed. "Benwa, like those balls a girl can push inside her pussy?"

"Not usually, but for you, yeah. Especially if that's a promise of where I'll end up tonight."

She nipped his earlobe and squeezed his cock again. "Do you have condoms or should we use mine?"

He took her to the club's dark "VIP" room; he led her back into the tiny room, like an old photo booth, usually reserved for taking drugs or indulging in a quick semiprivate fuck. The mirror above the narrow shelf reflected an image of them, her pretty brown back bisected by the yellow bandeau blouse. His face, tight with lust. Nostrils flared like a bull's. The girl immediately slid her hands under his shirt, pinching his nipples and raking her short fingernails over his muscled chest and belly. Benoît shivered.

"Nice," she breathed.

Benoît shook her hands away. "Later." His dick was about to explode out of his pants. "Jesus."

She only chuckled at his frustration, a breathy and heavy sound that didn't disguise her own want. The jeans were nice to look at, but they were hell to get off. Instead of struggling with them to get at the face-to-face fuck he wanted, Benoît peeled them off her gorgeous backside, tugged them down and turned her away from him. She sighed and reached back for him, her hand fumbling for his zip and the heavy weight of his dick in the same moment he slid seeking fingers into her from behind. She pushed out her ass even further, bracing her arms against the small ledge. Benoît tore the condom packet, sheathed himself, and shoved into her pussy.

Fuck, she was wet! His fingertips nudged her clit.

Their moans sounded chorused in the small room.

In the mirror, her face was a wonder of sex. Lips parted and moist, tongue peeking out, lashes low and fluttering. Though he didn't bother to look, Benoît knew his face was equally rapt. She felt so fucking good. Incredible.

"Fuck me," she gasped. "That's why we're here, right?"

She arched her back, widened her legs as much as she could in the prison of her jeans. The wet smell of her pussy engulfed his senses. And caught in the snare of denim, with her bent back and round flanks tilted up and the harsh fluorescent flooding over her brown skin, she was beautiful. Benoît was harder now for this American girl than he'd ever been in his life. And he wasn't high tonight, so it had to be true. He laughed at the thought, thrusting fast and deep into her heat.

"Jesus!"

Once he was there, once he saw the look on her face in the mirror, he couldn't stop. Wet heaven. The bass line from the music pounded against the walls, dim but certain. A perfect counterpoint to his thrusts, swift and deep, and her gasping breaths.

"Faster!"

He fucked her faster. Brought his fingers into play, but hers were already there, strumming her clit in time to the music that vibrated the walls. She hissed his name, pushed back into him, meeting him fuck for fuck. Her face in the mirror glowed. Her pussy around his dick pulsed. Clenched tightly. A vise. The pleasure-pain shoved him roughly over the edge.

"Fuck!"

He dropped his face into the damp space between her shoulders, trying to recapture his breath. Benoît held on to her as she shivered against him.

"Guh." He swallowed and tried again. His words didn't emerge any better the second time. He contented himself with a steadying hand under her belly. Its tight plane vibrated with laughter.

"Yeah, it was." A breathless laugh escaped her.

She gently nudged him away and Benoît took the hint, pulling his now-limp penis from her warmth. He tore off the condom and tossed it in the trash.

It felt like he had spent forever pressed inside her, but lifting his head to pay attention to the music he could still hear through the overhead speakers, Benoît realized that it had only been a few minutes. It had taken him less than fifteen minutes to achieve the hardest come of his life. He licked his lips.

"Listen, I have to—" he jerked his head toward the DJ booth beyond their sight, "I have to go, but can you stick around for a minute?"

"For what?" Her laughing gaze held his. She jerked up her jeans and buttoned them. Fluffed out her feathery Afro.

He shrugged, brain still fogged and trapped in the sensation of her, tight and clasping around him. His inner voice asked the same question. After you got off, you got gone. That was it. He'd played this way as often as most guys and girls he knew in the club life. But something about this girl made him want to see her again.

Benoît palmed the full curve of her ass. "Just do it, okay?"

She shrugged, adjusted the tube top around her breasts, checked the fly of her jeans. "We'll see." Her tongue peeked from between her bitten red lips.

It was then that he realized he hadn't properly kissed her. Her ass had slapped against his belly, he'd seen the deep pink center of her, felt it around his fingers. But he hadn't kissed her. Her lips became suddenly like food to him, the most delicious meal he'd never eaten but would give his life for. He leaned in.

She pushed firm palms against his chest. "Get back to work, baby." Her eyes dropped to his mouth briefly before she stepped back. Then she turned and unerringly found her way out of the room and back to the dance floor with him close at her heels.

"I hope that shit was good," Sergio said when Benoît slid back into the booth.

He cleared his throat but said nothing. He wasn't one to fuck and tell. But he flashed Sergio a wide grin before kneeling to pack up his gear. *Oh yeah, it had been more than worth it.* If he had the chance, he would probably try to make it last for more than a few hot minutes. The iPod streamed the last of his set, a weak mix by his standards, a practice one that he hadn't intended to use, but the girl . . . Benoît's gaze moved automatically to the crowd, but he didn't see her.

Using the club's rear door, he loaded his heavy turntable, records, and CDs into the small black Peugeot. When the iPod finished, he turned it off, leaving the club swamped in Sergio's edgier beats, and shoved it into his pocket. It was only a few minutes after three o'clock, right on time for Sergio to take the second shift and carry the party on until seven in the morning.

"Later, man." He squeezed Sergio's shoulder and got a distracted nod in return. The other deejay already had the headphones on, his body dipping in time to the music.

Instead of slipping out the back door and going home, Benoît wove himself through the crowd. He didn't bother fooling himself into thinking he wasn't on the lookout for the American girl. Her smell still lingered on him, and he wanted more.

"Where are you heading so fast?"

The catgirl from earlier stopped him with a hand on his chest. She shook thick brown curls out of her face, brought her cleavage closer to him for inspection. "Now that you're down here with the rest of us, the party can really start."

She slipped her arms around his waist, dancing close. Her mouth smelled like someone else's cock. "Come on, baby. Loosen up."

"I'm definitely loose, honey. But I got someone else to check for tonight."

Her breasts pressed against his chest, dropped her hands to his ass. "Maybe you can check out both of us."

Benoît gave her his killer grin, sexy but dismissive. "It's not that kind of party." He shrugged off her wandering hands. "Another time."

The girl gave an exaggerated sigh of disappointment, quite a feat with the almost deafening music and the press of bodies on them from all sides. "You don't know what you're missing." Her cock breath fanned his nose again.

"I think I do." Benoît pulled away from the girl. "See you around."

He dove back into the crowd but got waylaid again. Nearly two hours and half a dozen different conversations passed before he got anywhere near the club's front doors. All the while, he looked for the American girl. She was nowhere to be found.

Finally with disappointment sinking into his belly along with the slow realization that she had left, Benoît pushed himself out the club's front door and into the winter chill. *Ah well,* he told himself, *it was only pussy.*

Between checking IDs and the girls' legs and tits, the security guys at the door gave him a nod of recognition as he passed. Benoît veered away from the long line of people queuing to get into the club. He could just as easily get to his car from here anyway.

"Hey, loverboy. Forget about me already?"

He turned, thinking the voice was a mistake. But it wasn't. The girl sat on the bench near the club's entrance, drinking what looked like water from a clear plastic cup while her gay boyfriend from the dance floor smoked a cigarette next to her. Watching Benoît, the boy flicked the ashes off his cigarette, then blew a stream of smoke away from the girl.

"Impossible," he said in response to her glib question. The two of them made room for him on the bench. He sat pressed against her warm weight in the cool air.

"Aren't you cold in that?" She gestured to the loose muscle shirt that left his arms bare.

"Not really. I don't feel it yet. I got pretty worked up inside the club. All that sweat. The heat." He teased her with his smile, the one he knew girls liked. A tilt of his mouth, a lowering of his lashes to make them imagine what he was like in bed.

She had already covered up her little blouse with a thick down jacket sprouting fur around the collar. Even with her hands shoved in her pockets and over a dozen warm bodies around, she still looked cold. Her mouth spread slowly in a smile. Then she looked over when her friend poked her in the side. She laughed.

"Sorry." She rolled her eyes. "DJ Ben, my friend, Anthony."

Anthony looked him over again, unashamed, his mouth slightly pursed. "A pleasure," he said, taking Benoît's hand in an exaggeratedly limp-wristed handshake. "Or at least it was Kenna's pleasure as far as I could tell when she got back from whatever back room you took her to."

Kenna. So that was her name.

Beside her friend, she cringed but quickly recovered. "Don't hate, bitch." She flicked dismissive fingers through her hair. Twisted her lips. "If you wanted him to give you the VIP treatment I'm sure all you have to do is ask."

"Oh!" Anthony's mouth formed a perfect red circle. His thick halo of blonde curls and kinks bobbed around his head. "I didn't know I could get a turn."

Benoît shook his head. "You can't. Maybe if I was drunk enough, but not tonight. Tonight I'm really . . . focused." He made sure that Kenna took his meaning. He dropped a hand to his thigh and leaned forward, a pose he knew accentuated the lean muscles in his arms.

Anthony fanned himself with a wilted hand. "You need to stop, honey. I'm delicate." But he watched the flex of Benoît's arm anyway, looking very indelicate with his mouth wet and unsmiling.

Benoît raised an eyebrow, gaze grazing over Anthony to rest firmly on Kenna and her large doll's eyes. "Can I ask you for coffee?" he asked. She only looked at him. "A cappuccino?" When her gaze remained blank, he tried again. "Whatever you'd like to drink or eat?"

Anthony laughed, stubbing out his cigarette in the ground at his feet. "I see that you're in good hands, doll. I'm off." He turned his eyes once again to Benoît. "You will see that she gets home safe, right?"

"Definitely."

With a twitch of his hips and a mild look at Kenna, Anthony got to his feet. He leaned over to press kisses on her cheeks. "Call me if you want to escape."

"Thanks, love. I will." She grinned and slid a hand over his thick hair. The boy playfully shook off her touch and hitched a hip at Benoît.

" 'Bye, hot boy."

They both watched him forge a path through the growing crowd, his route taking him toward the large parking lot across the street.

"So," Benoît murmured, already imagining her spread out in his bed, her soft mouth open to his kisses. "How about that coffee?"

Suddenly Kenna looked shy, lowering her eyes and glancing anywhere but at him, as if all her inhibitions returned with the departure of her friend. She looked toward where Anthony had disappeared. Then she turned back to Benoît. "Sure," she said.

Benoît smiled.

2

Saturday morning

At his car she stepped shyly inside. With the doors closed the smell of her nearly overwhelmed him. The smoke of a dozen cigarettes, her mint chewing gum, the faint scent of sex lingering against her skin. Did it make sense that he found her so desirable, so mind-numbingly appealing that all he could think of was fucking her again and making her gasp his name? Benoît imagined what she would let him do if they were alone, if there was no danger of discovery, no work to rush back to. He swallowed and started the car.

"There's a café near my flat that I think you'll like. I'm going to park the car, then we can walk over. Okay?"

Kenna nodded. "Yeah, that's cool."

He drove the short distance to his place, told her to wait while he quickly lugged his equipment into the small apartment—no sense in leaving it out on the street to get stolen—then came back down the small elevator and crossed the cobblestoned sidewalk to find her leaning against the car waiting for him. Benoît pulled his jacket out and shrugged it on in preparation for the short but nippy walk to the café.

"That's a lot of shit you got there," she said, watching him with a slow smile. "Is that how you get all those muscles, lugging all that up and down stairs?"

"No, but I can show you how. Later."

It was pretty weak, he knew. But she laughed anyway, and in that moment they were like any other Friday-night couple getting to know each other with their teasing laughter and jokes no one else would find funny.

"Come on," he said and took her hand.

In the café, Kenna peeled off her jacket and sank into the straight-backed chair. "God, it feels good in here!" She unwound the scarf from around her neck and looked around. The few people already there leisurely sipped their drinks, smoked cigarettes, and held low-voiced conversations as if trying to preserve the sanctity of early morning. "That cold outside is no joke," she said with a slight shiver.

With his own jacket off, the heat from the café's vents washed over his neck and bare arms. Benoît leaned back, taking in the curve of Kenna's breasts through her blouse, the simple joy she took in being out of the cold.

"I think you're the only tourist in Belgium this time of year. Most people wait until summer to visit Europe unless they have family here to spend holidays with."

"And then there are the rest of us who can't afford to travel any other time. The tickets to Europe are really cheap in the winter." She spared him a quick glance before giving her full attention to the menu. After a long moment wrinkling her forehead, she raised her head. "The only thing I recognize on here is chocolate milk. I think I'll have that."

He looked at the menu. "That's actually hot chocolate, and it's the perfect choice."

Just then the waitress came to their table, slim and dignified in a long white apron over her dark blouse and slacks. He ordered hot chocolate and crepes with sugar and lemon for them both. They didn't have to wait long for the waitress to return. Giving them a slightly crooked smile, she set down two crepes sprinkled with powdered sugar, a tiny saucer of lemon wedges, along with their hot chocolates and two pieces of chocolate wrapped in silver foil.

"What's this?" Kenna asked after the woman left, pointing to a small shot glass of lemon cream.

"That is an option." Benoît unwrapped his chocolate. "You can dip your chocolate in it, eat it naked, or leave it alone." He dipped the small shell-shaped candy into the lemon cream, then reached across, angling it toward Kenna's mouth. After only a moment's hesitation, her lips parted. Instead of biting into the chocolate, she licked experimentally at the lemon cream, then, when she found it to her taste, sucked it completely off the sweet brown surface.

Her tongue darted over her lips. "Hm. That's nice." Benoît could almost taste the lemon on her breath.

"Yeah, it is." For a moment he was irrationally jealous of that piece of chocolate. He cleared his throat and drew back, plopping the candy into his steaming cup. "You can also dissolve the hard chocolate into the hot chocolate. That's my favorite way to have it."

"Hard and hot together." She grinned, a devil in yellow, and peeked at him from beneath her lashes. "I'm pretty sure I like it that way, too."

It took Benoît a few seconds to get his breath back after that one.

"So," he murmured, adjusting himself in the chair, "what made you come out with me tonight?"

Kenna laughed, incredulous. "Have you looked in the mirror lately?" But she didn't give him a chance to answer. "You may not like me saying so, but you're the most beautiful man

I've ever seen." Her gaze appraised him like she was about to buy him at auction. "Your skin is pretty, though a little light for my usual taste, and those lips of yours make me think of all kinds of sinful things. And—" her mouth stretched into a private smile,. "—from what I saw and felt a couple of hours ago, you have damn quick fingers."

His face heated in a blush. Though she said nothing he hadn't heard before, it was the way she had said it. Leaning close, her eyes devouring him. Benoît wanted to be that for her, a quick-fingered superfuck that she wouldn't regret going home with. But he didn't want to give that away.

"That's it?" he teased, lounging back in the chair. "Are you sure it wasn't my intelligent eyes? Away from the smoke and the music, you don't really seem like the kind of girl who'd go after things like that."

Her eyebrows rose. She paused with her cup halfway to her mouth. "What kind? A slut?"

It took him a moment to recall the meaning of the last word.

"No, no." Benoît shook his head. "I mean someone so free, with no . . . ," he chased down a word of his own. ". . . inhibitions."

"I'm hardly that." She smiled over her cup of hot chocolate. "Just a girl on vacation." Kenna fingered the rim of the cup, skimming a thumb over the spot stained brown from her lips. "It's only normal to try things away from home that you wouldn't do in your own backyard."

Was that true? Benoît wondered. He'd traveled to Spain and France for school and to Ibiza with his wealthy friends when he had the time between jobs, but he'd never done anything in any of these places he wouldn't do in Antwerp.

"At home would you feel ashamed of being seen with someone like me?"

"What? Someone hot?" She leaned over her crepe, studying it with intent before mimicking his actions and squeezing lemon juice over its layer of powdered sugar. Amusement lay in her gaze. "I don't think so. I'm a shy girl. Or something like that. I think I'm the reliable girl everyone knows at home. I do things. I give. My door is always open. I'm in school and I work. I visit my parents and help them with whatever they need. Now that I'm away from home, I just want to find out what it's like to do things for myself. To give to someone so I can get back. To open my legs to a hot boy and not regret it." Knife and fork in hand, she sliced into the crepe and brought a bite to her lips. "Umm. I like this."

His own crepe didn't taste nearly as good as hers if Kenna's reaction to it was anything to go by. She savored each bite as if ambrosia lay on her tongue, holding it in her mouth until the last possible moment before indulging in a luxurious swallow. "I *really* like this."

Benoît smiled indulgently at her absolute enjoyment of the food. He wondered if she loved sex just as much.

"I hope you don't regret what happened at the club," he said.

"No." Kenna licked sugar from her fork. She tilted her head as if turning off an annoying voice. "I loved it. I'd love to do it again." Her long pink tongue appeared again to lick away a spot of white powder from her bottom lip.

"Now?" He sipped his hot chocolate, only half joking.

Kenna folded another slice of crepe into her mouth, slowly chewed it, swallowed. "Okay."

They barely made it out of the coffee shop without touching each other. On the way out the door, their shoulders brushed as they passed through the threshold, then she turned lightly toward him so they could go through it together. Her breasts brushed his chest. She steadied herself with a fleeting grip on his arm. His pulse began a deep, uneven rhythm.

In the tiny elevator leading up to his third-floor flat, she stood with her back to him and Benoît barely stopped himself from reaching out to squeeze her small waist and pull her to him. He needed to distract himself from her, from the drum of arousal in his dick, before they started something in the elevator they couldn't finish.

Kenna must have had the same thought, too. "God! This is the smallest elevator I've ever been in." She stepped slightly away from him. Never mind that her face was nearly pressed into the door. The car trembled and groaned as it moved steadily up. "And the oldest." She traced the Dutch writing on the copper plate, eyes flickering around the space that was big enough for two well-acquainted adults and *maybe* one small child. "I feel like I should be taking the stairs." Kenna turned slightly to him, a faint smile on her mouth. Her gaze darted down to his crotch, then away.

"Don't do that," he said and gave in to temptation. He pulled her back into him. "I've ridden it a thousand times. Relax."

He made a show of soothing her, moving his hands down her denim-covered thighs. Benoît had never fucked in an elevator, but he seriously thought about it now.

She pressed her bottom into him, and Benoît dipped his head. Her skin tasted like salt. And woman. And sex they would have as soon as they made into his apartment. He tongued the side of her neck, nibbled on it, felt the vibrating moans against his lips. In the small moving lift with its ancient jolts, the familiar blue paint, and smells of previous generations that he hadn't noticed before now, Benoît could feel himself losing it. His hands pressed more deeply into her skin. She made a soft noise, slid back even more into him, rubbing her ass against his dick.

Her head fell back against his shoulder. She unzipped her jacket and pulled his hands up to her breasts. Under the thin tube top, her nipples were firm, prodding back at his fingers in smooth, voluptuous dips. Benoît brushed his thumbs over them, squeezed them.

"Harder."

He dragged the blouse down, baring her skin to his blind and grateful touch. Benoît stroked harder, pressed the firm flesh between his fingers. The elevator clattered open on her broken moan. Somehow, she had the presence of mind to grip the edges of her jacket closed before the sleepy blond couple waiting for the lift could get an eyeful. Benoît cleared his throat under their curious and suddenly alert gazes and gently pushed Kenna out the elevator toward his flat.

Their laughter tumbled them into the apartment, back against the door. In the privacy of that room, everything else abruptly fell away.

"So, Ben." Kenna laughed, breathlessly bold again. "This is your place, huh?" Her hands dipped into his pants, popping open the buttons and freeing him. Grasping him in her hot fist.

Words died in his mouth. Leaked from him in incoherent sounds.

"You want to show me around?"

But she didn't wait for an answer from him, only dropped to her knees and dragged his pants low. Kenna placed a hot kiss on the head of his painfully hard dick. He flinched at the quick, pleasurable contact. She kissed him from balls to tip, her mouth soft and wet, his dick getting fatter in her hands, the blood rushing to his groin in a dizzying flood. He shuddered when she took all of him in her mouth. His belly trembled and he gasped, bracing himself on the door to look down on her, to savor the heated suction of her mouth around his cock.

"I can—I can show you around—" His fingers slid into her hair, flexed against her scalp. "—anytime you want," he finished brokenly.

Her cheeks hollowed as she advanced and withdrew around him, pulling him all the way out to the swollen head before swallowing him again, the messy and wordless language of sex between her and his dick. Benoît felt the familiar pull at his balls, the tingle of impending orgasm. He pulled himself away from her. "Not yet," he said, gasping. "I don't want to come yet." He gently pulled her hair back so he could look in her face. "I want to be inside you."

She released his dick with a soft *pop*. "You *are* inside me, lover." And she dipped her head to swallow him again. But Benoît pulled away, his dick stabbing at the cool air instead of inside her heated mouth. Shaking his head, his knees shaking, too, Benoît tugged her to her feet.

"The bed," he said, breathless.

Kenna only sucked on her bottom lip, watching him like she longed for the taste of his cock in her mouth again. She pushed him away from her, a feminine version of rough, and walked backward away from him, keeping her eyes on Benoît all the while. Her lips twitched beguilingly from side to side. "Fine. Where's your bedroom?"

He pointed and she went, discarding clothes with every step. Shoes. Jacket. Her blouse. By the time they made it to his bedroom, everything she had on when she first stepped into the apartment was clenched in his fist, and she stood stark naked by his bed. He felt as if his bones had turned to steel. His vision sharpened, narrowed until he saw only her. The coyly posed knees, thick thighs with the furred jewel at their apex. Her curved belly. Kenna's high and lush breasts. Her mouth. Benoît dropped her clothes on the armchair by the door and surged forward to claim what she offered.

Their time in the club had been fast. A quick fuck and release that instead of sating his need for her only made him want more. To touch her again. To feel her pussy around him again. To kiss her, finally. Slowly.

He gathered her close to him like air.

"I want to make this last," Benoît whispered.

And he tried for slow, pressing his mouth to hers, meeting that longed-for flesh, but she licked his mouth. She said something as she arched her breasts into his chest, and his hunger raged once more. *Maybe later,* he thought, as his senses caught on fire and the need to feel every inch of her mouth took over him. She tasted like lemons and sugar.

He fell to the bed, aware suddenly of his nakedness and the sheets at his back and her climbing onto him, their mouths still wetly locked. His cock nudged her damp curls, aching to get inside.

"Shit! *Condoom.*" He gripped her hips, pressing her to him. "Condom."

"Where?" she gasped, breasts heaving as she hung over him.

He heaved backward, slammed his shoulders against the headboard, dragged open his bedside drawer. The pack was in his hand, torn open, the rubber rolled on. Kenna slid closer, trapping him against the headboard, half sitting, half lying down. She clambered onto his lap. Mounted him fiercely, hissing her pleasure.

"Fuck!"

"That's definitely—uh!—what we're doing." She gasped the words, her sweet heat engulfing him. Jerking against him. Dancing in his lap. Swallowing him. Fucking him.

He pulled her nipples into his mouth, tonguing them, sucking them as she rode the breath from his body. She grabbed the headboard behind him, using it for leverage as she moved, twisting like an uncontained storm, breath heaving, sweat washing over her skin, dripping between her breasts. Her ass moved in his hands, winding, moving, igniting the fresh flame of orgasm. Benoît gasped. *Not yet.* He gripped her ass, trying to slow her down. *Not yet!* If anything, she moved on him faster, forcing the pace, shoving him closer and closer to the fire.

Her pussy gripped him like a vise. Teeth clenched. Her face tight with concentration. Kenna wanted him to lose control. She wanted him to—Benoît pushed her back onto the bed, following her with his body to keep their connection.

He flinched when Kenna dug her nails into his shoulder. "Why did you move? It was perfect. Oh!" He slid deeply into her, firmly, in control.

"Yes." She grunted. Meeting him thrust for thrust. The rising scream in her voice took him back to the searing insanity in the club. How the smell of sex and sweat had risen around them. The enfolding darkness of the small room and the way her gasps rang like prayers in his ears. Their fuck session in the club had been hot. But this was beyond anything he'd ever felt.

She was even more incredible in a bed. God! Sensation wrung out of Benoît. He arched his back, feeling the sweat flood down between his shoulder blades, the grip of her legs around his waist, the velvet of her pussy around him. He gripped her hips, slammed into her. She gasped, bit her lip. Gasped. Her body urging him on. She pulled him deeper inside her. Grunting. Beast to his beast. Slapping. Flesh against flesh. The bed squeaked, protested their combined weight, their heaving bodies.

"You're fucking—uh! amazing," he panted into her shoulder, deaf to everything but the liquid kiss of her pussy around his cock. Her gasping moans.

"Ben!" she gasped. His hips bucked at the pleasure-pain of her nails raking his back. Friction and the goal of orgasm scotched everything else from his consciousness. The explosion froze him. Then he was shuddering, hips jerking uncontrollably, her pussy milking him as she came, too. They lay together, breathing heavily.

Though he was soft inside her, Benoît lazily rolled his hips, squeezing the last ounces of sensation from their joining.

"You're heavy," she muttered, pushing at his sweaty shoulder. And he reluctantly rolled away to flop onto his back. He pulled off the condom, tied it off, and threw it toward the trash bin. Dropped back down to blink at the ceiling in amazement.

"Your pussy must be magic."

"What?"

When she looked at him, wiping the dampness from her nose and cheekbones, he realized he had spoken in Flemish. Yeah, she definitely put something in there. He repeated what he said in English this time.

She sat up in the bed to lean over him, scoring his chest with her nipples. In the light from the windows, her body shone like polished mahogany. Like a love goddess risen from the earth itself. Kenna fluffed out her hair until it puffed around her head once more like a dandelion. "I think we make magic together, B. I wasn't exactly unaffected by your skills."

Kenna slid her hand down, touching her wet pussy, sliding fingers between the thick, wet folds. "I haven't had it like this in . . . a long time. I like how you feel inside me. I like fucking you."

Although he'd come too recently to get hard again, his cock twitched. She eased a finger into her pink hole. He imagined the sound of her pussy snacking on that finger, wanting something bigger. Kenna bit her lip. Closed her eyes. Like she wanted to fuck again.

He moved from under her, watching her play with herself, feeling an interested heat settle in his groin. *Oh yeah.* She wanted to fuck. He kissed her breasts. Leaned into her still-damp skin and flicked the wide aureole with his tongue. She sighed. He took the thick nipple into his mouth, working his tongue around it until she hummed deep in her throat. He teased her other breast with his thumb, squeezed it, until it plumped. Dimly, he was aware of her fingers, two now, steadily working at her pussy, slowly fucking, a slow and steady in-and-out motion, while her thumb worked her clit.

He pushed her fingers out of the way and dove down, pushing her on her back. She squealed as she fell, laughing. The laughter abruptly ended when he sucked her clit into his mouth.

"Oh," she breathed. "You would be good at this, too." Her legs widened around his head and her salt scent seduced him even deeper into her weeping pussy. "Yes, baby." Her hand settled on the back of his head, encouraging. "Yes."

Because she'd just come, Kenna wanted it easy. Benoît knew that much. He slid his tongue between her pussy petals, drinking her juice, then up again to lap at her clit, down again, circling her hole with his tongue, playing with the sensitive nerves at her entrance, then lightly probed her, flickering, fucking her shallowly.

"God!" Her hand tightened on his head.

The smell of her made him want more. To smear the thick cunt juice all over his face, suck on her clit, tongue-fuck her, until she gushed over his mouth like his own personal watering hole. Benoît pushed his hips into the bed. Gasped his pleasure into her cunt.

The bedroom door creaked open. "Hey, Benoît, your friends—oh shit!" It quickly slammed shut.

"Fuck!" She grabbed the pillow to her chest, too late, and rolled away from him, snapping her legs tightly together. "Who was that?!"

Benoît sat up. *That was awkward.* He wiped his mouth on the sheet. "Ah, that's my brother. He lives here, too. Sorry." He'd forgotten about Cristian. Nearly forgotten his own name under Kenna's spell.

"Doesn't he knock?"

"Normally. Usually. I think." Blowing out a breath, he scrubbed a hand over his bald head that was getting bristly and in need of a shave. "Sorry."

"It's okay. Well, not really, but don't sweat it." She fell back in the sheets with a groan, pressing her legs together as if trying to relieve the ache. "Fuck." Then Kenna rolled her head to look at him. "I hope you're not inviting him in here with us. I'm kinky, but that's too much."

Benoît choked on his laughter and shook his head. "*Neen.* No." He laughed, imagining the look on Cristian's face if he ever suggested something like that. "There's a better chance of that happening with your friend from last night."

She punched his arm, playful though the look in her eyes was not. "Never."

"What? Is the thought of having two men in your bed that repulsive?"

"It's not two men, that could be interesting." Her devil's smile emerged again. "But not with Anthony. I know what he's into, and that's just not for me." She wrinkled her nose.

"Have you ever been with a woman?" he asked, only mildly curious.

"No, but I've thought about it." Kenna paused. "Have you been with a man?"

He found himself smiling. "Once. When I was a boy. With another boy."

"Really?" She sat up in surprise. The stars on her necklace slid from the hollow of her throat to her chest. "You European men are amazing. Why didn't you lie to me?"

"Why should I? It's just sex. Nothing to be ashamed of. The fact that I fucked another boy years ago doesn't define who I am. It makes me know what I want and what I don't."

"Well, if you put it like that—"

A sudden hard knock shook the bedroom door. "I put coffee on," his brother yelled out in English. "Since I know you're in there with somebody, it's considered rude to hide away without coming out to make introductions, or at least share."

Kenna giggled. "I guess that proved your theory wrong. Your brother *is* that kinky."

"He must be drunk," Benoît muttered.

But he pulled himself away from Kenna anyway, kissing her laughing mouth once before pulling on his jeans. "Come on, you can clean up in the bathroom if you'd like. It's right across the hall."

"I'd definitely like." She clambered from the bed and reached for her clothes. "The taste of coffee and spunk don't really go well together."

"Oh, really? I thought spunk went with everything."

Clothes pressed to her naked front, she peeked out the bedroom door to make sure no one was coming. "How would you know? Oh, I almost forgot. Your childhood days of nibbling the sausage." She looked over her shoulder with a grin.

He threw a pillow at her retreating back.

"Cris, you fuck." Benoît hissed as soon as he got into their small combination kitchen/dining room. "I know you heard me in there, you could have just knocked."

Cristian, in a threadbare Converse T-shirt and jeans, didn't look up from washing the dishes. His jacket was tossed on the couch near his sneakers. He must have just come in after spending all night out with his friends.

"Shut up," his brother said, keeping his voice equally low. "I thought you had the television on or something." His thick black curls slid over his shoulders and into his face, but Benoît still saw the smile.

"No fucking way you thought that," he said. "I don't watch English porn."

"You should've locked the door, then, dickhead."

Yes, I should have. Benoît made a disgusted noise and shoved his brother out of the way to soap and wash his hands in the sink.

With dry hands, he reached for the packet of croissants in the cupboard and took down three plates to join the mugs Cristian already had on the table.

His brother stacked the plates in the drainer by the sink. "Like I was saying when I interrupted your dining experience earlier, your friends have been trying to call you all night and all morning. After they struck out with your mobile, they started calling me. Quentin, Troy, and the others want to meet up with you tonight at Café au Lait. I told them I'd pass the message along."

"Thanks," Benoît muttered.

Last night he had vague memories of tucking his phone in the bag along with the iPod. Why, he had no idea. *Kenna on the brain*, his inner voice chimed in. The mobile was either in the car or in the closet with his DJ equipment. "I'll call them in a few."

"Yeah, whatever." Cristian looked up, mischief on his face. "That girl is sexy. I hope she's not as crazy as that fucking Saskia." He put the last of the plates away and began wiping up the counter. There was after all a lady in the house.

"She's no Saskia," Benoît said, although obviously he knew next to nothing about her. But he could safely say he didn't get any of that clingy vibe from her. After all, she was just visiting Belgium and had no plans to stay in the country, much less with him. Saskia had shot off warning bells the day they met, but her gorgeous face and even more incredible body had silenced them once he'd managed to have a taste.

"You're just thinking with your small head and you know it." Cristian grinned. He poured coffee in all three mugs, then set a small gold box of Leonidas chocolates in the middle of the table. "And there's nothing wrong with that. Especially since you're leaving soon."

Benoît nodded. Yes, he was leaving soon. He exchanged a glance with his brother. Cristian would finally get the place to himself, at least for another year before he joined Benoît in America. Walking past to get the microwave, Benoît squeezed his brother's shoulder, hard. Half empathy and half "I can't believe you saw my girl naked." Down the hall, the bathroom door squeaked open.

"Is it safe for me to come in?" Kenna's laughing voice came from around the corner followed by her thick halo of hair.

Benoît switched to English. "*That's* the proper way to come into a private space, Cristian."

"Fuck off." His brother pulled out a chair. "Come in and have a seat, lovely lady."

When Kenna emerged, safely dressed in her low-slung jeans and yellow blouse, Cristian's face said it all. *Gorgeous.*

"Don't get any ideas about her," Benoît muttered in Flemish as Kenna thanked his brother and sat down.

Cristian took the platter of warmed croissants from the microwave. "It's not polite to speak another language when someone in the room can't understand."

"Fuck off." Benoît said that in English so there would be no misunderstanding.

"And I thought you were a nice boy . . ." Kenna grinned.

"I am very nice," Benoît said. He put cinnamon, cream, and sugar on the table for their coffee before claiming a chair. Reaching for the butter for his croissant, Benoît formally introduced Kenna to his brother.

"A pleasure to meet the lady my brother was paying such careful attention to."

Benoît kicked at his brother under the table, but Cristian neatly moved his leg out of the way.

"Oh, the pleasure this morning has been all mine," Kenna murmured, tearing into her croissant.

Benoît nearly choked on his coffee.

Cristian laughed and shoved hair out of his face. "Very nice," he chortled after he got his breath back. He turned to Benoît, his pale brown eyes glittering. "Where can I get one of these for myself?"

After breakfast, Cristian showered and left again. To go see a girl, he said, but Benoît suspected it might be a job. Ever since they had decided that Cristian would follow him to America after a year, his brother had been finding extra work and saving his money in preparation. Benoît was proud of his little brother.

With the apartment to themselves, Benoît washed the dishes while Kenna called her friend, Anthony, to let him know that she was safe, then they fell back into bed to finish what had been interrupted earlier. This time, he locked the door.

3

Saturday afternoon

Though huddled inside her thick down jacket on the bench beside him, Kenna still shivered. Benoît knew how she felt. The warmth from the hot chocolate and fresh baked *suikerwafels* they'd gotten from a street vendor had worn off a long time ago.

They'd reluctantly left his apartment and lust-inducing heat of their shared shower more than two hours ago. The tram took them to the Meir, where they walked side by side, sharing meaningless conversation.

Though Kenna told him bits and pieces about herself and her life in America, he was aware of holding himself back from her. They weren't just any couple out for a Saturday afternoon stroll. Kenna and he were strangers. Strangers with no shared future ahead of them. There was no point in talking about a life they did not and could not have in common.

"It's cold," he said and got to his feet. "Come on." His

breath puffed out in short streams. "We'll be warmer if we walk."

"I think we'll have to walk all the way to America before I can feel warm again." But she slid her arm through his and fell in step beside him.

"It won't take quite that long."

He pulled her close and gradually felt her body lose its shiver. They ambled along the sidewalk, weaving through the thick crowd walking briskly toward its business. It felt good to have her at his side, their hips gently bumping, the easy conversation about nothing, Kenna's curiosity about anything she didn't understand.

"Why does everything in this city seem to close at six?" she asked.

"Because there's no reason to stay open any later."

"What was up with those three guys staring at me like that?"

Benoît smiled at that one. "You're a nice-looking girl with an amazing ass. If you weren't walking with me I'd be staring, too."

Before leaving the flat, Benoît sent a text to his friends to confirm their meet for later that evening. Though it was tempting to stay in bed with Kenna until it was time to leave for the Café that night, Kenna, with a bit of hesitation in her voice, had vetoed the decision before it was voiced, saying she wanted to see the city with him. So they bundled back up and headed out to the Meir, Antwerp's biggest shopping street, which even in the middle of a gloomy winter day ran steadily with a constant stream of people.

"That window display is nice." Kenna pointed to yet another store window showing off clothes for the New Year party season. A pale mannequin in a black tux complete with sequined bow tie, and his two window companions, both wear-

ing large butterfly wings—black and sequined, of course—
tuxedo dresses and high heels.

"For some reason I can't see you in any of that."

As feminine as Kenna was in her tight jeans and body-hugging
shirt, Benoît found it hard to picture her in a dress.

She made a soft noise. "We need to work on your imagination, then." They walked on, leaving the window display behind.

"I love wearing dresses. I have a whole closet full of them
back home. It's just that I can't stand to have my legs bare in the
winter. And it's really too bad this time." She paused and glanced
up at him with mischief in her eyes. "I'd love to lift my skirt for
you. I'd love to have you somewhere raw and nasty with my skirt
shoved over my ass and your dick buried in my pussy." She bit
her lip, cutting her smile in half. "Wouldn't you like that?"

Benoît swallowed. "Shit! Only a fool wouldn't like that."

At his side, Kenna laughed and pressed closer. She was teasing him. Benoît willed his blood to simmer down, but the
heavy pulse low in his belly was difficult to ignore. He deliberately focused on their surroundings and not on the soft curve of
a mouth only a few tempting inches away.

The smell of sugared waffles and simmering seafood soup
from the roadside stands followed them past the dress shops. In
front of a leather goods store, a man dressed as a harlequin and
painted all in white with startling crystalline gold eyes played at
being a statue for an amused crowd. A little boy, with his
mother's laughing permission, tottered close to the statue man,
who stood as still as stone. The boy dropped one euro into the
box built into the pedestal the man stood on. Seconds later, the
statue blinked, startling the little boy into laughter. With each
robotic and graceful movement of the harlequin, more money
dropped into the box from the onlookers' hands, more laughter

and applause erupted until the harlequin moved fluidly, turning somersaults and contorting himself into inhuman shapes.

"That looks like a great way to make a living." Kenna leaned back into him as they stood watching.

"Didier would rather be in school than performing this bull-shit in this cold-ass weather."

She twisted around to look at Benoît. "You know him?"

"He used to live around the corner from us when my mother was alive."

"Oh."

If anyone took the time to look past the mask and white paint, they'd see that Didier's eyes were dead. Flat gold in a face that rarely smiled. He was just wading through life, knowing that at some point, he would inevitably drown.

Benoît didn't want to deal with any of that. He'd battled the state of things in Belgium for years now before finally making the decision—and getting the opportunity—to leave. After being in denial about it for years, he faced the truth that limit-less opportunities in this country existed only for native-born Belgians. If he'd wanted to, Benoît could have sold himself to the highest bidder like his cousin Paolo. Ever since his cousin lost his virginity to a diamond dealer with a big apartment near Groenplaats, the boy had been passed from one rich Belgian man to another, but he never lacked for anything. Anything Gucci, Prada, or Louis Vuitton was his for the asking. But that broken look in his eyes was something that Benoît could never forget.

"I'm leaving for America in a couple of days," he said, un-able to look away from Didier's empty movements. "It'll be good to leave this behind."

Before Kenna could speak, he took a deep breath and leaned down. "Come on," he whispered into her ear. "Let me take you someplace we can both warm up."

The *Schipperskwartier*, the city's police-regulated red-light district, was only a few streets away and Benoît guided Kenna there unerringly, tracing the same path he'd worn many times throughout his years living in Antwerp. His friends had all visited the area for at least one of their birthdays, taking advantage of the pleasures a thick wallet and youthful stamina could bring.

Kenna looked around with curiosity as they passed through cobblestoned alleys, shops selling Belgian lace and silk scarves, and passed under old stone-faced buildings with their gold roof-bound statues that had been a part of the Antwerp cityscape since the sixteenth century.

She startled when a man abruptly emerged from around a corner and ambled toward them. He had a balding head. A gut. And wore the clothes of a construction worker. The man laughed, a sound of exhilaration, of renewal, as he jerked his pants into place around his hips, yanked up his zipper. Moments later, a girl strolled out from the same dark corner, her walk more leisurely. She flicked a glance to the man before walking off in the opposite direction.

The man continued past, barely giving them a glance. Up ahead, the girl wound her way through the trickling flow of men, catching quite a few eyes with her hip-twitching walk and her tiny red dress that burned like a flame against her dark skin.

"Oh, baby, you shouldn't have!" Kenna glanced around with a false look of bashfulness on her face.

They emerged onto a street studded on both sides by brightly lit windows. In each window, a beautiful woman sat perched on a stool or leaning provocatively against the glass. Kenna's eyes flitted from one side of the street to the other in curiosity. She veered toward one of windows and the girl, posing like a pinup in a neon picture frame, straightened, shoving out her breasts in the pale lace bra, trailing a hand down her bare thigh. She parted her lips in pink invitation while bright lights corrupted her skin.

Kenna's arm slid from Benoît's and she slowed down.

"It's three o' clock in the afternoon. I thought they only did this kind of thing at night."

"People don't save sex just for the nighttime." He quirked an eyebrow.

"Really?" Her sarcasm wasn't lost on him. With him in her wake, Kenna walked past the first girl, her expression going quickly from curiosity to fascination.

"I'd always heard about these kinds of places but thought they only existed in Amsterdam."

"Prostitution is legal in most countries. It's only the United States and a few other hypocrites that don't have it as a real and legally protected profession so the women can carry on their trade without having to worry about cops, unethical pimps, and STDs."

"You sound like you have a special love for hookers."

Benoît shrugged. "People should be allowed to do whatever they want with their bodies. It just makes sense. For some, that's all they have to barter with. The government might as well make it safe for them."

She looked at him. "The longer I know you, the more surprised I get."

"After less than twenty-four hours, I hope that's a good thing." He chuckled.

"So far, yes." Kenna looped her arm through his. "But all this talk about hookers is a bit too much for me. Let's go over there instead." She tilted her head toward the next street with its more subtle use of neon, advertising peep shows, sex cinemas, and toy shops. "I think that's more my speed."

He raised an eyebrow. *Really?*

"Come on."

She pulled him into the first shop advertising peep shows. The big blond guy at the front counter nodded at them once in greeting before settling his gaze back on the street. Deeper into the shop, in a labyrinth of booths and pink-doored private rooms etched with numbers, men glanced at Kenna, their eyes surprised and hungry, before carrying on with their own business. The tiled floor was clean, Benoît noticed with relief. A red bucket and mop sat outside one of the closed doors.

"You can get change from that machine," an African-accented voice sounded behind them. The big man attached to the voice approached them from a side hallway. His black jacket shone nearly the same color as his skin.

"Thank you." Benoît leaned toward Kenna. "The booths only take coins."

"That's cool, I have plenty of change." She grinned and reached into her pocket, brought out a round cloth purse. The coins jangled joyously.

But Benoît changed five euros anyway. *Just in case.* "Where do you want to go?"

"I don't know. Let's just pick a door."

She chose and he followed. But he checked the floor before he allowed her to close them inside the booth. With the door shut behind them, they could hear things they hadn't before. The raucous voices of men yelling out to each other and probably to the girl who waited for them behind the closed window.

"Have you done this before?"

"When I was younger, yes."

"And?"

"And it was fun. In the right frame of mind or in the right company, these places can be very enjoyable."

Her doll's eyes watched him, considered him, before she shoved two euros into the coin slot. Giving her room to enjoy the upcoming show, he leaned back against the closed door. She stood in front of him, her mouth slightly open, as the partition before the window slid open. On a slowly rotating bed, a blond girl danced while crouched on her knees. Something about her pout and the way she arched her body, clad only in white lingerie and heels, reminded him of an old girlfriend. The men's voices grew even louder, chattering loudly in Flemish and what sounded like Italian.

"She's not very pretty," Kenna murmured, turning to him without taking her eyes from the girl. "And why is she wearing clothes?"

The girl cupped pert C-cups through the lace, tossed her hair. A hand slid down her flat belly and into her panties. She aimed another pout toward the rowdy men, who sounded close, as if one stood in each of the rooms surrounding her and the turning bed.

"She's only wearing clothes for now," Benoît said, unable to hide his smile. The more money you spend, the more naked she gets."

"I don't know if I want to invest that much in her." Kenna narrowed her eyes at the girl and frowned. "At the rate she's going I'll be broke before she even takes off a shoe."

The window slid shut.

"That's all we get for two euros?" Kenna looked up at him, incredulous.

"Pretty much. You may be able to buy sex, but it's not cheap."

"Ugh! She was boring anyway. Only the other guys got her attention. She barely looked at us."

Benoît shrugged. "Maybe we weren't loud enough for her taste." He enjoyed how she got into the spirit of their little adventure.

"Or flashing enough cash." Kenna jiggled her coins. "She had no idea how good we could have been to her." It was her turn to shrug. "Let's go to another booth. Maybe we'll get to see a cuter girl."

"I have a better idea." Benoît led her out the door, down the hall, and to the right toward another set of booths, these with dark red doors. "Here."

He peeked in two of them before finding one that would work. Instead of a window into another room, the booth had video monitors, four small screens below a full-sized one, and a red pleather armchair snuggled close to the door.

"Why do you keep checking the floors?" Kenna closed the door behind Benoît.

"Cum."

Kenna shuddered. "That's so gross."

"I thought you might feel that way about it." He took out a packet of disinfectant wipes he'd bought from the front and wiped down the coin slot, door handle, and chair. It never hurt to be careful.

With a faint smile she turned to look at the blank screens. "So is this going to be better than what we just saw?"

"I'm sure you'll let me know in a few minutes." He reached past her to drop money in the coin slot underneath the monitors.

The screens flickered on.

"Are you serious? People pay to sit in here and watch porn?"

"And other things," he said, stretching out in the red chair. Kenna took off her jacket and sat on the chair's arm to watch.

Four separate movies played on each small screen. On the first one, a blond couple in a bed fucked vigorously with the woman on top. On the second, three lesbians lay twisted together in front of a fireplace, eating each other's pussies and sucking on silicone-enhanced breasts. The next was a solo show, a caramel-skinned woman and her crystal dildo. A foursome took over the last screen. The scene on the first monitor also played on the large one.

"Do you think they enjoy all this?" Kenna asked, gesturing to the naked images flashing behind her.

"That last girl isn't," he said.

Pressed between three men with one man's dick gagging her throat and another spearing her pussy while she jerked off yet a third, the dark-haired girl wore equal parts pain and boredom on her face.

"Would you enjoy yourself if you knew she was into it?"

"Yes. I always prefer it when my woman has a good time. Otherwise there's no point."

"I wish all men felt that way."

As if in agreement, they watched the other four videos in silence. On the big screen, the long-haired woman rode her man while she faced the camera and her ass tilted toward her lover. The length of the man's dick appeared and disappeared at her pussy's entrance as she fucked him. She panted, squeezed her breasts and nipples, all the while licking her lips and pouting for the camera. Arousal trickled into Benoît's lap. He became even more aware of Kenna near him, her slow breath, and the press of her breasts against the blouse. She still smelled like his soap. But underneath it was her woman's scent, a pleasant musk that made his dick twitch.

Was it his imagination or was Kenna leaning more into him? Her breasts were suddenly close enough to press his chest against. Under the cotton, her nipples were hard.

She stood up to lean back against the monitors. "You love this," she said. Not a question, but a statement with her eyes steady on the thickening bulge in his jeans.

"I'm only human," he said, his libido fast losing interest in the porn smorgasbord behind Kenna. Instead it focused on her full presence, the *doucement* of her smile.

Kenna slid her foot between the sprawl of his thighs, booted leather gently nudging his balls.

"And the real thing? Does it excite you more? Or is it all the same?"

"What a question." He gasped from the pressure of her foot on him.

Kenna pulled away, drew back to lean against the monitors, accidentally jolting the licking lesbians to the main screen. Their moans filled Benoît's ears.

"That's no answer." She flicked open the top buttons of her jeans, then her eyebrows arched in question.

"Keep going," he said, his voice thickening with arousal.

She smiled, all predator. One more button. Then another. With her head back, she watched him from between slumberous eyes, sex-heavy eyes. Kenna wriggled the jeans down her thighs, baring her thick bush of pussy hair. Before her, Benoît had preferred his women shaved, their slits and clit bared to him for easy access and enjoyment, but with the pearl of pussy juice clinging to the curling dark hairs between her thighs, he didn't want her any other way.

"Can you—" he cleared his throat. "—can you take your pants off?"

She shook her head, lightly combing fingers through the curls guarding her cunt. Her clit stood out hard and thick. Kenna touched it, and she shivered, leaning back even more with closed eyes. The monitors behind her went blank. Their time had expired. She widened her thighs, tilted her hips to get at her pussy despite the jeans at her ankles. Two fingers. She slid two fingers inside her pussy. Groaned in her pleasure. Benoît felt hard enough to burst.

"Where's my show?" she growled. "I paid, too."

The chair squeaked as he moved lower in it, opened his thighs wider, undid the buttons straining over his erection. He pushed back his briefs, groaning at the accidental friction.

"Perfect," she whispered, pushing the slick fingers deeper inside her furred pussy. Her thumb agitated her clit. "Show me more."

She fucked herself slowly, eyes locked on his dick. He squeezed himself once, watching her. Smoothed his thumb over the thick head of his cock, lubing himself with the precum.

"Show me what you do when you're watching porn alone. Show me."

He gave a few experimental twists of his fist, realizing that yes, he could do this in front of somebody else. It felt good. The tight cave of his slow-moving fist. He wanted to feel her around him, not this substitute he could have anytime he wanted.

"Come sit on my lap, baby," he pleaded.

"I don't have any condoms."

"But I do." He reached for his wallet. Pulled one out. "Please. I'll make it good for you." Although Benoît was so hot for her right now he wasn't sure how long he would last.

Kenna shoved off her boots and jeans, shoved them into the small shelf above the monitors, and, steadily watching his face, sank into Benoît's lap, swallowing his cock in her cunt. A long singing groan left both their throats.

"Jesus!"

She was so tight. So wet. Shit!

"Pull down your—yes!" Her breasts popped out of the yellow blouse. He eagerly opened his mouth for them, sucked the thick nipples, licked the soft flesh while they both filled the air with their sounds—the liquid kiss of his mouth on her breasts, of his dick in her pussy, the hissing, growling sounds Kenna made at the back of her throat.

"Fuck me," she gasped.

And he gripped her hips, shoving up into her, straining as if his life depended on being buried, again and again, inside her melting heat. Sweat prickled under his clothes, and pleasure's vise tightened even more in his belly, in his balls. He gasped her name.

The chair squeaked. Her panting little gasps, his grunts.

These sounds formed the symphony of their sex as he thrust and she clung and the chair slid across the floor and her hair bobbed around her face. Kenna screamed her orgasm into his mouth. And he drank it up. Her pussy squeezed him, stroked him until he was coming, too, and howling his joy at being in a place he never expected to be, with someone he never expected to find.

4

_____

Saturday late afternoon

"Do you believe in destiny?"

Kenna lay wrapped up in his sheets, her body hidden from him after all they had done. She traced her name in the sweat cooling on his stomach. After the peep show it had only seemed natural that they end up back here, in his bed. Fucking with the door locked. Their shouts rising and falling. Sweat-soaked skin sliding against sweat-soaked skin.

"No. I'm not even sure if I believe in God," he said in response to her question, not quite sure where she was going.

He lay naked beside her, not bothering to reach for his usual post-sex cigarette because she's asked him not to. "Do you?"

"I want to believe in something else, something greater. How else could you explain us connecting like this?"

Though Benoît had only gasped his amazement at finding her while his dick was buried in some hot and moist part of her anatomy, in his precoital moments he believed it, too. She must have seen the agreement on his face.

"Some things are only meant to happen for a short time, Kenna. A storm. An orgasm. Maybe even you and me."

"I don't want to believe that." She sat up. "At home, I'd always been a little on the cautious side. My roommate called it careful on days when she liked me and uptight when she didn't. There had always been men. Nice men who offered me things, who I had fun with. But I was always cautious, even afraid. I'd always seen how my roommate was with men. She played with them, got her heart broken, told me stories that belong in *Playboy* magazine, or *Hustler*. And although she had so much drama along with that, I secretly wanted to be a little like her."

She put her palm flat against his belly, and Benoît's muscles jumped.

With a slow smile, she splayed her fingers against his skin. "I want to fuck a guy so hard he'd never forget my name." Kenna leaned closer. Her breath brushed his lips. "These days I think so much that, for once, I want to be in my body. I want to be comfortable sharing it with a man who I know will appreciate it and share his body with me, too. You have no idea how hard that is to find. I've found it with you and that can't be an accident."

Her large eyes, filled with the conviction behind her words, captured and held his.

Benoît swallowed. He wanted to believe her. That whatever this thing was between them, it was far greater than a weekend of incredible skin-to-skin contact.

"But how do you explain the rest of the world outside this room? It all looks like one giant accident to me. A mess."

"I'm not talking about the rest of the world, I'm talking about us."

"I think we are a happy accident. There's no fate in it, no destiny. Just incredible chemistry and bad timing."

She pouted. "You're not the romantic I thought you were."

"Oh, when did you think that? When I begged you to suck

my dick and make it last?" Grinning and sly, he shoved her hand lower to the weighted curve of his cock. "Or when I grabbed—"

Kenna climbed on top of him, touched her lips to his neck. "When I saw my favorite book on your nightstand." Her tongue licked his ear.

Benoît pulled back in surprise, his lustful mood interrupted. His well-thumbed copy of a Pablo Neruda poetry collection sat next to a half-empty glass of water. The cover, a reproduction of Gauguin's *Woman with a Mango*, had initially drawn him to the book. It was the poetry, naked and deceptively simple, that made him buy it.

He leaned back into her, eager again for a taste of her pouty mouth. "It's just a book, baby."

"No, gorgeous." She took his dick in her hand and gave it a long, delicious stroke. "It's destiny."

5

Saturday night

Benoît opened the door for Kenna and stepped into the café behind her. The noise and bustle of the small space immediately enveloped them. A few heads turned, tracking the two of them as they walked deeper into Café au Lait. The bartender, slim with a cascade of inky curls around his freckled face, nodded at Benoît in greeting. He nodded back, scanned the drink menu written in flowing script on the wall.

Beside him, Kenna pulled off her jacket and crushed it between her belly and the bar as she leaned forward to look at the menu, too. Her arm brushed Benoît's. He shivered.

After they woke up in his bed that last time, she said she wanted to go back to her friend's for a change of clothes, but Benoît hadn't wanted to let her go. Instead he took her back to the Meir, where he bought a dress and tights that she picked out. The long-sleeved green dress faithfully followed her curves from throat to waist before flaring out in a flattering cascade of fabric to her knees. The tights and boots kept the rest of her warm.

"The usual?" the bartender, Michel, asked.

"Most definitely."

"And you, *cherie*?" Michel directed a warm look at Kenna.

She asked for a mojito, head swiveling to catch every detail of the café. The slowly thickening crowd of black, white, and all shades in between. Wooden African masks and statues on the small randomly placed built-in shelves. The gigantic painting of a beautiful brown girl taking up an entire wall.

Benoît paid for the drinks, then guided her to his favorite spot at the rear of the café. The group at the pool table paused for them to pass before resuming their game. He and Kenna sank into the black leather booth against the wall, adjusting the red cushions at their backs.

"This spot is pretty cool," Kenna said.

Three stationary disco balls hung from the ceiling above them among a cluster of white Japanese lanterns. Against the dark red walls the pale light refracting from the disco balls shone like tiny open-mouthed kisses.

The café was half full tonight, but it was early yet, barely seven o' clock. Music thudded in the air, a new Moroccan hip-hop tune that had everyone in the place bobbing their heads.

"People here seem friendly." Kenna settled next to him with her mojito, drinking in the atmosphere.

"Everybody is friendly when they want to fuck you." He leaned back in the booth, only half joking. The people in the café knew him and liked him well enough. By extension they would welcome anyone he brought, especially if they looked like Kenna.

"Is that why you're so nice to me?" She turned to him, light spilling over her high cheekbones and round moon face.

"Of course."

Her plump mouth, which, in his short and happy experience, was perfect for dick sucking, pursed as she looked him up and down. "I have to figure out how to get something out of this deal, then."

Benoît licked his lips. "You mean you haven't been so far?"

"I want more."

"I can give you more." A pulse thudded once, heavily, in his dick at her suddenly voracious look. Benoît opened his mouth.

"This place is so fucking empty." A slim figure with the look of Africa stamped clearly on his handsome features dropped into the empty space on the other side of Kenna. "Hey, DJ D. *Ca va?*" An orange scarf fluttered at his throat as he lifted his head in a reverse nod at Benoît. "You're here early, man."

"I was enjoying the company of a beautiful woman before you guys got here." Benoît briefly nodded in Kenna's direction. She sipped her drink and watched the two of them with an interested smile.

For the first time, his friend seemed to really notice her. He took his time looking her over before leaning close to kiss her on the cheek.

"My name is Quentin, lovely lady. A pleasure to meet you."

Kenna laughed with delight. She tongued the straw and looked from Benoît to Quentin. "Are all Belgian boys as beautiful as you two?"

"Of course," Quentin murmured, taking the compliment as his due.

Like Benoît and most of their other friends, Quentin was a half caste, or more precisely, a mixed breed. A Dominican mother. Belgian father. French sensibilities. His short, curling hair and dimpled cheeks and limitless charm disarmed everyone he met. He used those looks to sleep through most bedrooms and back alleys in Antwerp. Quentin would fuck anything, not simply because he could, but because there wasn't an experience in the world that he didn't want to try at least twice. Sitting between Benoît and Quentin, Kenna looked ready to be charmed. Benoît could easily imagine her walking away from him to spend the rest of her holiday weekend with his friend. She wouldn't be the first girl to leave him for Quentin.

Benoît ignored the pang in his chest.

"Hey, Benny. What's going on?" Martijn, the pretty Asian boy in Benoît's group of friends, bounced up to them. He pressed his cheek briefly to Benoît's in greeting. "I knew you'd come early." He leaned down to slap Quentin's back, then squeezed in between Benoît and the wall. Grinning, he winked one blue eye at Kenna.

Bart and Hugo followed behind, practically vibrating with energy. Spanish dark and identically good looking, the boys were often mistaken for brothers. When a couple of cute girls were involved, they were often slow to clear up the mistake. Benoît laughed, happy to see his friends. As they came close he smelled the liquor, something sweet, on their breaths. *Peach schnapps?* The guys noisily pulled up two chairs to the table, scraping the wooden legs against the floor, and sat down.

"What's up, boy? We came to celebrate with you."

Hugo squeezed Benoît's shoulder. "We'll miss having you around the neighborhood, *maat.*"

"You guys are making me tear up," he said in English to bring Kenna into the conversation.

They looked at him with curiosity. He gestured to the girl at his side.

"Ah. A pretty English girl."

"American," Kenna corrected with a smile. She introduced herself and all of Benoît's friends stood up or leaned forward to kiss her cheek, offering their names for hers. Every one of them dropped their eyes to her breasts as soon as she stopped looking in their direction.

Hugo was the first one to break out the compliments. "Benny's getting better taste every day."

"Damn right," Benoît said knocking back his *mazout*. The salty-sweet of the beer and cola concoction made his tongue curl. "She's fucking fantastic and you can't have her."

"Interesting choice of words," Quentin said in Flemish, flashing his Adonis smile at Kenna.

Her eyes went wide at that blatant bit of flirtation, but she only pursed her lips for no one in particular and put the frosted mojito glass to her mouth. Under the table, Benoît lightly squeezed her thigh.

Nearly four hours later, the five of them stumbled out of the café and into the street, laughing.

"And Quentin had no idea the condom was stuck to his ass!" Hugo roared with laughter as he stumbled against Kenna. "You should have seen his face when we told him."

Benoît's friends spent the last four hours buying Kenna drinks and telling old stories about him. Reminiscing. Smoking all their cigarettes down to the filter and unwrapping new packs. Their way of showing that they would miss him. This was their last time together and even though Kenna's presence had initially thrown them off—compelling them to play to the female audience suddenly in their midst—as the night wore on she became one of them. Her shy-sexy charm, ability to tell a dirty joke, and the startling fact that she could play a decent game of pool despite being pissy drunk, drew them in.

When Quentin bought her a drink, leaning close over the scattered balls on the table to offer her some bit of unsolicited advice, Benoît stiffened and tried to prepare himself for it. But Kenna had only chuckled, subtly pushing Quentin back. She didn't make that gradual slide toward his friend that Benoît had grown used to seeing. Instead she'd looked at Benoît with amusement in her eyes before leaning over to make her shot. The yellow ball slammed decisively into the corner pocket.

"I need some smokes." Outside the café, Hugo patted his pockets, produced a crumpled red pack. He stuck the last cigarette between his lips, crushed the pack, and threw it toward a nearby garbage can. He missed. "Unless somebody's got one for me."

Benoît laughed. "You know better than that." His own cigarette pack was only half empty and he planned on having it stay that way until he was ready for one. Being around Kenna and her crisp, clean smell made him cut down on his smoking. At this rate he wouldn't have to buy another pack until he was in America.

Martijn lit his cigarette, squinting against the lighter's flame. "Yeah, take your ass to the nightshop. You can't have any of mine."

"Fuck you," Hugo muttered.

But they all moved as one toward the lone store with its fluorescent lights burning steadily through the glass doors and windows.

At Benoît's side, Kenna shoved her hands in her pockets. "I don't know how you can function when all the stores shut their doors at six o'clock like they're keeping prison hours."

Benoît glanced at her and saw his friends do the same. Their six pairs of footsteps tapped wetly against the damp cobblestones as they crossed the street.

"What? It's true," she muttered. A tiny grin sat at the corner of her mouth.

"Yeah, I heard in America, you can get anything you want at any time of the day or night."

"Not anything," Kenna said. "But damn close. These night shops you have are ridiculous, though. They don't even stay open past eleven."

"They're *nachtwinkelen,* not *dagwinkelen.*"

"Night shops, not day shops," Benoît translated, nudging Kenna out of the way of a passing bicyclist.

She rolled her eyes and chuckled softly at the weak joke.

Benoît pushed inside the store, sending the bell over the

door jangling, and Kenna walked in ahead of him. Hugo followed behind, laughing. "Dagwinkelen. That's funny."

Martijn snorted and pushed past him into the shop.

The Pakistani guy behind the counter looked up as they came in, ignoring Kenna's greeting. Instead he watched the shift of her ass as she walked past, at the same time reaching down to dial a number on a mobile, not once taking his gaze from her. Benoît moved up to shield her with his body. *Take your fucking eyes off my girl.*

"Give me a pack of Marlboro Reds."

"Me too." Martijn joined Hugo at the counter while Benoît and the others scattered to different parts of the store.

The guy at the counter reached for the cigarettes while speaking in Urdu to someone on the phone. His eyes darted around the store, trying to keep track of everyone who'd just come in.

At the ice cream fridge, Quentin reached for an ice lolly about a foot and a half long with alternating rainbow stripes. "Can you handle something like this?" He dropped the dessert to crotch level and directed his laughing question at Kenna.

"Come the fuck on!" Benoît said, irritated now at his friend's blatant attempt to steal, or at least share, his girl.

"Don't worry about me, baby. I'm getting this and more from my boy toy." Kenna grabbed the ice cream from Quentin's hand, stripped off the white plastic covering, and wrapped her lips around the head of the cold stick. "Don't be jealous."

"You going to pay for that!?" The irritated voice came from the front of the store.

"Don't worry about it," Quentin barely looked over his shoulder to give his reply. "We're not gonna steal shit from this place."

"Then pay for the stuff before you open it."

The front bell sounded and another man walked into the store, brown-skinned and zipped up in black against the cold. He said something in Urdu to the guy behind the counter.

After a rapid exchange, the newcomer stormed to the back of the store.

"Buy what you want and get out!" he shouted, words partially distorted by a thick accent.

"Fuck off," Quentin said dismissively. "We can damn well take our time if we want." But he turned to face the newcomer with hands already clenched into fists.

The tall guy unzipped his jacket and stepped even closer. "But leave. Hurry up! There are too many of you niggers in here."

Benoît felt Kenna stiffen. "What the fuck?" Her mouth gaped open at the slur.

He swung around. "You don't say that shit to us!"

But the guy didn't back off. Instead, he pulled the edge of his jacket back as if reaching for something hidden inside.

"Don't be stupid!" Kenna reached blindly for Benoît's hand. "We're going to pay for what we take."

At the counter, Hugo and Martijn, who had turned to step outside the store, swung back inside. Surprise and anger rushed into their faces. "No fucking way," one of them said. "Give us our fucking money back." Two packs of cigarettes flew across the counter and hit the clerk, who lifted his arm too late to block his face. "We don't have to shop here. Give us back our *nigger* money and we'll leave."

"Too late, too late. Get out!"

Running up to the front of the store, Quentin spat. "Fuck you!" He hurled something hard at the glass door, a can of beans. The glass shattered.

Benoît pulled Kenna toward the door. This was going to get very ugly. "Come on!" He threw two euro at the clerk for her ice cream and rushed them out the store. The night air immediately shot into his lungs; only then did Benoît notice his own rapid breath and his heart's heavy beat.

"Shit! He's coming. Run!"

His friends scattered. A bell clanged noisily. The sound of someone chasing them from the store. Benoît didn't look back to see who.

"You gonna pay for that!" The voice chased them as they ran down the slick stone sidewalks, darting across the road through traffic, swerving into and through an alley. Kenna panted heavily at his side.

Their footsteps beat against the cobblestones as they ran. Pulling Kenna behind him, Benoît dodged streetlights and bright storefronts. Dashed down another darkened alley and ran fast and faster. Their breaths panted in the night air. Puffed steam into the evening's blackness.

He whipped into alley after alley until he was sure no one followed them.

"Oh god! That fucking—" Benoît's words jerked to a halt when his breath failed him. "—Quentin!" A damp wall supported his heaving length, the stone leaking cold into his palm. "Fuck."

"That was crazy." Kenna's laughter had a touch of hysteria in it. She flung herself against the wall, her head leaned back, breath huffing at the sky. Her necklace of stars winked in the faint light. "I didn't know shit like that happened here."

He waited until his breath calmed down before responding. "There are assholes everywhere."

In the aftermath of his adrenaline rush, the flutter of Kenna's eyes came to Benoît. Her open mouth as she pulled in more air. His slowing pulse began to speed up again.

"Those guys could have totally fucked us up!" Kenna quickly unzipped her jacket with shaking hands. "Are your friends crazy?"

"Sometimes."

Their harsh breaths mingled, steam meeting in the air.

Benoît's attention narrowed until all his awareness focused

on the full pout of her lips, the heaving press of her breasts against the green dress.

"That was actually kind of hot, too," he said.

She licked her lips. "Yeah."

"Yeah."

She tasted of the chase. Fear-bitter breath. A dry mouth he quickly made wet with his tongue. Kenna growled, fumbling for his belt and zipper. Cool air washed over his dick. Her warm hand cupped his balls, stroked the hardening length of his cock.

"Fuck me," she hissed at his ear.

Need bubbled up in his blood so fast, Benoît reeled, suddenly dizzy. With his last bit of common sense, he reached for one of the condoms in his back pocket. Rolling it on almost killed him. Her hands, so warm. Soft. Kenna. Kenna. Kenna. Endlessly intoxicating, she flooded his veins. He tongued her breasts through the thin material of her dress, sucking hard until the cloth was dark and wet from his mouth and her nipples stood stiff and responsive, begging to be naked to his touch.

"Fuck me."

He shoved her dress out of the way, but her tights stopped him from going further. Benoît made a sound of irritation. Ripped the cloth. The scent of her pussy flooded up to him. Thick and loamy. Ready for his hands, his dick. "God!"

He lifted her, hands under her ass. Her fingers around his dick, and—fuck! It was perfect, the feel of her sweltering pussy around him. Slick and damp like she was made for him.

"Wait!" she gasped, pressed sweat-damp fingers against his mouth. Her pussy clutched around him. "There's someone. I think I heard something."

They froze. Only the sound of their faintly panting breaths, dirt crunching under his sneakers as he adjusted his thighs under her weight. No other noises. Then he heard it. Another set of breaths. A low groan. A whispered question in Flemish. "Why did they stop?" Someone was watching them. And getting off on what they saw.

He whispered his discovery in her ear. But the shift of her body on him, the slight twitch of her pussy pushed out his words in an urgent gasp.

"If it's not the cops," Kenna pushed against him, biting at his lips, "then I don't care." Her internal muscles flexed around his dick, squeezing a tremor from him. "Fuck me." Her tongue stroked his ear.

She didn't have to tell him twice.

Benoît slammed her back into the wall, grunting. *So good.* Balls deep inside her. The cloth from her tights rubbing against his cock with each thrust. Her gasping and moaning his names. Legs locked around his waist as Benoît slowly died. Knees trembling. Pleasure flashing in his belly, coiling low and ready to spring. Kenna panted, licked her lips, gasped his name softly as she jerked against the wall, her slender neck arched back while she blinked at the dark sky, eyes glazed as if the pleasure had taken her to another place.

In the darkness behind them, he heard similar noises. Grunts. Quiet pleas. The rhythmic slap of flesh against flesh. Benoît couldn't tell who was watching them, he only knew they were having fun. The sounds of their fucking urged him on. Thickened his dick inside Kenna.

An animal grunt spilled from his lips. Benoît squeezed Kenna's breasts through the dress, scraped the rigid tips with his teeth. Benoît panted. His dick driving into her, hips beyond his control as she groaned his name.

"I see them," Kenna gasped. "—watching us. A guy and his girl." She groaned. "He has her bent over. He's fucking her from behind—oh!"

Her words drove his hips faster. Benoît imagined their dark shapes in the alley across from them, the girl's bare ass turned up, her boyfriend slamming his dick inside her while she moaned quietly, trying not to make a sound. Both of them on the edge of excitement as they watched him and Kenna fuck. Benoît slammed into her hot pussy. The friction already working to bring him close. His balls tightened.

"Do it now, baby." She clutched at him, legs tightening around his waist. "Ben!"

He didn't know what *it* was, but his body apparently did. He went even deeper, slamming in, then pulling almost all the way out before colliding into her again and again. Benoît gripped her hips. Biceps and thighs and ass muscles straining to hold her up, to keep the pleasure coming and make sure they both got what they wanted.

"Ben!" Her guttural screams. Her pussy sucking him toward his own orgasm.

Jesus. He jerked against her, spending himself in the condom. *Jesus.*

He staggered. Her legs fell from around him and she sighed, laughed, leaning back into the wall. When her eyes turned to search the shadows down the alley, Benoît turned. Their voyeurs were still at it, partially clothed in darkness with only shafts of light from the street lamp penetrating their hiding place. Benoît could make out the pale skin of the girl's ass, her boyfriend, equally pale, equally skinny with his pants around his ankles, fucking towards their orgasms. Benoît turned away.

"Well, that was nice." Kenna licked her lips and watched him, already dismissing the nearby couple. He'd never seen a more beautiful thing.

"Yeah, nice." He leaned against the wall next to her, fighting the sluggishness in his limbs to pull off the rubber, tie it off, and throw it into the darkness. With a smirk, she knelt to help him zip and buckle his pants, her knees on his sneakered feet. Of course, her hands wandered. Benoît couldn't bite back a groan as she handled his twitching and damp cock, tucking it back

into the briefs and zipping up. She ended her tender loving care
with a squeeze before standing up.

"You weren't very quiet a few minutes ago, so I suggest we
get out of here and back to your place. I'd rather the cops find
them—" She jerked her head toward the other end of the alley.
"—and not us." She nipped at his chin with her sharp teeth.
"Come on."

6

Sunday morning

"Your city is very beautiful, very complicated." Kenna ran her finger along the stars at her throat before picking up her tea. "Like you."

At the kitchen table, wearing his oversized sweatshirt and nothing else, she stretched out her legs across his lap. Benoît nudged aside his empty bowl of muesli. The table did its familiar rattle and dance as he leaned against it, propping his arm on its edge.

"I don't think there's anything complicated about living here. It's just life in a different country. People, I'm sure, would say the same thing about America."

Kenna slid the stars along the silver line of her necklace, back and forth, watching him. "And do you think America is beautiful, like your Belgium?" A smile toyed with her lips, making him realize he was being too serious again. He shook his head, chuckling, and leaned back in his chair. Her toes wriggled against his belly.

"In my limited experience, yes. America is very beautiful."
He gently squeezed her toes with their deep orange polish.

She settled back in her chair and took a sip of her tea, satisfied.
Benoît laughed again. With her hair in plaits and the soft glow of
morning still on her face, Kenna seemed already part of the relaxed beginning of his day. A sight he could get used to indulging
in every day. But after tomorrow he'd never see her again.

The smile fell from his face.

Kenna tilted her head, looking at him with a question in her
eyes. "What's up?"

"Come here." Suddenly he desperately wanted to feel her
skin again. To press his face into that sweet spot at her throat
and keep her close to him for as long as he could.

She chuckled. "What are you, fourteen?" But she came anyway, abandoning her tea and moving gracefully into his lap.

"I don't always want to fuck, you know," he said.

"Really?" She wriggled in his lap, provoking a groan and the
heavy pulse of arousal in his dick. "Then what's this I'm sitting
on?"

He didn't bother to answer, only reached up to pull her face
down to his. Kenna tasted like jasmine and honey. Like other
mornings they would never have together. He groaned again,
this time for a different reason. It didn't seem fair that he
should find this girl when he was leaving. But he would make
the most of this. He had to.

Benoît moved his hand under the sweatshirt, squeezed her
bare breast, and felt the nipple harden under his palm. She
sighed into his mouth.

The doorbell rang.

Kenna lifted her head, nibbling at his lip once more before
pulling away. "Do you think that's your brother warning us before he bursts in?"

"I'm not dreaming, so no." Benoît set Kenna on her feet to
get up and answer the door.

"Thank God you're here!" The woman in the doorway rushed inside the apartment, her pretty face a mixture of irritation and relief.

What the hell was she doing here? Benoît reluctantly closed the door behind his ex-girlfriend. He hadn't seen her in weeks and hadn't expected to see her at all before he left.

"What's up, Saskia?"

"I thought something happened to you." The dark hair around her face snapped in the air as she quickly looked him over as if to confirm that he really was okay. She grasped him in a firm hug, jumped back, then stepped in to cling to him again. The cold, crisp scent of outside clung to her hair. "I've been a mess thinking that you've been run over by a tram or something." She spoke quickly as she flitted around him, a dragonfly in her iridescent green jacket and tight black pants.

"I don't know why you'd think that," he said. "I've been here, just busy."

"But I've been trying to reach you all weekend." Saskia grasped his arm, then pulled away as if burned. Her smile held a touch of nervousness in it. "It doesn't matter now, anyway. You're safe and everything." She paused. "Now that I've found you, can we have a conversation?"

"I'm a little busy, can it wait?"

She turned, for the first time seeming to notice Kenna's presence in the small open kitchen. "Oh, sorry." Saskia stretched her mouth at the other girl before turning back to him. "It won't take long. I just have to ask you a small thing."

At the kitchen table, Kenna looked watchful, drinking her tea that Benoît was certain had gone cold, her face neutral.

"We can talk in the room," he said, wanting to spare Kenna what his old girlfriend had to say. Knowing Saskia, it could be any damn thing.

When he met her three years ago at university, he had been captivated by her slim brown body and the way she intellectually demolished everyone else in their class, even the professor. But shortly after they became lovers, he discovered that her manic energy came from cocaine and that she was as stupid about life choices as she was smart about academics. Ahead of him, Saskia opened the door to Benoît's bedroom and stepped inside. She sat on the low bed, waiting for him.

"*Ca va*, Saskia?"

"*Ja, ca va*," she murmured, shoving the dark hair from her face. "Well, no. I'm not really doing so well."

"Is it something to do with Pieter?" he asked.

"Sort of."

Something about Saskia's gaze made Benoît back away. He leaned against the wall and crossed his arms, waiting for what was to come. Saskia was a beautiful girl. Vibrant and enthusiastic about everything she did. She was an only child; her parents adored her and gave her everything that she even thought about asking for. When he and Saskia had been together, her parents often sent them to Ibiza, Barcelona, Paris, and anywhere else Saskia even hinted she wanted to go. Stefan and Elke Janssen had hopes that Benoît and Saskia would get married, but the relationship, under the pressure of Saskia's relentless drug use and clingy behavior, fell apart after the second year.

If he'd wanted a free ride through his life in Belgium, Benoît would have stayed with her and inoculated himself against her stupidity and limpet personality with regular infusions of cash from her family. That's what his friends had advised him to do, but Benoît had turned away from that option. He didn't want to be trapped with her and her parents in that way.

A year ago, Saskia found someone else. A young diamond dealer more on her level. Good looking, though not as nice as Benoît, and courteous enough to please the parents. Their wedding was less than one week away.

Saskia stood up. "What we had was good, right?" She walked toward him, her eyes wide pools of need. "Remember how things were with us? How we couldn't get enough of each other?"

"In the beginning, yes, things were good," he replied, cautiously unfolding his arms.

But in the end, things had gone badly. On their last day together, Saskia gave away most of his records to another DJ who had come to Benoît's apartment claiming to be a friend. Her naïveté had been staggering. Infuriating. But more so was the fact that she'd been high on coke damn near the whole day and if she'd taken the time to sober up before letting some stranger into his place, she would have known she was being played. And all the while Benoît raged at her, Saskia cried, saying she had only done what she thought he wanted her to. He walked away from her that evening, hardening his heart against her and her later attempts to get him back.

"And now, what about now?" Saskia asked him. "Can't things be good between us now?"

"You have a wedding coming soon, and it's not with me. There's nothing between us."

"But what if there could be?"

She came close, closer, close enough for him to grab her arms, preventing her from snuggling up to his chest, or worse, kissing him.

"That's not a question you should be asking," he said gently.

This was coming out of nowhere. The last time he'd seen Saskia she giggled to him about how happy she was with her fiancé and his Mercedes and access to the exclusive crowd of young-sexy rich kids running wild all over Europe.

She came by Orgy with two of her girlfriends when Benoît was playing and stayed after his set ended. He took the girls back to the quieter VIP rooms and they insisted on buying him drinks, flirting with him and each other until the club closed at six thirty in the morning. Flashing him hints of their breasts, touching each other teasingly while he watched. Practically grinding their asses in his lap each time one of them slipped past him in the booth to go the toilet. That night, Benoît wasn't sure what Saskia had been after.

Later, she told her friends to go home and asked him out for breakfast, then a lift back to her flat. Over coffee, she told him about her wonderful new life, her upcoming wedding, how happy she was that he'd gotten this opportunity to go to America. It had all been perfectly amicable and normal. A good-bye.

Now, Saskia pressed her palms against his chest. "I'll leave him if you say we can get back to how we were. I'll leave him. Today."

What? Benoît drew back. *Did she just—?* "No! Saskia, there's nothing for us to get back to. It's over."

"But you haven't been with anyone else since me. I know it's because you miss what we had."

"Come on." He gently squeezed her arms to get his point across. "This is not something you should do. Go ahead and get married. Have babies. Invest in someone who actually has something to give you."

"But that's you, Benoît. It's always been you." She sighed, a soft exhalation of sound, and slipped from his grip, dropping to her knees. "Don't deny how good things were between us." Her hands fumbled for his zipper, yanked it down.

"Saskia!" He grabbed her again and dragged her to her feet, ignoring his body's automatic response to warm fingers enclosing his dick through thin cotton, to her mouth a breath away from enveloping him. "Snap the fuck out of this. You're not doing either of us any favors right now."

Suddenly she sagged against him. "You don't want me, do you?" Her wet face pressed against his shirt.

"No, and you don't want me either." He rubbed her back in slow circles. More tears came, silent sobs that jerked her body against his and hooked her fingers in his back through his thin shirt.

Long seconds slipped by before she drew away, silently wiping at her eyes. "I just made a complete fool of myself, didn't I?"

Benoît tucked the hair out of her face and behind her ears, hugged her briefly before stepping away. "Define 'complete.'" He deliberately made his voice low and teasing.

Saskia chuckled weakly, unconvincingly. "Dammit, I swore to myself I wouldn't humiliate myself over you again." She pounded his chest once with a small fist, then backed up to drop heavily onto the bed.

Suddenly Benoît winced, another concern popping up out of nowhere to occupy his brain. Was Saskia able to smell the two days' worth of cum and sweat trapped in the sheets? He cleared his throat. "Come sit over here." He gestured to the thick leather loveseat against the wall. "I think the chair would be more comfortable."

"Why? I already smelled the sex when I walked in. Sitting in the chair is not going to make a difference at this point." Her big black eyes blinked wetly at him.

Benoît willed himself not to blush.

"That girl out there, is she the one you've been ignoring me for?" Saskia didn't get up from the bed.

"She's the one I've been spending time with, yes."

Hurt flickered across her face before she shielded it behind a cascade of hair. Then she scooted back in the bed and lay down in the sheets, pressed her face into a rumpled pillow. The one Benoît had used to prop up Kenna's ass as he fucked her from behind.

"I'm going," she said, voice muffled, eyes closed. "Good luck in America. I mean that."

Unease scuttled under Benoît's skin. He resisted the urge to jerk her from the bed and out of the apartment. With her laying there, wallowing in the remnants of something she would never have again, he was reminded of the end of their relationship. Saskia showing up at his gigs, at his classes, too many times on his doorstep, begging him to reconsider, until Cristian snared one of his friends into taking Saskia out, fucking her, until she forgot all about Benoît.

Saskia breathed deeply into the pillow again before getting up. She straightened her blouse, zipped up her jacket, and walked out the bedroom door, all without looking at him. By the time he had the presence of mind to follow her into the living room she was already out of the apartment.

"That looked pretty intense." Kenna used the remote to silence the television as she turned to him. She twisted on the couch and the hem of the sweatshirt crawled up her thighs.

Benoît turned to lock the front door, using those few seconds away from Kenna's eyes to push aside the unease that Saskia had stirred up.

"Yeah, but it was nothing really. Just an old girlfriend," he said. "Like you heard, she wanted to talk."

"Talk?"

She threw the remote aside on the sofa and came for him, brows raised. In her eyes blazed a thousand questions, the usual feminine ones that arose at the unexpected appearance of another woman. But she didn't voice these questions. She shoved lightly at his chest and he allowed it, realizing after a few surprised moments that she pushed him toward his room. Walking backward with her steadily prodding at his chest, he bumped into and bounced off the doorframe. Once inside, she twisted around to slam the door shut. Her eyes never left him.

"To *talk*, you take her into your bedroom?" Her smile was both tease and poison, as she pushed him onto the bed.

Sprawled on his back, he gave her the quick and clean version of what happened between him and Saskia moments before.

She climbed into the bed, planting herself between the sprawl of his legs. "Are you that good?" she asked.

"You tell me." Benoît resisted the urge to grin.

He liked where she was going with this. He liked it very much. Benoît watched her from beneath lowered lashes, sheets shifting against the bed as she crawled toward him, discarding her sweatshirt along the way. Her breasts. He licked his lips at the sight of her naked breasts, the dark tips already hard and tasting the air.

"I'm not sure." She tugged at his jeans, pulled them completely off. "Refresh my memory."

With a sigh of pleasure from them both, his dick was hard and hot in her hands. Expertly, she quickly reached for a condom in the bedside table drawer and slid it on without leaving him. She leaned down to wet his lips with her tongue, her nipples scoring his chest. Sensation quivered down his belly and he was helpless to the curl of his fingers at her waist. The tilt of her hips.

"Did she give you a hand job while I was waiting for you out there?" Kenna knelt above him, her pussy close but not close enough.

His hips jerked at the unexpected question. At the growl in her voice, as if she wanted him to say yes.

Benoît's silence damned him.

"She did, didn't she?"

"No, it was—ah!"

Kenna took the tip of his penis inside her, squeezing lightly around him, hot sucking kisses on the head of his cock.

"Go on," she urged, softly.

"She wanted to. I said no." He forced out the words around the heavy pulsing of blood in his hears, in his cock.

"Did you get hard for her?" She cupped his balls and lightly scraped her blunt fingertips against them. "Did you?"

The combined heat of her pussy and her eyes, the sure way she handled him, brought arousal, sure and powerful, surging through Benoît. He heaved up, but she neatly eluded his possession, taking his dick in just far enough inside for him to know the promise of her sex, but not for it to satisfy. *God!*

"Yes." He pushed the truth between his teeth. If he lied she would know and he'd never get to feel her fully clasp around his him. Not now. Not today.

"If I hadn't been here, would you have fucked her?"

"No." *God, no.* "Only you," he gasped, aching for her mercy.

"Good." Her pussy opened up and swallowed him.

Oh yes, she was good. Heat exploded in his belly and his head hit the bed. A groan arched out of him. Benoît didn't know he had been watching her, tense, until he felt the tension ease from his neck. "You feel so fucking *good,*" he whispered as her thighs flexed under his hands. "Incredible."

Kenna rolled her hips on him, squeezed. "I'm going to make sure that you never forget it," she hissed.

"Benoît?"

He froze at the incongruous voice. The bedroom door cracked open and a dark head peeked through.

"Fuck!" He shot up in the bed, grabbing up a sheet to cover Kenna's nakedness. She hopped off him and Benoît dragged a pillow across his lap. In the doorway, Saskia stared with wide, unblinking eyes.

"I—I just came in to give you back your flat key. You should have it back."

He should have had it back a long time ago—or had she taken the original and made a copy?—but this wasn't the time to discuss that. What the fuck was wrong with this girl that she thought it was okay to walk in here like this?

"Just leave it on the chair." He gestured vaguely to the armchair by the door, heart still racing.

"Why are you here?" Kenna's voice jerked him out of his shell shock.

Saskia dropped the key on the chair, then after a moment

when Benoît thought she wouldn't answer Kenna's question, repeated in English what she just told Benoît.

"I don't believe you," Kenna said. "Only an idiot wouldn't know what we were doing in here without having to walk in to see for themselves." Her eyes bored holes into Saskia. "Did you just want to see who has him now that you don't?" With the sheet still pulled up to her chest, she left the bed. "Or did you want to fuck him one last time before you go off to spend the rest of your life with some loser?" The sheet dragged across the floor with each step she took toward Saskia, then past her to shut the bedroom door. With a slightly raised eyebrow, Kenna looked back at Benoît.

He understood where she was going without her saying a word. Benoît shook his head. "This is *such* a bad idea."

But neither of them was listening to him. The women looked at each other, Kenna with curiosity on her face, Saskia with naked jealousy.

"Come in. Take one last look. If he lets you, taste him one last time. I don't blame you." Kenna's eyes flickered over him. "He's any straight girl's idea of a real good time, and he knows how to use the gifts God gave him. But you must know that already. That's why you're back here."

She secured the sheet under her arms and came up behind Saskia. Kenna pushed the other woman toward the bed. "Go on. You're getting one last chance to taste what you'll never have again. Go ahead. Taste."

"Wait a minute. Don't I have a say in this, too?" But his dick was immediately hard again, like stone, at the sight of Kenna behind Saskia. His ex-girlfriend with her unashamed longing that made her seem as naked as Kenna under that sheet. Kenna watched him with both amusement and an odd kind of determination.

"Move the pillow, baby," she said. "Let her see what she wants to."

His cock throbbed. When he lifted the pillow away, it rose, the mushroom head throbbing and purple, seeking.

"He can't help himself," Kenna crooned. "See. Little Ben wants you to have a taste, too." She gently nudged the girl forward until Saskia's knees hit the edge of the bed. Saskia glanced between him and Kenna, as if uncertain about what to do. Ducking her head, she pushed her hair behind her ears, allowed her eyes to meet his for the first time. There was no reason in those eyes, only desire.

"Kenna . . ." His voice was low and pleading. But he didn't know exactly what he pleaded for.

Saskia crawled into the bed toward a frozen Benoît, her eyes drinking in all of him, flickering over his face, chest, and the thick stalk of his cock. His entire body felt heavy, making it impossible to move, but he felt everything. The soft sheets under his thighs. The waves of warmth from the radiator heater under the window. Saskia's hands fisted around his dick, one over the other. Her hot mouth teased its thick head, hovering just over its jutting purple thickness. Then her tongue. *Mother of God!* Benoît groaned and only barely stopped himself from falling back into the bed. He locked his elbows. He wanted to watch the action in his lap. He wanted to watch Kenna.

Behind Saskia, Kenna dropped the sheet. She walked around the bed, closer to him, watching his face, watching his ex-girlfriend slurp his dick.

"Slow down," she murmured to Saskia, "Ben likes you to build up to it. You shouldn't have forgotten something like that."

He nearly exploded when Kenna walked Saskia through tasting him, guiding her to lick the long vein running the underside of his dick, swirl her tongue around its head, roll his balls in her hand, tongue the slit until his eyes squeezed shut and his world rolled on the verge of exploding.

Kenna was using Saskia to make love to him, to show his ex

what she would be missing and how well someone else would take care of him.

Jesus!

He buried his hands in Saskia's hair, his hips moving, the wet length of his dick appearing and disappearing into her mouth.

"He's going to fuck your mouth hard now. Just open your throat. Don't gag. That's good. But slow down, I don't want him to blow just yet."

Through eyes narrowed to slits, he watched Saskia yank down her zipper, plunge a hand inside her jeans to finger-fuck herself while her throat did its best to swallow him. His hips bucked.

Kenna climbed on the bed and firmly shoved him on his back. "Pay it forward, baby. You don't want to waste inspiration like this." She crouched over his face. Her pussy lips glistened. Kenna parted, then caressed her clit. And he was in heaven.

In his whole life, Benoît never thought Saskia would do anything like this. Never. She'd put him in her mouth often enough to get the job done, but never like this. With her crouched low over his lap and the wild musk of Kenna on his tongue it was like being trapped in a dream. Trapped because he knew Saskia would make more of this than it was. A dream because Kenna was the one crouched over him, murmuring soft words of encouragement as he ate her pussy.

He slid his tongue between the thick cunt lips, licking through the dense forest of hair that tickled his nose and chin. Her hips began to move above him, rolling like a lariat in the air as he lavished her clit with licks and sucks and hums of pleasure. Pushing her toward her orgasm even as Saskia's mouth sucked him toward oblivion.

Without Kenna's guidance, Saskia's technique faltered. She slowed down when she should have sped up. She licked when all he wanted her to do was suck him deep into the back of her throat. But the taste of Kenna on his tongue, the earthy flavor of her flowing down his throat, was enough. Her panting gasps of "oh God, yes, right fucking *there*!" pulled the tension tighter in his belly, caught him in *that* place.

He shouted his orgasm into the drizzling pussy above him, shouted and licked. Shouted and sucked. Shouted and gripped Kenna's hips until she was coming too, nearly drowning him in her joy. He was dimly aware of Saskia swallowing around his softening dick, of her mewling softly, a sound she only made just after she came.

Over him, Kenna sighed, pushed her pussy once against his face before taking her sweetness away. As Saskia's mouth released his dick, letting it fall heavily against his thigh, Kenna moved down to kneel at her shoulder. His ex's eyes shone brightly above her flushed cheeks. She licked her reddened lips.

"Did you enjoy him?" Kenna asked.

"Yes." Saskia's megawatt eyes found him, greedily opened to swallow the sight of him sprawled and vulnerable in the bed. The two women sat close, shoulder to shoulder, with Saskia's dark hair falling over Kenna's shoulder. They were close enough to kiss.

"Then I think it's time for you to go," Kenna told her. "Go home to your man. Ben is being well taken care of, so you don't have to worry about him anymore. Remember that last taste of him. Take it with you on your wedding night. Do whatever you need to do to get over him because today is all you're ever going to get."

"You're very lucky," Saskia said.

She wiped her mouth on the back of her hand, then shakily stood up from the bed. The look she gave Kenna was an oddly grateful one. She looked more satisfied than when she'd left the room nearly an hour before. This time she didn't say good-bye. She didn't have to. It was in the way she looked at him with finality before straightening her clothes and walking silently from the bedroom. Seconds later he heard the front door close behind her.

Shit. Benoît scraped a hand over his face. "I can't believe that just happened."

"What? You just had your dick sucked by a woman desperate to have you. That shouldn't be anything new."

"Trust me, that was definitely a unique situation." He groaned at the remembered intensity of it. Saskia's mouth on his dick. Kenna's voice in his ear. *God!*

"I take it you enjoyed yourself?" Laughter hovered around her words.

"Very much. I don't know whether to thank you or throw you out." He pulled up a pillow and shoved it under his head. "Why did you do that?"

Kenna's mouth tilted in a smile. "I've seen women like her before. And I always thought if these girls just got one last real look at the thing they want, if they got the chance to touch it and taste it in a setting that sets up the finality of that encounter, then they'll get over it. In your friend's case, you allowing her to suck you off without a trace of reciprocity while you channel all your energy into pleasing another woman shows her what a selfish prick you are. If she gave up her man to marry you she'd never have your respect, or your attention."

"So that was your solution to getting her to leave me alone, show her what an asshole I am?"

"It worked, didn't it? Not to mention you got a decent blow job out of it."

"Like I said, I don't know whether to thank you or throw you out." He sighed the words, lethargic while his senses lay in a puddle in his lap.

She chuckled and flopped down next to him in the bed. The mattress dipped, then settled. "You better hold on tight to me, cutie. You'll never get this lucky again."

That was his cue to laugh, but Benoît found himself swallowing instead. He had gotten truly lucky when he found her on Friday night. She was everything he'd wanted but had never been ready for. Smart. Vibrant. Perceptive. Sexy. Very sexy. After this weekend was over, would he be able to carry on with his life as if nothing significant had happened to him?

"So what do you think this is, this thing between us?"

He looked up, startled at Kenna's question. As if she'd read his mind.

She settled on his chest, her soft body draped over his, waiting.

"This has been one of the best weekends of my life," he said.

Despite his earlier thoughts. Despite that she was an incredible woman he would probably never meet the likes of again, Benoît wasn't willing to pursue this thing any further. He knew the role of a vacation fuck in the bigger scheme of life. Hit it, get on that plane and never look back. He'd seen too many horror shows—people who wanted to keep that endless orgasm after the vacation was over. It never ended well.

His father had been a vacation fuck. His mother imported him to Belgium from Haiti and once Claude had gotten his Belgian citizenship and gotten her pregnant, he was gone. On to the next white woman who could satisfy his parasitic thirst for a new experience.

Kenna's face slowly closed itself off from him. Eyes lowered, the caressing fingers over his skin stilled.

"It has been fun, hasn't it? When I get back to the States I'm going to be so pissed that there aren't more boys like you." Her smile flickered on, then off. "That's how it goes sometimes, right?"

7

Monday Predawn

A shaft of gray light slanted through the bare window, filling in the faint shapes and colors of Benoît's room. The sofa covered with discarded clothes in tones of green and dark. On the bedside table, his small stack of books, including the Neruda collection Kenna said meant more than it did. Monday morning.

Beside him, she lay still, snoring gently through her open mouth, chest moving up and down with her breath.

He had set the alarm but woke long before it, getting barely two hours of sleep. His body knew today was the last day it would be with Kenna. The plane taking him to America would leave the Brussels airport at ten and he needed to be at the airport no later than eight thirty. Benoît ignored the not-so-silent ticking of the bedside clock.

On the pillow, Kenna's face seemed steeped in innocence, oblivious to everything but the dreams parading behind her twitching eyelids. It seemed a shame to wake her.

Since they'd gotten together, by silent and mutual agreement they hadn't talked about their future or their past, except for in the most generic way. Kenna hadn't shown any interest in why he was leaving, he hadn't asked about her life in America. But suddenly Benoît was curious. He wanted to know about her. What her dreams were. If she believed in God or Allah or nothing. If she had her mother's smile or her father's eyes. If she believed in a future for them. He wanted to know.

He toyed with a plait curling around her ear. With a soft moan, she shifted and turned over. Her eyes flickered open.

"Hey, cutie," she rasped.

He smoothed her hair again. "Morning."

"Is it? I feel like I just fell asleep."

"You did, but it's still morning." He manufactured a smile for her. "Unfortunately."

"Yeah." She buried her face in his neck. "All I want is one more day."

"Then another and another. I know." He trailed fingers along the back of her neck. "But we don't have that."

Curled against his, her body felt perfect, as if it had been made to fit, for her to live here in his arms. He drew in the scent of her, of their sex on her skin. Last night she'd burned candles in mourning for their last evening together. As he'd moved inside her clinging wetness, ass clenching, his whole body intent on pleasing and savoring every drop of her, Benoît had been aware of sadness hunting for him. It found him now. In the early morning, with her soft weight pressing down on him and her breath playing at his throat, he already felt bereaved. Without.

His fingers curled into her neck.

8

Monday morning

The warm length of her pressed against Benoît's side as they walked through the chill, quiet streets back to her friend's flat. Their breaths frosted the air. Footsteps slapped gently against the cobblestoned walk. Only an occasional car passed, twin headlights piercing the dark as it growled past. In an hour, the trams would start rumbling through the streets again, signaling the official awakening of a new day.

Kenna looked up at him. "After this weekend I'm glad I came here in the winter. Being here with you in this weather feels special. Like it's just me and you on the streets, sharing this . . . whatever it is." Her mouth tilted in a far-off smile.

Whatever it is. Benoît squeezed her to him in answer. Wordlessly agreeing. In the summer, all they had experienced over the last couple of days would be a cliché. Summer love. Summer lust. But this heat between them in the middle of winter was hard to dismiss as "usual." Benoît never thought he'd look back on Belgium with regret, but now that he'd met Kenna in his last days there, he regretted not meeting her sooner. Not getting the chance to spend more time with her. Not being able to take her warmth with him.

Approaching her friend's flat, their steps slowed. Light in the third-floor apartment glowed weakly in the gray morning. A few early travelers pushed steadily through the predawn, most with one hand shoved in their pocket, the other occupied with a cigarette while their breath and smoke clouded the air. Cold nipped at Benoît's face. He and Kenna stopped in front of the building, staring steadily at each other. There was no way he would be able to find someone else like her as long as he lived.

"I don't want to say that I'll miss you, even though I will." Kenna said finally.

Benoît wanted to tell her everything that was sitting on his chest and making it hard to breathe. But he said nothing. They were flying away from each other and he couldn't do a damn thing about it. America was a huge country. He didn't even want to disappoint himself by asking her where she lived. It seemed impossible.

"You'll get over me," he said with a slow smile, swallowing past the lump in his throat.

She clenched her hands in the front of his jacket and leaned close. "Yeah."

Benoît closed his eyes. Her hair still held the scent of his bedroom, the candles she'd burned as they made love for the last time. The coffee and cakes they shared in bed before reluctantly getting up to make their way to her friend's flat.

"You came at the worst possible time," he said, allowing the sadness to finally take over his face. "I want this to last longer."

She made a sound that muffled against his jacket, between a sob and a laugh. Then she pulled away. "Shut up and leave or you're going to make me cry." But her face was already wet.

"Take this." Biting her lip, Kenna shoved a piece of paper into his back jeans pocket.

"Copping one last feel?"

"It's my address and phone number in America. If you're ever in my neighborhood, give me a call or something."

Benoît paused. "Okay."

They both knew he would never look at her address, never call her number. Already, Benoît could feel the paper crumpling in his pocket, halfway to the trashcan. He kissed Kenna. Offered that simple press of flesh that was the last thing they would ever share.

She closed her eyes, pushed weakly at his chest. "Go. You have a plane to catch."

"Okay," he said again. "Okay."

His words had run away from him. An incredible woman would soon be out of his life forever. Once he left her here, in front of this squat marbled building, things were finished. And he couldn't even tell her what their time together had meant to him.

"When it's your turn, have a good trip."

The meaningless words fell heavily off his tongue. She flinched from them, stuffed her hands in her pockets, and backed slowly away until her back pressed against the building's front door.

"See you around." Kenna bit her lips together, gaze flickering away, anywhere but at him.

He forced himself to watch her wrestle the keys from her pocket and unlock the building. She ducked inside and quickly closed the door. Behind the thick frosted glass, her silhouette paused with its head down, frozen for a moment in thought or pain, before disappearing completely.

Asshole. He hissed the curse at himself, but it didn't make her reappear at the door.

I love this woman. The thought floated through his head, but he ignored it. *This is just a vacation fuck. Move on.*

He turned away from the building, cupping his hands around a cigarette to light it. If he tried hard enough, maybe he could convince himself that it was the trailing gray smoke from the cigarette that burned his eyes. Maybe he could convince himself that it was the smoke and not that last image of her behind the glass. Frozen and alone. Away from him.

9

Atlanta, Georgia: Spring
Monday afternoon

A Georgia Power truck honked its horn, startling Kenna into looking up from the depths of her shoulder bag. The light was still red. It wasn't their turn to cross the street.

Beside her, her friend and roommate, Doreen, narrowed her eyes at the slowly passing truck. "What's his problem?"

"I'm sure he's just showing his appreciation for your fine form." Kenna said, her hand emerging from the bag in triumph. She slipped on the newly found sunglasses. Behind the amber tinted lenses, her eyes relaxed their squint against the noonday sun.

Doreen sucked her teeth. "Well, he needs to show proper appreciation instead of beeping at me like some hood rat."

Kenna didn't know how that proper appreciation would look like since the man *was* cruising past in his work truck. "You're asking for entirely too much," she told her friend, adjusting the oversized black handbag on her shoulder.

The light changed and the two women surged across the street with the rest of the downtown pedestrian traffic. With her sunglasses out, the bag—now carrying the books from her two morning classes, her purse, and some paperwork for her internship later that afternoon—actually felt heavier. Kenna sighed. The day was half over but still felt like it had a long way to go. She sighed.

"Come on, honey. It can't be that bad," Doreen said.

The heels of her stilettos attacked the pavement as they crossed the busy street. Her low-cut natural, slim physique and silky black skin attracted more than a few admiring stares on the way. Doreen strutted, stepping quickly and gracefully, as if moving across a catwalk.

At twenty-four, Doreen was an assistant bank manager and steadily working her way up the corporate ladder. Although she could more than afford her own place, she chose to share the Candler Park condo with Kenna, saving most of her money but spending the rest on expensive indulgences like her 3 Series BMW convertible and the lunch she and Kenna were on their way to.

"Of course it's not that bad," Kenna said in response to her friend's earlier comment. "But I—"

A burst of French from close by whipped her head around. Kenna's palms, suddenly damp with sweat, slid down the handle of her bag while her frantic gaze searched the crowd of faces for someone familiar. But it was only a group of kids from the university. They poured from a nearby building, their voices raised in laughter and excitement, sprinkling a medley of French, English, and some other language she didn't recognize into the air. No medium-height, light-skinned boy walked among them.

"Oh, shit," Doreen said. "I know that look." She peered at Kenna through the dark lenses of her shades. Reached over to squeeze her waist and urge her to keep walking. "You need to get over that foreign Negro. Right now."

Heat rushed into Kenna's face. Yeah, she was a mess. After three months she was starting to think she'd never stop seeing him in the faces of strangers.

The first few times it happened her heart literally skipped a beat. She thought it was him. She was *certain* it was him. But the pale skin, long lashes, and curving mouth resolved themselves into someone else, never as compelling as the original, who returned her stare with an interested smile, or simply walked past her as she if wasn't there. She felt stupid for looking. For trying to find someone on the streets of Atlanta she'd left behind half a world away.

A group of office workers, like a storm cloud in their shades of gray and black, poured from the doors of the Jewish deli and onto the sidewalk, nearly pushing the women into the street. Kenna and Doreen shoved their way through them, bumping shoulders and arms. They didn't bother with apologies.

"Girl, that must have been some good dick 'cause your head hasn't been right since you got back."

Kenna playfully shoved at her friend. "Stop getting in my business."

But Doreen was right, as usual. School already started for the spring semester, her last semester at Georgia State University, and she was barely able to focus long enough to finish her homework. Kenna felt stupid. She bet that wherever Benoît was, he wasn't wasting his time obsessing about her.

She'd given him her number, although she felt embarrassed about it immediately afterward. He never contacted her.

These days, other than her helpless obsession with the boy, her internship at CNN was the only thing that demanded and kept her attention. Mainly because it was a *paid* internship and she really needed the cash right now.

When Kenna first got back from Belgium, she hadn't been

able to talk about him. He was a secret dream she kept close until her best friend and roommate finally wore her down, interrogating her about the lost look she wore. With Benoît she had become another person. Done things, felt things, that the Kenna in Atlanta never even dreamed of. She missed that Kenna. She missed him. She spilled everything and for a long time Doreen only stared at her with her mouth hanging open.

"You did *not* do that shit!" her friend finally screamed, laughter riding on her voice.

But Kenna had done all those things and she relived every moment in the privacy of her dark room every night before she fell asleep. The way he looked, how he kissed her with his whole body, his distinct accent that made every word he spoke an invitation to sex.

"Well," Doreen said with a flashing grin. "Hopefully this fabulous lunch that I'm about to buy you and that damn good job offer you just got will help you through nights without your stud."

Cutting through the afternoon lunch crowd ahead of Kenna, Doreen stepped neatly through the revolving glass door of the hotel lobby. She waited for Kenna to catch up with her before she headed for the elevator that would take them to the top-floor restaurant.

"Anything's possible," Kenna said, meeting her friend's smile with a tentative one of her own.

"You know, I think you need some hair of the dog," Doreen said.

As they stepped up to the hostess's station, Kenna forced herself to snap her mouth shut. The girl, voluptuous in a black dress and high heels, gave them a professional but friendly smile before showing them to their reserved table. As soon as they were left alone, Kenna swung around to face her friend.

"What?!"

"You heard me, girl. You need some new local dick to make you forget about that old foreign dick."

"Jesus."

"He's got nothing to do with this." Doreen took her time looking around the restaurant filling fast with the business lunch crowd. She was single and very much on the prowl. "I guarantee if you take my prescription you'll be all better in no time."

A waiter appeared at Kenna's elbow with menus and an inquiry about what kind of water they'd like. He darted off and was back with superhuman quickness carrying Kenna's tap water—no ice, no lemon—and Doreen's Voss. In a crisp and clear voice, like a stage actor's, he informed them of the restaurant's specials and the wines that went with them. Having studied the menu online ever since her friend told her she was taking her there for lunch, Kenna already knew what she wanted. They both ordered their entrées and sent the waiter on his way.

When they sat alone again, Kenna sighed. "Everything isn't about sex, Doreen."

"But your vacation obviously was, so you need to get over it." Her friend tilted her head to consider Kenna, her nearly black eyes pinning her like a bug. "Look, girl, I've never seen you get this messed up over a guy. Before all this, you had your head on straight. Your European fuck isn't even thinking about you."

Doreen unfolded her napkin and draped it across her lap. Took a sip of her bottled water. "Before you left, I was proud of the way you kept yourself above all that shit. When you get with a guy you keep it light. If he starts drama you drop him and move on. I wished I was like that. But the way you're acting now, it's like you've been saving up all that drama and fucked-up anxiety for this one Negro. Get over him. This is Atlanta. There are a thousand guys here just like him."

Kenna nodded. She knew her friend was right. It wasn't worth torturing herself over Ben. She thought they'd had a connection walking around the streets of Antwerp sharing tiny pieces of themselves with each other.

"I know."

"Good. The one thing I hate is to see a sister down, especially you." Doreen reached over and squeezed her hand. "Now look around this place. Don't tell me with all these fine specimens of black manhood you can't find something to take home with you some night."

"You don't have to keep pushing men on me, Doreen. I get it. Get over him. I will. We can drop the subject now, I promise."

"Really?"

"Yes."

"Good. Then we can talk about me." Doreen wriggled in her seat, smiling. "I met this *fine* brotha in the bank today. Can you believe he had the nerve to slip me a note asking if I had any panties on?"

Kenna shook her head and chuckled.

Doreen's nagging aside, their lunch was incredible. The pan-seared trout on a bed of steamed broccolini and shiitake mushrooms went perfectly with the side of whipped sweet potatoes. Kenna ate every single last bite. From the way she moaned with nearly every forkful, Doreen's herb-rubbed grilled scallops were just as good.

"Thanks for lunch, Doreen." Kenna patted her mouth with the napkin. "When I get my first paycheck I'll take you somewhere nice, too. For dinner."

Her roommate laughed. "Don't feel like you owe me, Kenna. After everything you've done for me, you deserve more than a nice meal. If I wasn't leaving tonight for Charleston to go to that damn conference, I'd have taken you out to dinner."

"This was perfect. With lunch prices this high, I can't even imagine what this place charges for dinner."

"It's manageable, believe me."

Their magical waiter made another appearance. "Was everything to your satisfaction, ladies?"

"Yes, everything was perfect. Thank you."

"Can I get you anything else?"

Doreen put her wallet on the table. "No, just the check."

He produced a small black folder from behind his back and placed it in the middle of the table.

Talk about service. Kenna looked on in amazement.

"I can take that whenever you're ready."

"We're ready now," Doreen said. She slipped four twenties into the folder and handed it back to him. "We don't need any change."

"Thank you, madams. It was my pleasure to serve you this afternoon." He sketched a brief bow and revealed a row of crooked teeth. "Enjoy the rest of your day."

They thanked him again and stood up to leave.

"That was nice. It's too bad we couldn't stay a little longer. There was a lot of eye candy in that place," Doreen said.

Even Kenna had to agree with that. The restaurant had a fine share of suits and ties and $100 haircuts, if a girl was into that kind of thing. "I'm surprised you don't make this your regular lunchtime hangout." She smirked.

"Uh uh, honey. I'm not going to spend my money cruising these boys when I can sit in the park with my sandwich and watch them for free."

"But at least in the restaurant they'd ask for your number. In the park, I dunno. They'd probably just ask for a blow job, no matter how nice you dress."

Doreen laughed. "You might have a point."

They moved through the thinning crowd toward the door, their arms looped together, laughing. As they approached the elevator, it chimed and the doors glided open.

"Perfect timing."

About half a dozen men, more suits, spilled from the elevator.

"Excuse me, ladies," they murmured politely and let Kenna and Doreen pass.

One of them held the elevator for them. Gray suit, not very tall, with a silver star-shaped lapel pin. She got into the elevator behind Doreen.

"Thank you," Kenna said with a smile. "I just love a Southern gentleman."

Startled light brown eyes jerked to hers. She gasped.

"Kenna?"

The elevator doors slid shut.

Doreen pulled a packet of mints from her purse, popped one in her mouth, and offered the pack to Kenna. "He's cute. You know him?"

"I—" She shouldn't but she did. Those clear brown eyes. The way he just said her name. "Oh my God! I have to get back up there." Kenna pushed the button for the top floor. She pressed a hand to her chest. Her heart raced, felt as if it would burst from its cage any minute. "Oh my God!"

Doreen grabbed Kenna's shoulders. "Are you okay?"

"That was him!"

"Him who?"

"The boy from Europe. The one."

Doreen straightened and the worry left her face. "Are you shittin' me? You know that's next to impossible, right?"

The elevator dipped toward the ground floor, agitating her

suddenly nervous stomach. "I don't care. I have to get back up to the restaurant."

"Are you sure you're not hallucinating?"

The way he said her name. "I'm sure."

Of all the times she'd thought of Ben, she never pictured him this way. In a suit, with his hair grown out. In a restaurant with dozens of other men who, except for the fact that he made her heart hurt, looked just like him. This was no hallucination or nighttime fantasy.

The long ride down to the lobby with several stops in between to let people on and off helped to calm Kenna's racing pulse. Doreen stood next to her, alternately rubbing Kenna's back and checking her face for signs of insanity.

"I swear I saw him."

"Do you want me to come up there with you?"

"No, no, it's okay. I know you have to get back to work." Kenna glanced at her watch. It was almost two o'clock. She had to be at her internship by three.

"You sure? It's no big deal if I'm late." Doreen's tough-girl facade fell away in the wake of her concern.

"I'll call you. And—" Kenna trembled. This seemed so impossible. Why would he even be here? In her city?

Doreen squeezed her shoulder. "I don't even know why I ask you." She pulled out her phone and dialed a number.

"Ricky, I'm going to be a little late from lunch, maybe fifteen minutes or so. Could you let everyone know? Thank you." She closed the phone and put it back in her purse.

Kenna bit her lip. "Thank you."

The elevator finally made it to the lobby. It slid open and more people got on. Kenna pressed the button for the top floor again.

"Hold the elevator, please."

And he stepped on.

Ben, this new Ben, stopped and looked at her as if he didn't know what to do now that they stood face-to-face.

"It *is* you." She twisted her fingers together to stop herself from touching him.

"Kenna." He said her name with a throbbing urgency.

The other people on the elevator looked at him, looked at her. Beside her, Doreen drew a quick breath.

"Damn. Now I see why you couldn't forget him."

But this was not the man she left behind. Not this elegant gentleman with skin tanned to a luscious caramel, hair in a riot of short curls on his head, long enough to be sexy, short enough to be neat. He looked like he'd just stepped off the cover of a magazine. Too beautiful.

"Do you live here?"

She could only nod.

He reached into his jacket pocket. "I have to go back to my meeting, but take my card. Call me tonight, okay?"

She turned the card over in her hand, remembering when she had passed him her address and phone number a lifetime ago. Despite that scalding memory, Kenna drank him up. She felt the elevator's blind rush back to the top floor, made no effort to stop at a lower floor to get off the elevator and continue with her day. He watched her, his honey colored eyes intent, never once leaving her face.

Kenna wanted to peel off his clothes, to get to the familiar body, destroy the suit that made him a stranger. She wanted to feel him under her hands to know that he was real and this elevator encounter was no hallucination.

"Okay. I'll call."

The elevator bell sounded, the car jerked to a stop. She stared after him as he walked out and disappeared around the corner into the polished wood interior of the restaurant.

Kenna sagged against the wall.

"Shit." Doreen dragged out the word, watching for the last

signs of his straight-backed figure melting into the restaurant crowd. "That's one sexy motherfucker."

In Kenna's palm, the card Ben gave her shone white against her skin. She read the neatly stamped black script for the first time.

Denis Benoît, Architect.

She stared at the closed doors of the elevator. Had she really known anything about him?

10

Monday evening

For the first time since Kenna had started her internship at CNN, she wished she was somewhere else. Among the TV monitors and frenetic rush of activity and constantly smiling faces she'd once found exhilarating, Kenna now felt resentful. All day, Ben's card burned her skin through the hip pocket of her slacks. The imprint of it felt like his hand, warm and compelling, urging her to run away from work to be with him.

Antwerp nights haunted her. While Kenna made phone calls, booked guests for shows, ran to get coffee, she remembered. His hands pressing her thighs open, while his mouth hovered an aching millimeter away. How he laughed, throwing his head back, with his pale eyes still sparkling on her face.

One evening he'd read to her. He picked at random from the Neruda collection, easily wrapping his tongue around the Spanish words before offering her the English translation of "Algunas Bestias," then the Dutch. When the last words of the poem were nothing but memories in the air, Kenna finally acknowledged that she had fallen in love with him.

When it was time to leave work, she rushed out of the building, her thoughts running in circles, her feet on automatic pilot through the downtown rush. Skyscrapers rose up around her from all sides, the noise and filth of traffic, exhaust in the air, the occasional burp of a car horn. She brushed shoulders with other pedestrians, most dashing toward the train station, others meandering under scaffolded buildings as if they had no particular place to go. The workday was over.

Kenna clutched her shoulder bag, finally fighting the rising sense of excitement. He was really here. In Atlanta. But did it mean anything? The excitement died in her just a little. Only when her idle footsteps took her before a revolving glass door did Kenna realize where she wanted to go. Home would be an empty, meaningless place with Doreen already gone to her conference. Even her friend's mindless chatter and inappropriate questions would have been a welcome respite from her whirling thoughts.

She stepped into the copper-walled elevator. Nodded at the others already waiting inside. At it rose, Kenna faced the transparent rear of the car showing the city. Spring was just beginning to burst on Atlanta. Branches that had been naked when she first got back from Europe now nursed tiny budding blossoms. Women had already abandoned their thick coats and slacks for Capri pants and twinsets. The men not sporting suits strolled alongside them in designer jeans and sweater vests over short-sleeved shirts. This was the first time she noticed any of that.

When the elevator's bell chimed she turned away from the view. Instead of heading into the restaurant, she went up the spiral staircase to the less formal lounge.

Today, he was here. At the bar, she ordered a whiskey sour, took a sip of the drink's sweet heat, then went up another set of stairs, truly the top floor of the building with its transparent glass dome cover that deflected most of the sun's heat. A few giant palms lay scattered around the solarium, the fronds hovering over chairs and tables to provide even more protection from the sun. Below, the city sparkled like a newly polished stone.

Kenna had read about the solarium online and thought that the idea of it was beautiful. The reality of the place was even more so. The few people in the room seemed too caught up in their own worlds to pay attention to anyone else. Their conversations, their solitary drinks, the palm trees' friendly shadows swaying in the air-conditioned breeze, all these things held their separate attentions.

A pair of familiar eyes found and held hers. She crossed the room, conscious, suddenly, of the sway in her hips, the way the slacks clasped her ass, how the pale green blouse sat over her breasts, hugging and releasing her flesh with each breath.

"After this, you can't tell me you don't believe in destiny," she said.

He'd watched her walk across the room, no surprise in his face. His jacket gone. The tie loosened. A glass of beer the same color as his eyes held loosely in one hand.

"Right now, I'd believe in Saint Nicholas if he was the one responsible for bringing you here."

At the words, her heart faltered in her chest. Then accelerated. Kenna took a slow sip of her drink, feeling the same bubbling heat begin to rise between them. She licked the sticky rim of the cup, felt the glass's smoothness under her tongue, felt the way he watched her with that familiar hunger. His eyes darkened. Suddenly, their surroundings ceased to matter. His suit became just another covering over the body she knew so well three months before.

"I think you did this all on your own, baby," she murmured.

Benoît smiled and reached for her hand.

It was the same. The press of his palm against her palm brought a rush of electricity, not static, but active and fierce, under her skin. She felt every nerve, every molecule of her body respond to him. It was the same.

"Come home with me."

Kenna tightened her fingers around his. "No." She flinched from the hurt that flashed in his pale eyes then quickly disappeared with a flicker of his long lashes. "What I mean is," and she stepped close to feed him her body's warmth, "*you* should come home with me. I want to share some of myself with you."

His lashes lifted, and she saw the smile in his eyes long before it materialized on his lips.

"I think I can do that."

11

Monday night

His skin tasted the same as before. Peppery musk. The sweat of a hard day's work. And his scent was the same. But his kisses burned more deeply when he pressed her into the bed, rediscovering her mouth with his tongue, sucking on her lips, biting them. He was liquid between her thighs, fucking her with long, thorough strokes, holding her down, keeping the control that she'd fought him so hard for in the past.

Ben pressed into her and she clung to him. The vise of his hand around her wrists, welcome. His dick angled perfectly to skim her clit with each stroke. Every breath she took in was his. Kenna gasped under him, moaned deep in her throat as he fucked her, grunting through their kisses.

There had been no preliminaries when they stepped into her apartment. No appreciative glance around her apartment from him. No offer to see more from her. They stripped each other quickly, tongues and mouths meeting in frantic haste. Somehow they found a condom and fucked on the living-room floor like animals. Her leg thrown over his shoulder and him guiding himself urgently into her juiced and waiting pussy. Her fingers sinking into the back of his neck. Short, stabbing jerks of his hips. Both of them coming quickly. Shouts. Screams. Pleasure lashing their flesh. Then they untangled themselves, grabbed up their clothes, and stumbled to her bedroom for more.

The three months apart had made him ravenous. He ate her pussy like he thought he'd never taste it again. Lapping up her juices, fucking her with his tongue until Kenna wailed in orgasm, then twitched, crawled backward to get away from his insistent attentions to her sensitive clit. Ben didn't let up. He buried his face in her pussy, smearing her cum all over his face until he was hard again. That's when the kissing started. That's when they began to make love.

Afterward. After the sweat dried and their gasps died away, they lay together under the thin sheet. The air conditioner droned quietly over them.

Kenna buried her face in his throat. Bit his skin. It felt so good to have him close again.

His warm breath blew softly against her ear. "I didn't know you lived here," he said.

"I didn't know you were an architect."

In the dark his honey eyes burned into hers, alive and loving. "There's a lot we don't know about each other." He paused. "But if you're willing, we can take the time to learn."

Kenna laughed, caught off guard by the surge of happiness in her chest. She hovered above him, smiling. "I'd like that," she said. "I'd like that very much."

Driving My Man Wild

Sydney Molare

1

"Uhmmm."

I was close.

So, so close.

Tingling in my clit; tightening of my pussy. Thighs bunched, unbunched as legs searched for the best position to reach nirvana.

Eager fingers stroked, rubbed, rotated faster up and down, side to side, over my slick, viscous tissue. I widened my thighs until they caressed the sides of the tub, gave me better access to my watery triangle.

In. Out. Shallow. Deep. Mash. Pinch. Brush. Slide.

Middle finger pushed past labial lips swollen in desire, stroked deep inside my hungry pussy, let the walls contract, release around slick fingers, before sliding up to cover my clit. I diddled my nub; mashed back and forth across the stiff minipenis. My head rolled backward as needle pricks flowed upward from my feet; forced me to stroke fast—

"Honeyyyy!"

Shit! Jare's home!

I was close, but I wasn't close enough to enjoy finishing my-self off before he hit the bathroom. And the last thing I wanted was for my husband to catch me pleasuring myself. The one and only time he did, the resultant conversation was one I didn't care to repeat again this lifetime.

But just once, I wanted Jare to see me pleasuring myself, his cock hard watching me as I loved me and knowing it took nothing away from us. Just once. Instead, I lurched upright, the wake extinguishing some of the candles I'd placed around the sides. Great. So much for planning.

I'd *planned* to be laying here in the tub, seductively secluded in bubbles, candlelight hiding all my flaws, waiting to "show him what I'm working with." Instead, he's late—four hours late to be exact—the water is cool and the candles are just about on their last sputter. Hence, the masturbation since I was *past* ready and he wasn't available.

Hearing his steps grow closer, I slide lower in the tub, arch my back—elevating my breasts in the cloudy water—and plas-ter an inviting smile on my lips.

This will have to do for now.

"Babe, why you got the lights all off?" Jare flipped on the switch, the aura created by the candles immediately extin-guished.

Damn! My flaws were itching to jump up out of the water and reveal themselves. "Well—"

"And all these candles. You've got them all over the bed-room and you're in here. Are you trying to burn the house down now?" He looked around, eyes wide and uncompre-hending. It's obvious the sight of the half-moons of my breasts floating above the water were *not* exciting him in the least.

I lifted my breasts higher while ignoring the ache in my lower back. "Ah . . . well—"

"You still in the tub at this hour?" He glanced at me then

back at the candles. "I'd of thought you would be in bed by now."

Me too, with you wrapped around my body. The thought never had a chance to reach my vocal cords as he continued.

"I'm beat." He looked it. I could see the tiredness lines wiggling across his forehead. "We really got a lot done tonight. I probably should have skipped the last basketball game, though. I'm too out of shape." He patted his rotund belly before slipping his shirt off.

Watching him, I winched, thinking back to when his now "early pregnancy" belly was trim and sporting a six-pack. I pinched my own abundant inches beneath the water. *The pot talking about the kettle.* Well, at least he's got eight inches—that he knows how to use—to make up for it.

Turn around, baby. Just turn around.

But his back stayed to me as the underwear slid down his skinny hips and pooled at his feet. His love handles jiggle as he turns the knobs of the shower. "I'm just gonna grab a shower and hit the sack."

I tried to relax my face and smile, but my eyes snatched control and squinted anyway. So much for butt-romping sex. My back sighed in relief as I let the arch out and my breasts slid beneath the water again.

"Jare?"

"Yeah, babe?" He looked back at me, still fiddling with the knobs.

"You hungry? I cooked." And did I. Pan-roasted steak, mashed potatoes with gravy, candied yams, and collard greens with cornbread. My mama would be proud. Maybe this is just sex delayed. My breasts lifted again at this thought.

"Naw. I ate over at Mike's."

Great. Just damn great. Two hours slaving over the stove, *then* heating and reheating the mess until it ought to be stuck to the pan, and he's already had dinner. Wonderful. My breasts slid back out of view.

The shower door closed and he began that awful whistling that raked my nerves raw. I snatched the plug from the drain and rose, ignoring the mirror that beckoned me to look. I didn't have to look to see Jare wasn't the only one that needed to put a little more exercise in his day.

I slap-dried off, grabbed my nightgown from the bed, simultaneously slipping it over my head while stepping into my panties. I blew out the candles on the dresser and walked back in the bathroom to extinguish those. At that moment, Jare cut off the water and opened the shower door, fanning the steam into the bedroom, which took its cue in this travesty and drifted into the hallway. In seconds, the smoke detector began its annoying scream.

I rushed from the room, my hastily grabbed towel flapping all around the irritating whining device, trying to silence it before our son, Lucky, woke up.

"Berze! See!" Jare was coughing, his face scrunched tight. "All these doggone candles. You 'bout to choke me to death!"

Puh-lease! The smoke was bad, but it wasn't *that* bad. I fanned and kept the harsh comments my mind was zinging to my mouth to myself.

"Mommmmy!" The scared cry comes from down the hallway.

This is just beauteous. Add Lucky's crying to the mix.

"You woke up Luck. We won't get a drop of sleep with him crying and whining now," Jare cried and whined himself.

"I know. I'm sorry. I'll get him," I spit out, walking quickly down the hallway to Lucky's bedroom. Lucky was sitting up, eyes wet, little whimpers from his mouth. My heart softened. "It's all right. Mama's here, baby," I cooed, taking him into my arms.

"What's that noise? Are we going to die?" His wide eyes stared into mine. Mercifully, the smoke detector goes silent.

"No. It's the smoke detector. Mommy set it off by accident." I heard Jare enter the room, but I don't turn to look at him.

"Daddy!" Lucky jumped from my arms and into Jare's waiting ones.

"Hey, big guy! I know we gave you a scare, but it's all right now." Jare hugged him to his chest, Lucky's behind perched on that protruding belly.

"You sure?" Fright still laced Lucky's voice.

"Yeah. Everything is just fine." Jare's voice is silky smooth. "If you want, I can sit here with you while you go back to sleep."

"Please! Please! Please!" Lucky grabbed Jare around the neck, squeezing tightly.

"Sure will." Jare settled them both on the bed. Our eyes met, his tired and accusing; mine, irritable. "Say good night to Mommy."

Definitely no sex tonight!

"G'night, Mama. Sleep tight," Lucky sang out.

"You too, baby." I kissed his forehead before he plopped back on his pillow. "Y'all want the lights on?"

"Naw. We'll be fine with just the night-light," Jare answered, his voice thick.

"All right then." I walked stiffly through the door and back to our bedroom. The smoky smell was strongest there, but I don't even try to shift the smoke anymore as I snatch back the covers and pull them over my head.

Hell, if I die . . . I'm just dead.

2

"How much?"

The tall woman lifted the vase from my hands, turned it side to side, then looked under the bottom before handing it back. "Five dollars."

"Sold." I fished out five dollars and handed them over before she changed her mind.

"Don't leave yet. Look around," she encouraged before helping another customer.

I turned the vase over in my hands before storing it inside my huge purse. This was the reason I loved yard sales. Most people didn't have a clue as to what things were worth. I'd be able to sell this vase on eBay for more than a hundred dollars. With that thought, I fished out the vase and smiled at it again.

I wandered through the rows of items—clothes, toys, housewares, linens, bikes, even a motorcycle—with nothing specific in mind, just seeing what I could make a dollar from. I stopped beside a Tiffany-styled lamp.

"I'll sell it for a dollar," a guy wearing a bandanna offered before I asked.

I smiled. The lamp wasn't my focus. It was the trunk I saw peeking through the sheet beneath the lamp which had caught my attention. "Is the trunk for sale?"

"Everything you see here is for sale." He waved his arm wide.

"Great. Could you move the lamp?"

He set the lamp to the side and I slid the sheet back. There was dirt encrusted on the top of the trunk and as I brushed at the finish, plenty of rust beneath.

Hmmm. It's seen better days.

Paper stickers were glued beneath the handle. The nearest one was faded pink with the top of a building evident. I leaned closer, trying to read the writing on the top sticker. It was torn, but I could make out I-S-T-A-N that was left. Istanbul? That intrigued me. Looking at the other stickers, I saw France, Italy, Morocco and others whose destinations had long since faded away. This trunk had traveled the world!

"How much?" My gut told me this was a once-in-a-lifetime find.

"You don't want to see what's inside first?"

I didn't care if it was full of rat droppings, I wanted that trunk! "Sure, let's open it up."

Bandanna Man turned the trunk around and popped the ancient clasp by hitting it with the palm of his hand. I hid my wince, glad he hadn't ripped it off. He flipped the top upward; I caught it before it had the chance to travel too far backward and break the hinges.

Crinkly paper covered whatever lay inside. I slowly peeled the paper away, saw the edge of white lace, and froze. I leaned forward, began coughing, hacking, a hand grabbing at my throat.

"You okay?" Bandanna Man fanned at the dust. "You want some water? I've got some here." He fished water from some hidden stash and handed it to me.

I took the proffered water as he slammed the lid closed. Good.

"You must be allergic to dust." A chuckle.

I blinked rapidly and cleared my throat. "Whoa. Must be."

He shifted from foot to foot. "Guess you aren't still interested, huh?" Hopeful eyes.

I coughed some more before answering, "How much?" I kept my voice low.

Fingers scratched under the bandanna before he replied. "Three dollars."

Hot dog!

I stared at the trunk for a moment, pondering, before answering. "I'll take it."

Bandanna Man exhaled the lung full of air he was holding in. I passed over three ones and asked him to help me get it into the Jeep. He made small talk as we walked through the maze of stuff, but I tuned it out. I just needed him to get that trunk in my Jeep! He slid it in and shut the back door before helping me into my car.

"Hope you'll stop back by when we have our next sale. We'll try to have things aired out a little better next time."

I certainly hope not.

"I do plan to be back."

"Have a nice day."

I left him with a wave. I then drove two blocks, stopped, and screamed like I hadn't since childbirth. The lace I spotted appeared to be the Egyptian kind that costs thousands of dollars a yard! If that guy had seen what treasure was in the trunk, it's no telling how much he would have wanted. And I'd gotten it for three measly ones. Dollar signs swam around in my head. I was about to make a mint on eBay.

I whistled off-key as I continued on home. Who knew what other treasures awaited me in the trunk?

*   *   *

No one was home when I arrived. I lugged the trunk from the Jeep, happy to find it wasn't as heavy as I'd feared. I made space in the middle of the laundry room floor and prepared to delve into my latest buy.

I lifted the top slowly, not wanting to stir up the dust again. The paper crackled as I pulled it back. I sighed. It was definitely an exquisite piece of antique lace. My fingers slowly pulled it from its resting place and held it high.

A wedding dress. Oh my goodness! This was way better than I'd expected.

I couldn't resist holding it in front of me like a schoolgirl. It looked like it could fit me. On impulse, I shucked off my clothes and pulled the stiff crinoline underskirt of the dress over my head. It floated over my body like a cloud. I stared down at the gorgeous lace bodice and skirt and admired how it flowed in front of me. Just as I reached behind me, felt for the pearl buttons to close the dress . . . the world *tilted.*

My fingers stretched for the washing machine that bounced around in my vision. It seemed miles away. I leaned toward it, dizziness increasing, when . . . I felt a hand brushing the back of my leg.

I stopped, stunned. The room spun faster. I pushed down on my nausea as the hand moved up and around my calf, rubbing, kneading slowly. I swallowed, suspended between vertigo and disbelief. The hand never stopped its caress. It skimmed higher, just behind my knee.

The spinning room decelerated a bit as warm lips pressed against the indentation of the back of my leg. The lips were soft, oh so soft. My legs trembled from the touch. I moaned as a wet tongue traced up and down, making my legs jerk and tremble more. The smoothness of the tongue and the friction of the fingers . . . my clit tingled.

The hand moved higher, seated between my thighs. They pressed into the juncture, spread me wide. My panties were pulled down; air blew across my pussy lips, made me gasp, arch my back. I panted as fingers tiptoed upward, rubbed at the edge of my moisture.

A digit slowly slid between my lubricated lips, parted me. A warm wetness covered my lips, surged into my pussy. I mewled as a tongue pushed inside my wet folds, shivered as the stiff organ lapped the length of my pussy lips . . . then farther still. Arms encircled my thighs and the mouth buried itself in my pussy, tongue pistoning.

I closed my eyes on the slowly spinning room, squatted, and rolled my pelvis over and over the wet mouth-penis, caught up in this unusual moment. Hands gripped my thighs as I slide back and forth, allowing the wet tongue to caress every crevice in its path. I bounced on the stiff tongue and bit my lip as pussy juice poured from me like a fountain.

It was when a finger wormed itself into my anus that the prickles began at my toes and shot upward. My heart pounded. My legs clenched as the sensation moved higher and higher. Then . . . a firecracker exploded in my clit.

The world went completely black.

"Berze?"

I opened my eyes, saw a laundry basket full of clothes inches from my face, which was pressed into the floor.

"Berze?" Jare walked into the room. "Berze? You okay?" He crossed the floor and gathered me into his arms.

I blinked rapidly, trying to come up with some type of explanation. "Yeah." I rubbed at my head. "I just . . ." I looked at him, "I don't know."

"What are you wearing?"

I looked down. *Shit! I was still wearing the wedding dress.*

I giggled. "It was in this trunk I bought at a yard sale." *And it comes with a fucking ghost, too.*

"And you put it on? Girl, it could have cooties." Jare held me away from him.

"I couldn't resist. You know, girlie-girl stuff and all that."

"No, I don't, but then again, I'm not a girl." Jare shifted. "Here. Let me help you out of it."

He helped me to my feet and kneeled in front of me, his hands skimming my calves as he pulled the dress higher.

Déjà vu.

"Be careful. This is expensive."

"I will."

Jare pulled the dress slowly over my head, then stopped. "What the hell?"

"What? What is it?" My eyes bounced around.

"You tell me." His nose flared as he stared up and down my body.

From his facial expression alone I didn't want to look down, but I finally did. I then gulped a room full of air. My underwear was bunched around my knees and my viscous juices were smeared all in my pubic hair.

This won't be good.

"You've been sexing yourself again." Jaw hard, lips thin and pinched.

What could I say? No, I put on the dress then some... some *phantom* ate my pussy out? I wasn't that crazy and he wasn't that believing.

Instead, I said nothing.

He threw the dress down and huffed, "I'll be out late."

"But we're supposed to go to a movie tonight." We rarely spent alone time together as it was!

"Plans change." He grabbed his keys from the counter. In seconds I heard his car pulling out of the drive.

Damn.

3

Six years and counting.

That's how long we'd been married. From the moment I spotted the curly-haired, athletically built brother at a college party and he peeped me in my leopard mini and high arch-your-calf-to-the-sky killer sandals, the sparks were shooting from the heavens. I've never felt anything like it before or since. It didn't help that he pursued me unmercifully. Flowers. Clothes. Jewelry. Every week it was something new. We were an item within a month. Married by the time the diploma was placed in my hands.

The first two years were pure bliss. He was so attentive, so loving. Anything I *thought* I wanted, he gave to me. In fact, we seemed to have that psychic connection. He got me things before I even expressed that I wanted them.

Then along came Lucky.

My mother used to say a child would cement your marriage, draw you closer. Not in this case. Instead it seemed to have separated us. Jare was jealous of the time I spent taking care of Lucky. Oh, I'm not saying that he was a bad father by any means . . . he just wanted the attention I was giving Lucky and sometimes acted like a two-year-old to get it.

I don't know, it just seemed like after I returned to work, things got in a rut. Work. Cook. Clean. Sleep. Repeat. Sex was a luxury, not a necessity. Truth be told, after working all day, then coming home to run after Lucky, pick up the house, and get us fed, I was too exhausted to put much into Jare and me. The days of picking up at a moment's notice, eating out and roaming the parks hand in hand were a memory now.

And Jare . . . *changed*, too. He wasn't as laid back as he once was. He was finicky about little stuff—the way the towels were folded, all the cans facing label out on the shelf, his socks paired up in his underwear drawer and a too-starched collar irritated him all day. Sometimes he fussed worse than any chick I'd ever known. I'm on edge more than comfortable a lot of the time and it was easier to keep the peace than work at *us*.

Shoot. I was just too tired and numb to see what effect it was having on our marriage. But now that I realize our relationship was not like it used to be, I'm trying to do things differently. Hence, last night's fiasco. I'd cooked his favorite dinner, got Lucky in bed at eight—and that in itself was a feat for a child that doesn't even want to *think* about sleeping until eleven or so—ran a bubble bath, and lit scented candles around the bedroom and tub in preparation for a night of love. Why? So he can stay out late working or hanging with his friends and who knows who else, missing a chance at romance . . . again.

I sighed to myself. What actually happened when I put on the dress? Did I go back in time or something? Who knew? I will say the orgasm was off the chain, kind of like the ones I *used* to have with Jare.

Lucky was with my mother since we'd planned to have a night to ourselves and I'd managed to screw that up. There was no telling when Jare would sex me again.

I pulled the trunk to me, deciding to go through it since it appeared I had plenty of time on my hands. I smiled as I pulled out three antique corsets with boning and some frilly bloomers. Thick ivory stockings were rolled in balled atop a garter belt.

Sexy.

It was obvious I had a treasure trove of historic clothing. My fingers tingled as I continued. Beneath all the clothes were bundles of letters neatly tied with string. I pulled a bundle to me with anticipation. I was hoping these letters would give me insight into the original owner of the trunk.

The first envelope was so brown and brittle, I couldn't make out the name on the outside. The paper inside was fragile. After a corner broke off in my hand, I handled it carefully. The handwriting was beautiful, the old calligraphy you never see anymore. The writing was clear:

8 January 1867
Wolfchase, England

My Dearest Frieda,
　I dreamed of us last night. We were at the King's party. Your midnight hair was pulled high framing your beauteous face. Your ripe breasts pushed at the edge of your bodice, indeed, beckoned for my lips. I imagined your Eden was wet, wanton for me as it always is during our trysts. The vision of you forced me to submit to my lust. I pulled your nipples free, suckled you like I was a babe fresh from his mother's womb.
　Your hands tangled in my hair, held me close as I pulled your dusky nipple deep. When you moaned, I felt as though my rod would burst. I threw your dress high, ripped the seat of your bloomers like a ferocious animal, pushed deep into your wetness. My member hardens even now as I think of your heat surrounding me as I humped

inside of you. I could manage only a few strokes before my rod exploded and my seed scattered inside of you.

My lonely bed is constantly wet with our unborn. I shall return soon. I miss you terribly.

My love always,
Eduardo

Wow. That was a sexy letter. Who would have thought people were writing sexy letters a few hundred years ago? A love letter, yes. A sex letter? Previously unimaginable.

My curiosity was naturally piqued. I pulled out another letter.

19 January 1867
Berkinshire, England

Eduardo,

Your letter was again so tame compared to the lion you are, my dear. Since reticence is not my strong suit, I shall get straight to the point. I want to fuck you until the walls shudder with their own orgasm, the dogs howl at the moon, the plaster cries for its own liquid release, and the King sends out sentries to find the source of pleasure. I want your red-tipped cock in my mouth, in my pussy, in my arse, making me shiver with desire, making me shudder with reluctance to end as you spill your seed inside of me.

How much longer must I pleasure myself with you only imprinted on my brain? How much longer will you make me wait to wrap my legs around your back and impale myself on your cock? How many more mornings will my sheets be saturated with my own wasted juices?

I want you anytime, anywhere, the public be damned!
Come home soon. I need you.
Frieda

Hot damn! Now this is what I was talking about! A woman who knew what she wanted and wasn't afraid to say it. The fact she masturbated and told him she did was a hell of a turn-on. My hands strayed to my own wet snatch . . . then stopped. The way my luck was going, the moment I came would be the exact time Jare would walk in.

But that was the kind of love life I wanted with Jare—a man who wrote me sex letters and enjoyed my sexuality in all its forms. Not this boundary shit. You do not pass this point. Ugh!

You can have that type of life if you want it. This thought niggled to the forefront of my brain.

My mind bristled with energy. I couldn't fault Jare completely for the state of our sex life. I *was* part of it. I guess I was expecting him to lead and me follow.

Step to the plate and guide your man, girl.

Guide him. I looked back at the letters. Hell, if Frieda could guide a man a few hundred years ago, surely I'd evolved enough to do it in the twenty-first century. Right? I just needed a plan. Like they said, plan your work, then work your plan.

I found a pad and pen and began sketching out what I had suddenly christened the *Drive Jare Wild Plan.* I played around with different ideas, facets I'd like to see implemented on the regular. After fifteen minutes, I had a bunch of good objectives and a goal. And this plan only had one goal: for Jare to be stone-cold crazy for me by the end.

4

Jare tied the knot in his tie and brushed at some imaginary spot of lint before peering at his forehead. He was thicker than years before, but handsome and attractive to me nonetheless. I lifted upright in the bed.

"Babe?"

"Hmmm?" He kept staring in the mirror.

"About last night . . ." His face wrinkled, but he didn't look at me. Not a good sign. I still pressed forward. "I know how things . . . looked."

He gave me a pointed stare in the mirror. "Really?"

I swallowed beneath his withering gaze. "Yeah, I do, but let me tell you, I wasn't sexing myself at all."

He turned around, gave me the withering stare head on with an eyebrow arch for good measure. "Berze," he looked at the floor then back at me, "stop me when I get something wrong here. Weren't your panties bunched around your knees?" I nodded. "Wasn't there plenty of *spent* juice from your pussy in your hair and running down your legs?" I nodded again. "Yet you want me to believe that you hadn't been masturbating?" I lifted my chin and nodded a third time. He closed his eyes, shook his head. "Berze, don't I give you everything you need?"

Yes, but not everything I want. I nodded again.

"You already know how I feel about the masturbating. I mean, I've told you how that makes me feel as a man, right?"

"Jare, I know what—"

A hand was raised. "Hold up. Let me finish first. I don't think I'm hard to live with," *depends on who you ask,* "but I do have a few things, *rules* some might call them, you already know I won't let you change. And behind sleeping with another man, masturbating and toys are it. It just says I don't please you."

"You do please me. I know what you've said in the past, Jare. I'm just saying that we're six years in and doing the same things." I heard the whine in my voice and hated it. "Just *when* are we going to push the envelope, take our sex life to another level?"

His face went blank. "You think there is something wrong with our sex life now? What? You want a ménage a trois or something? An open marriage? Sex clubs? What?"

Shit! Shit! Shit! This definitely was going in a direction I hadn't anticipated. I took a deep breath and spoke carefully. "Jare, I'm not saying there is anything wrong with our current sex life and definitely am not implying we need other people to sleep with. I'm just saying we shouldn't be passive; let's work at keeping things spicy and hot."

"So what are we now? Lukewarm?"

No baby, we're damn near barely defrosted. "No, I'm saying that I think we should be open to suggestions each of us come up with. My masturbating is something you were well aware that I did when we met. I stopped because I loved you and wanted to please you."

"Go on."

"My masturbating really has nothing to do with you."

"So you are thinking of another man when you are sexing yourself?"

"No, that's not what I'm saying or even what I'm wishing."

"So what are you saying, Berze?"

I took a deep breath before speaking. "Jare, I—I think we should rededicate ourselves to our relationship. You know, spend more time together, date each other, raise our intimacy level a bit."

He was already shaking his head. "And when are we supposed to have this extra time? You work, I work, we've got this big old house to keep up and the tons of bills plus making sure Lucky has what he needs. Just when are we supposed to get this more time?"

I saw he was refusing to see my point at all. "Jare, when a couple gets complacent, things . . . happen."

"Are you threatening me?" His eyes were hard.

Definitely treacherous territory. "No, I'm saying I want us to be all we can be together. Just keep an open *mind* and be ready and spontaneous sexually."

Jare snorted. "Sounds like you're planning on us screwing in the park behind the bushes or joining the mile-high club."

Sounded like good ideas to me. "Jare, I'm just saying I want to be all the wife and woman I can be for you."

Jare walked slowly over to the bed and sat down. "Berze, I love you. You are the woman I chose to spend my life with. I hear what you are saying,"—*but are you listening?*— "but I need you to hear me also. I love you like you . . . *us* like we are."

It's not enough. But I kept that statement to myself. I could see in his eyes he wasn't getting the whole reason for this entire conversation. I deflated. "I understand."

"Maybe we can squeeze a dinner in once a week but more than that, I wouldn't count on it." He patted my hand and stood. "I'm going to be late and I'm supposed to have a late dinner with a client, so don't look for me before eight."

"Have a good day, baby."

He gave me a peck to the lips. "You, too."

I lay back feeling bereft in this episode of My Life. Yes, I had a husband that showed all the requisite trappings of a good husband, but still, there was something lacking. Why was he so against the masturbation? It's not like I'm dry and unable or unwilling to sex him whenever he wants. Instead, I feel like he's bought into the married people's sex routine comedians always joke about. Where they can be smoking a cigarette or watching television while making love because it's so routine, monotonous.

I was well aware of those things I could not live without in my life and passion was at the top of the list. Sometimes the masturbating is to take me away from the rote, the sameness. Other times, I'm just horny and not wanting to wait. I want to sex myself *and* him. It really *wasn't* about him; it was all about me and getting my vast sexual needs met, having *me* done just like I liked it.

Shoot, I already had Jare's lovemaking habits down pat. Our lovemaking would most likely be at night, after a hard day of work, when I'm frazzled. He would take a shower before me, then start massaging my arms, kiss my neck, suck my breasts, lift my nightgown, and be inside. When he came, he would roll over and go to sleep.

Part of it was my fault. I never complained when it began happening. I was tired and it was easy. But the lack of real foreplay sometimes was getting to me. Masturbation gave me what he didn't. I could feel my vagina pulsing as I squirted the K-Y Jelly onto my fingers. See the juices beginning to ooze as I parted my lips and covered my clit. I close my eyes and allowed the sensations to wash all up and down my body, imagining that it's Jare's fingers, Jare's tongue that's loving me like I want.

Thinking about the masturbation actually made me flush with excitement. I rechecked to make sure Jare's car was gone, then walked over to the closet and fished out a shoebox at the bottom of a column of shoeboxes. I smiled as I pulled out the silver bullet. I'd bought it years ago despite Jare's protests. He would shit bricks if he ever found it.

I squirted the K-Y onto my fingertips, then lay back in the bed. My pelvis undulated as I coated my stiff button and smeared the rest up and down my inner lips. With the bullet turned on low, I pressed it beside my clit. I couldn't stand the sensation head-on but needed to acclimate my nub to the vibrations.

My nipples blossomed, my head rolled as I slid the bullet back and forth, around and around up and down my clit. This was how I liked it; my pussy spewed juice. I needed no scenarios, just the image of Jare, tongue extended, fingers pumping into me. I pinched a nipple, felt the resultant tug in my womb.

I then spread wide, pushed the bullet inside my wet snatch, pumping rapidly. The vibrations spread upward, niggled my clit. With the image of Jare's head between my legs, I bit my pillow, covering the yelp that escaped as my womb ejected juice around and around my fingers.

18 March 1867
Wolfchase, England

My loving Frieda,
There is no easy way to tell you this, but I have been detained with the King's business. My gut roiled as the orders were given to me. I had hoped to be nestled back inside your silky folds by now. Instead, I find myself farther away.
You came to me again last night as you do most nights. You wore the sheerest of gowns, the hair of your pube evident to my eyes. I hardened like a marble statue. I wanted to tear the fabric from your body, kiss you from your feet to the nape of your neck.

You smiled at me before moving towards me. I held my arms wide for an embrace. Instead, you kneeled in front of me, pulled my leaking rod from my breeches. My breath stuttered in my chest as your wet lips kissed the tip before engulfing it inside your mouth. It felt as though a string was pulled taut, bowing me backward as you pulled me in and out. My toes curled like the court jester's shoes, head spun as if I had consumed three tankards of ale as your lips and tongue loved me. When your fingers grasped my sac, I could not stop myself from spraying down your throat. And you swallowed all of me.

I must confess, my nighttime imaginations have necessitated that I have a room to myself. They complain that I grunt too loudly for them to sleep. Alas, they have not seen you, my dear Frieda. Then they would understand my longing.

My business should be finished here soon and I shall return home to you, my love. My dearest, I love you with all my heart.

Eduardo

I sat on the side of the tub and reread Eduardo's letter again. There was definitely something to be said about a man putting his lust for you down on paper. It made things . . . sexier indeed.

I knew if I showed Jare what I was talking about, he'd understand what I wanted for us much better.

Lead your man, girl!

That's exactly what I planned to do. I called into work and took the day off. I knew my mother should have dropped Lucky off at daycare, so he wasn't a worry. Besides, I needed a Berze Day and didn't want him underfoot, so I left him where he was.

I cleaned the house from top to bottom. I made sure the

floors shined, the rooms smelled good. I even did those things Jare liked—the can labels all faced outward; sorted the veggies with the veggies, the cereal with the cereal, the rice with the rice; the laundry was all done and carefully folded; the walk-in closet was walkable and the clothes were color-arranged. I wanted no "irritants" to insert themselves to stop our night.

I was exhausted when I finished, but I picked Lucky up at four, took him to the park, and played with him until his eyes drooped. That was the idea. I needed him in the bed and asleep by seven. After giving him his dinner and a bath, he was snoring by six. I was ahead of schedule.

Bubbles rose from my bathwater as I eased into it. I soaked for a bit before scrubbing myself and exiting. I rubbed the Victoria's Secret lotion Jare bought me—the scent one that I really didn't care for—into my skin and spritzed the cologne on top. I then pulled a sheer teddy over my body and admired myself in the mirror. Yeah, I needed work on some areas, mainly the waist and hips, but I didn't look half bad.

I applied a dab of makeup, pulled my hair up and let ringlets fall around my face, then waited. I was armed and ready for a night of lovemaking, Berze style.

Jare arrived at eight as he'd said. I'd run him a tub of water with plenty of suds floating on top to relax him.

"Hey baby." He was pulling his tie off as he came into the room.

I smiled and went to him. My lips pressed against his, tongue entered his mouth. He pulled back. "Whoa. You trying to get me hot?"

"What's wrong with that?" I rubbed my thigh against his. "You are my husband and we are legal and all."

He held me at arms' length. "Look at you." His eyes ran up and down the length of me. "You've got on that Victoria Secret's perfume I bought and I haven't seen that teddy since our anniversary dinner."

"Been way too long, lover." I nodded and rubbed back upon him.

"Ump."

He stepped away from me before I could wrap my arms around him and headed toward the bathroom. *Follow your plan.* Honestly, I was a bit piqued at his actions, but I trailed behind him anyway. He stopped when he saw the filled tub. I moved around him and stood in front of him.

"I ran you a bath."

"I see." His eyes didn't meet mine.

I began unbuttoning his shirt. "I thought you'd want to soak a bit, relax after a long day at work."

He stared at the water, then shook his head. He captured my hands in his. "Berze, baby, I'm not feeling the tub thing at all. I appreciate all this," he waved his arm around, "but really, I just want a quick shower." He smiled and pulled me to him. "I love that you were thinking about me though, but let me get a shower and I can be back to you pretty fast."

You got to be kidding me! But I pushed my hurt down and stepped back. "Sure. You do that."

"Okay. Just give me five minutes." He turned the knobs on the shower and began undressing.

I left the bathroom and threw myself on the bed. Why can't anything I plan come out exactly the way I want it to? I clenched my teeth, swallowed my own rising irritation and pulled out the bottle of massage oil. Surely he wouldn't turn down a massage.

Jare walked into the bedroom and headed straight for the underwear drawer. I said nothing as he slid his legs into his boxers. I did notice his cock wasn't even at half-mast. It was shriveled as a prune. Guess the sight of me in my teddy didn't excite him as it once had.

I forged ahead. I plastered a smile on my lips and held up the bottle of massage oil. "Come here."

"What's that?" He didn't move.

"I thought you might like a little massage." I shook the bottle and patted the bed.

Jare dragged his feet, but finally laid across the bed facedown. I straddled him, then poured a small amount of oil into my hands. I smoothed it across his shoulders.

"Wow, you are tight."

"Yeah, I've been tense all day."

"Is this a pretty big client you had dinner with?"

"The firm thinks so. The client wants us to design ten upscale shopping centers in large outlets across the country. *Major* opportunity. It's the inroad we'd been hoping for to get into the commercial side of things."

Jare was a junior architect in his firm. He knew if he landed a big client, he could be made partner and this was one of those *big* clients. I stood behind his goals, but at the same time, I knew making partner meant we'd have even less time together. At company gatherings, the partners always got together and joked about eighty-hour workweeks while their wives complained about loneliness on the other side of the room. I didn't want to be one of those lonely, irritated wives. Well, not more than I already was, anyway.

"Sounds good." I kneaded the tight muscles in his upper back.

"Ooh, baby, that's the spot." He pushed himself deeper into the bed as I used the flat of my palm to work over a tense area.

I took my time on the upper part. I karate chopped up and down his back, knuckled knotted areas, and kneaded muscles. I finally moved lower, pulled his boxers off, and sat my pussy directly on his ass as my arousal heightened. I was wet and wanted him to feel my wetness, wanted him to know the effect he still had on me. His ass clenched as I slid my wetness back and forth over his hips. This was definitely a good sign.

I drizzled oil down the center of his back, smoothing,

kneading as he encouraged me. I shifted off him, rubbed down his legs, massaged his calves, poured oil over his feet, and sucked his little toe. My fingers and arms were beginning to ache, but I kept at it. I wanted him pliable and ready for my lovemaking.

The back was finally finished. "Turn over." Jare didn't move. My nipples were buttons, my pussy was soaking, and I wanted to see his cock before I rode it. I patted his hips for encouragement. "Jare, turn over baby so I can get the front."

My request was met with a snore. *What?* I pushed myself forward, stared into his face. This was no joke. Jare was a-s-l-e-e-p.

I wanted to push him out of the bed, slap his ass, tell him to wake up and give me some loving. But what good would that do? The best his sleeping tail would give me would be some more of the routine married sex he always gave. Shhheeeeiiii-itttttt!

Frustrated beyond frustration, I stomped out of the bedroom, grabbed the carton of Caramel Sundae ice cream, and turned the television to Lifetime.

5

"Mommy, I'm hungry." Hands tugged at my arm. "Wake up, Mommy. I want some cereal."

"Huh?" I squinted. Lucky stood beside the couch in his Power Ranger pajamas.

Lucky pumped my arm a few more times. "I'm hungry. I want some Cap'n Crunch. Could you please wake up and give me some?"

I shook my head before slowly rising from the couch. Apparently, I'd fallen asleep with the television on and either Jare hadn't awakened and noticed I was missing from the bed or had noticed and left me here anyway. Not that it mattered. Both options were pitiful signs of the state of our marriage.

Cereal was poured into a bowl and milk followed quickly. Lucky smiled as his jaws bulged with the cereal. I stroked his head and kissed his cheek. He was adorable.

"I'm going to check on Daddy."

There was a mixture of emotions running through me—irritation, lust, love—as I strode down the hallway. Was it a crime to want to be all you could be in your marriage? I mean, I love sex. I want to be held, stroked, and fucked at least five days a week. Truly, it's seven but sometimes men need a breather, too. But damn, wasn't that every man's wet dream? A woman who loved sex, wanted to give him sex, and was good at sex? Yet, he's happily complacent with *whatever.*

Jare was still sleeping. I stood at the doorway and watched the rhythmic rise and fall of his chest. Most likely he hadn't awakened and noticed I was gone. Anyway, that's the option I chose to make me feel better.

I crossed the room and sat at my dressing table. The image in my mirror wasn't too bad—clear skin, few wrinkles, nice teeth, and the hair needed combing but had a nice healthy sheen to it. I would be considered attractive by the masses. But I seemed to be taken for granted by the one I willingly wanted to give myself to.

I turned my mind from those thoughts and grabbed another letter from the stack.

18 October 1867
Berkinshire, England

Eduardo,
   We are well. The babe grows larger in my womb each day. I fear I will soon resemble a female who swallowed a melon whole. My maid, Lycinda, grips my arm in viselike hands whenever we venture outside. She says she doesn't want me to fall and injure the baby and have you kill her upon your return. Such silly gibberish!
   My breasts have swelled considerably. The nipples are so tender that even when I wash them, I become excited. Indeed, they drip as an unmilked cow's teat as I pleasure myself. Oh, I can see your lips closed around the distended tips, suckling the milk before our babe arrives.
   Your mother refuses to look at me now. She sent a mis-

sive stating I should stay cosseted inside in my delicate state. I sent back a hasty reply: Kiss my arse.

You are well-loved by two bullheaded females. Come home to me soon.

Frieda

"Honey?" I jumped at the voice. I was so into Frieda and Eduardo, I missed him exiting the bed and walking over to me. Jare hugged my back, pulled me into his chest, and kissed my hair. "What's that?"

All my irritation evaporated as he rubbed up and down my arms. I even managed not to comment on his morning breath. "It's a letter from the chest."

"Interesting?"

I nodded. "Very. It's actually a bundle of letters dating from the mid-1800s."

"That was a long time ago. And you can still read them?"

"Ahuh. They are love letters between a woman named Frieda and her husband, Eduardo. Pretty sexy letters, too. Want me to read you one?"

"Sexy letters from the 1800s. Why not? Sure. Got one you really liked?"

Carpe diem!

I scrabbled to find Frieda's sexy letter, the one where she wrote about pleasuring herself. I thought if Jare saw it was natural, he'd understand the whole masturbating thing, just *me* more.

"You ready?"

"Go ahead." Jare sat on the floor, rubbing my calves.

I read the letter slowly, passionately. When I finished, I could see his robe tented in the front. "So what do you think?"

"Damn." His cock rose higher.

"That's all you can say? Damn?"

"Frieda was a helluva woman."

"I think so, too."

"Come here." He held his arms wide. I slid onto the floor and let him engulf me. We rolled onto our backs. "Baby, I know I don't tell you this enough, but I love you." He leaned up on his elbows and looked into my eyes. "You're a helluva woman also."

I could have melted through the floor. My hands caressed his chin. "You're a helluva man, too."

Our lips connected, tongues plundered, ravaged each other as hands stroked, brushed, and massaged our bodies. His teeth pulled at my straps until my tits sprang free. Those same teeth nipped in the valley of my breasts before claiming a dusky nipple between his lips.

I moaned as Jare suckled my hard berries. My hand tangled in his pubic hair, cupped his sac. I encircled his base, stroked upward slowly and firmly. Felt the precum slide over my fingers as I fisted the head.

Jare breathed deeply as his lips trailed down my body to my navel. I wiggled as the soft flesh was bitten and lapped. Around and around, his tongue swirled inside my umbilicus; I felt pussy juice extrude from between my lips.

I shifted, lay so that his cock stood inches from my face. I smiled as more precum pressed from the head as I stroked upward. I licked the head, tongue swirling and lapping rapidly.

"Damn, baby."

His breath was hot on my pube. A tongue slowly traced around the outer lips. My body involuntarily arched, tried to reach nirvana in a millisecond. As his fingers parted me slowly, I slid his cock to the back of my throat.

"Shit!" Jare's legs flailed outward, hitting the dressing table. The contents rained onto the floor. I didn't give a rat's ass. Instead I surged my mouth back onto his cock.

My hips lifted, tried to get the release my pussy needed from his mouth. No contact. I lifted again, needing for his touch to take me over the edge of madness. My hips pumped air over and over again while I sucked his cock.

"Berze?"

My mind was hazy, I was almost *there.* I pulled his cock toward me, hips still pumping air, when Jare lifted his leg across me, pulling his cock from my mouth. As I rolled toward him, thinking he was just changing positions, a hand to the chest stopped my motion.

"Berze." Firm. *Very* firm.

Glazed eyes met his. I was surprised to see they were hard, not half-lidded as they normally were during sex. As my eyes traveled to the left, my heart stopped as I saw what he held in his hand: the silver bullet. Apparently, I'd left it on the dressing table under a letter and it had fallen during the crash.

"Is this what I think it is?"

I refused to lie. "It is."

His body slumped; he held his head in defeat. "Even though I'd made it clear that I didn't like you using toys or masturbating, you still bought a vibrator. And hid it." He wiggled the bullet just beneath my nose. "How long have you had it?"

I supposed if I were a quick comeback thinker, I could have concocted a believable story in a few seconds. Unfortunately, I wasn't. "Jare . . ." I stopped, not knowing what else to say, what else could be said. He held the damning evidence in his hands.

He didn't wait for me to continue. "I'm going to get dressed." He stood up and entered the bathroom, leaving me sprawled on the floor. I slapped the floor in frustration. What did I need to do for him to accept me and my sexuality? Damn! Just when I was so close.

Jare didn't look at me as he reentered the room. I could tell he was irritated by the way he got dressed—yanking his shirt off the hanger, mumbling under his breath. I remained on the floor, naked and splayed wide for the world to see, watching him, wanting him to say something so we could make things right between us. He never spoke a word until he stepped over me. "I'll take Lucky to the birthday party, then over to your mother's like we'd planned afterward. I'll be late."

I didn't even bother to reply. It was obvious his mind was made up and honestly, I was irritable and no telling what I'd say, so I let things go unsaid. I stayed in the room as he dressed Lucky and they left, Lucky laughing at something Jare said.

Hours went by as I lay there on the floor thinking about *everything*. What changed us? What could I do? Why didn't the plan I concocted seem to be working? What was the real deal with the toys and masturbation? Dang, the way he was acting, you'd think he got hemmed up in a whorehouse when he was a kid and they'd used some toys on him. I already knew that wasn't true, so what was it?

We'd talked and talked *ad nauseum* about our past relationships before marriage. Not one time did he say he'd had such a horrible experience that affected him sexually. Not once. So what was the doggone problem?

The bigger question was: could I continue to live with a man that accepted only parts of me, not the whole?

You know he wants all of you, so stop this foolish thinking. He needs you to show him the way. Lead your man, girl! my mind chided unmercifully.

Okay. I found my pad, reevaluated my plan. I tweaked this idea, nixed another, but the main goal was still the same: Jare was to be totally driven wild by Berze.

Step one of my plan was the Ambush. I knew my husband well. Jare was a man of habit and routine. Break the routine and he floundered around flustered. I pulled a sheer red G-string from my lingerie drawer, then discarded it. Too tame. I needed that "freak me" outfit since it was past time for Jare to be flustered in my opinion. I knew he planned to stay out late with his boys, punishing me, coming in around nine or ten. But like he'd said before, plans change.

I sent Jare a generic text: *Hey, we need to talk. Don't stay out too late. I'll have dinner waiting. I love you.* I then grabbed my keys. I had a plan to implement and time was wasting.

6

Two hours later, I returned home quite satisfied with myself. In one hand I held a bag of Chinese takeout. No way was I slaving over a stove tonight. But in the other hand, I held the killer outfit I'd been hoping to find.

Jare always salivated over Halle Berry. When he'd seen her in that Catwoman outfit, he'd gotten a hard-on that made me jealous as hell. I knew I wanted that outfit or something along that line, minus the mask, of course. It was by chance I visited the new Leather 'N Lace Emporium. I'd told them what I wanted and they didn't have it in stock, but this spike-haired chick managed to suit me up in similar fashion. I'm talking leather bustier with my titties almost bursting over the top, leather pants, which we slashed along the legs plus removed the crotch, and my favorite—a fringed leather thong. Six-inch platform heels completed the look.

Oh, I was nowhere near as slim as Halle must be in real life, but before this night was over, Jare would definitely know "what I was working with," for 'sho.

I tell you, keeping secrets makes me giddy! I was as excited as a kid sniffing glue. I poured more than enough bubblebath in the tub before I soaked. I scrubbed every inch with sea salt, gave myself a facial, manicure, and pedicure, painting my nails in a color labeled Slut Red. My hair I pulled up in a haphazard yet sexy way. The makeup was dramatic. Jare always said he hated me wearing makeup, but I was wearing it when I hooked him and besides, look where not wearing it all these years has gotten me. B-o-r-i-n-g.

Then it was time to put on my new outfit. As I closed the last strap, I looked at myself in the mirror.

Shit, Halle Berry was cute . . . but I was thicker and cuter.

Eight forty-five. Jare was true to form. I expected him to come huffing in around nine. The food was on the table and I'd positioned myself seductively on the living room couch. No way could he miss me when he walked in.

At five after nine, I heard the car pull into the driveway. Showtime!

I checked my position on the couch. Then, unbelievably, I heard *voices* before he opened the door. Not good. I'd been expecting Jare alone. He knew I wanted to make up, yet he brought some friends with him? He shouldn't have done that.

You running or stepping to the plate, girlie?

The old Berze would have ducked into the bedroom and pouted. But that was before The Plan. Now, I stood, straightened my spine, but didn't budge an inch from my spot in direct view of the door. I felt my knees trying to knock together, but I tightened my thighs and stopped the involuntary movements.

His key opened the lock and Jare was turned away from me, high-fiving his buddy Shaw as the door opened. *Gracious! It was a Saturday night. Didn't his friends have a life?* I guessed the joke they were sharing was the bomb since it took a few seconds before they noticed me standing there. Then his friend Mike's head popped into view.

Three mouths dropped in concert.

Bet this will be one helluva discussion with the boys.

Boldly, silently, I began rocking from side to side without saying a word. You could feel the tension in the air.

Jare broke the spell. "Berze, wha . . . wha . . . what's going on?"

I gyrated my pelvis in small, erotic circles before I answered. "I told you we needed to work things out, didn't I?"

"Y—yes," he stuttered.

"Yet you dismissed my request and managed to bring Mo and Larry with you anyway, didn't you?" I whispered, making eye contact with the Two Stooges. Shaw licked his lips—typical—and Mike stared, wide-eyed.

"Yes," Jare now whispered.

I took this moment to palm my ass, making the fringe swing. It had a pendulum effect—all eyes were glued to it as it swung.

I loved the power I felt!

Hell had gotten its hooks deep in me and I pushed the envelope. "So . . . what? Are they staying?" I didn't want any part of Shaw or Mike, but Jare needed to be shocked.

"Hell, yeah!" Shaw yelled, taking steps toward me.

Jare grabbed his arm, pulling him back, "What the fuck is wrong with you, man? You know damn well you're not gonna do a damn thing with—" His speech cut off as I dipped low, legs spread wide, before rising upright just like I'd seen the chick do it in the *Tip Drill* video I'd overheard them whispering and giggling about one night previously when they were over.

"I tell you what. You've got fifteen minutes to get rid of Ike and Mike, otherwise . . ." I took this moment to stick a finger in my mouth and suck the tip, "I'm starting without you. And let me tell you upfront," I trailed the wet finger down the front of my body, "I'm horny as hell," and let it land over my crotch. I moaned in simulated ecstasy.

That did the trick. Jare turned, grabbed his boys by the arm, and yelled, "Time to go, fellas!"

Mike followed behind, but Shaw stayed in the same spot, watching me watching him. He rubbed the bulge in his crotch and licked his lips again, totally ignoring what Jare had said. Shaw took two steps toward me before Jare realized what was happening.

Jare grabbed the back of Shaw's shirt, yanking hard. "You got a death wish? Don't make me fuck you up!"

I could see from Shaw's eyes he was seriously considering the challenge. Tension was thick as chests swelled and fists balled. Then, Shaw turned and walked to the door . . . but stopped to give me a final look. Jare shoved him through the entry and slammed the door.

What they say is true: Pussy is a helluva drug!

It wasn't ten minutes before I heard the car return, tires squealing as it braked. I pushed a finger into my soaking pussy, was swirling it slowly as Jare ran into the room. Yeah, he could react like he had previously, but it was time he saw my sexuality for what it was. All of it.

"Berze, wait!" he yelled as I moaned from the sensation.

Jare shoved my hands to the side. His head dipped low, tongue extended toward my wet sex. I stopped his downward progress with a hand to his forehead. He stared at me in confusion.

I waggled my finger in front of his nose before smearing my juices onto his lips. "Not before we eat."

He licked his lips. "Shit. Food can wait." He pushed my hand to the side. I flipped my leg over his body and rose quickly.

"Not . . . before . . . we . . . eat," I stated firmly.

His cock bobbed in his shorts. I so wanted to pull it free, stroke it, lick it, but I had to remain in control. It took a moment, but he finally deflated. "Let's eat then."

I led him to the table and seated him. I knew he wouldn't play fair and he didn't. His hands were all over me, rubbing, stroking, pinching. I was tingling everywhere in anticipation of the sex ahead. His dick lifted, strained against the thin material and this excited me even more.

Just as I leaned over to place some shrimp fried rice on his plate, my nipple popped free of my bustier; my breast swung within inches of Jare's face.

"Hell!" Teeth clenched, sweat popping up on his forehead. "Sit the plate down."

"No." There was a new sheriff in town and her name was Berze. I shoveled more rice onto his plate.

Jare didn't reply with his mouth. Instead, he swung up out of the chair and pushed me against the wall, where the loaded spoon added abstract character to the paint job. Hot lips latched on to my nipple and he sucked it into the back of his throat.

I clenched and unclenched my pussy.

His fingers found the zipper, yanked it open. My other breast fell out to join the first one. Fingers grabbed while lips gnawed. My hands palmed his head, scratched across his chest, before dipping lower, searching for his cock.

He moaned as my fingers engulfed his stiff dick through the thin fabric, shivered as my wet lips followed suit. I teased the fabric from his hips, allowed his dick to spring free. Both of his hands braced against the wall for support as my hot lips teased the tip around and around . . . before I deep-throated him.

"Shit! Shit! Shit!"

Guess it's getting good for him, huh?

I palmed his sac before drawing one ball, then its brother, into my mouth.

"Oh, gawddamn! Gawddamn!"

This shit was turning me on! I sucked in earnest while fingering my own pussy. Jare grabbed two handfuls of my hair and began fucking my mouth. The back of my throat eagerly met his inward stroke; my tongue lubricated him as he pulled out. Rivers of pussy juice streamed down my legs as my fingers stabbed away.

I gave it my all—suck, stroke, suck, stroke—drawing him deeper than I'd ever done before. I needed him to *know* the extent of my skills. Needed him to understand that whatever he needed, whatever he wanted, I *could* give it to him.

My fingers tickled around his anus. His pumping increased. My nails dug into his ass. Jare stepped back, swung me upright, and turned me in one motion. He positioned me spread eagle like I was being arrested, a hand on the back of my neck holding me in place. He surged between my lubricated pussy lips. His fingers pulled on my nipples as he leaned back and pumped into me like we were in a race to the finish line.

The dick was so good, I couldn't do shit but fuck him back. I turned all the sexual frustration I held into pussy-clenching strokes. My back hurt, my lungs were bursting, my heart was thumping against the wall, but still I fucked. Even when I felt him stiffening up, making mewling sounds, I fucked. Even when I turned my head and saw his fuck face, I fucked. I fucked, Fucked, *Fucked,* and FUCKED until his legs gave way and he collapsed onto the floor.

Then I stopped fucking.

Leaning down, I checked his pulse—rapid but strong—and smiled. I loved it when a plan came together.

I slowly rose and walked into the kitchen. Turning on the tap, I filled a glass full of water. I knew I needed it to wake him up. He didn't realize it but . . . Mama was still hungry.

7

Men always talked about sexing a woman until the sun rose, but I didn't think Jare would ever participate in that type of discussion again. Why? Because I'd put that yakking to the test last night. I'd humped, pumped and slithered all over and around him, trying to see if he truly wanted to do what it took to claim the coveted title of King Cock. Guess not. For once, he was the one crying "Uncle!" and I'd loved every minute of it.

I had to smile as I looked at Jare sprawled across the bed, snoring to high heaven. My baby was pooped. However, I wasn't. I was as refreshed as if I'd spent a week at a spa. In fact, my pussy was itching to close around his fat cock again.

Girl, how many mornings did Jare wake you up with a kamikaze sex attack?

That was true. He'd snuck upon my tired body many mornings, expending his lust before I'd even gotten into first gear. I'd asked him to give me a heads-up, but no. He seemed to like taking it when I was most vulnerable.

I smiled again. One good kamikaze attack deserves another, right?

I slid closer to Jare, inhaled his sweaty scent through his T-shirt. He lay on his back, legs wide. That was good. I scooted downward, getting level with his pelvis. I touched him lightly. He jerked but resumed snoring in seconds. I let my hands brush his thigh. The snoring was constant. Good. I let my fingers slide higher, sneaking up on my destination.

Now or never.

I snaked my hand inside the opening to his boxers, pulled him free, and encased his soft head with my hot mouth.

"Baby, I'm tired," Jare grunted, hand brushing downward.

I nudged the hand away, sucked the tangy head slowly, methodically, refusing to release the growing cock from my wet prison. I cupped his balls as I licked up the side of his ever-expanding cock.

"Damn, babe. What are you doing to me?" Fingers gripped, ungripped the sheets.

My reply was to draw him deeper into my mouth until he touched the back of my throat. The copious saliva produced from my gag reflex lubricated his thick shaft. I licked up and down the side, then lifted the cock, sucked his balls. My tongue rotated around and around his sac. He moaned. I pumped on him then.

"Shit!"

Hands tangled in my hair, ass lifted as he pumped his cock into my mouth. I increased the suction; drew him into deeper, tighter depths.

"Baby, baby, baby, *shit!*"

I pulled back, spit on his cock, then slammed my mouth back on him. His eyes were closed, mouth open as I pistoned him like well-oiled machinery. My neck muscles ached. I ignored it and swirled as I bobbed, twisted as I sucked.

"Oh shit! Oh shit!" His toes curled, knees rose.

That's it, baby. Bring mommy the honey.

Two more pumps later, I felt Jare's salty juices shoot into my mouth. I swallowed and sucked until he was completely drained.

Jare's hands fell from my hair; his snores resumed in seconds.

Thank you, baby.

I lounged in the bed well past noon. Jare had gotten a sudden burst for the need for religion—probably scared I would hump his bones again—and jetted off to church. He'd informed me he'd pick up Lucky from my mother's and be home later in the afternoon. It was all good. I'd planned to let him have the day off anyway.

I stretched and yawned before pulling my nude body from the bed. After a quick shower, I decided to work my way through a few more of the letters. I was hoping each one would be sexier than the last. Randomly, I pulled one to me. It was from Frieda.

Berkinshire, England
1 December 1867

Eduardo,
    Life has been a bit prickly for me. I'm afraid I have upset your mother to the point she has asked me to leave. She found my cache of "improper reading material" and has been in a snit since that time. You should have seen her face. She looked as if Muffie had pooped on her silk shoes. I had to stifle my giggles as she fanned my copy of The Nude Gardener *beneath my nose.*
    However, when she called me a tart, I had no choice but to defend my honor, as you were not here to do so. I informed her that it was more than obvious she should take the time to read each page slowly and thoroughly. Then perhaps your father would smile more and she wouldn't appear constipated all of the time. Needless to say, there was a huge hullabaloo after that.

So it appears I will be finding other suitable quarters. I
shall write you with our new address as soon as I secure a
place. Come home to me soon so we may christen our new
home properly.
   Loving you more and more each day,
   Frieda

Banned books. Boy, her mother-in-law would have a coro-
nary if she read some of the "literature" being printed now.
Thinking about my collection of racy novels, I smiled. Mommy-
in-law would have put me out a long time ago, probably with a
boot in my back and a cussword on her lips, too. It was amusing
how history was actually made. I pulled another letter to me.

Portugal, Spain
3 January 1868

Frieda,
   Goodness, woman! What excitement you have brought
to my life! When I laid eyes on your bloomers, my heart
stuttered in my chest. I quickly shuttered myself away,
needing this experience to not be shared by any gawking
eyes. At the first whiff, I fell to my knees, weakened by
your glorious scent. My God, woman! What you do to me!
Blast this king's business. I yearn for the time I shall again
hold you close to me! It will not be much longer. I promise!
   Loving you always,
   Eduardo

Go ahead Frieda! Sending your man worn panties in the
1800s. And here we are thinking this was something new.
Humph. Looks like the only thing new was us getting with an
age-old program.
   Jare would probably have a stroke if he opened up his brief-

case and pulled out a pair of my . . . worn . . . panties? Hmmm. I nodded to myself as I added an addendum to The Plan.

I read through a few more of the letters, ideas flitting around and around. Eduardo and Frieda's love made me laugh, cry, shout, then they depressed me when I compared my love life to theirs.

Jare returned with Lucky deep into the afternoon. He then changed and headed out to "hang with his boys." I expected him to be late again, so I was pleasantly surprised when he returned less than an hour later.

He was smirking as he placed his keys on the rack.

"You're back early." I was munching on some popcorn, watching *Extreme Home Makeover*.

"Yeah."

I shifted my legs as he sat down beside me on the couch. "What happened?"

He rubbed hands across his face then looked at me. "You." The smirk widened into a smile.

"Me?"

"Yeah, you." He nodded and rubbed his chin. "The guys were ragging me so bad, I decided to leave."

I smiled now. "Last night?"

"What else?" He shook his head. "Girl, last night . . . I didn't know if that was you or some woman you'd hired at first."

I gave him an eye roll. "You know I'm not paying some woman to get with my man."

"I didn't think you would, but honestly, I couldn't get my eyes past the fringe on that dang thong to look up to your face." We both chuckled at that.

"That's a good thing, huh?"

He pulled my legs onto his thigh and began massaging my feet. Strong fingers rotated over the callus on the ball of my foot. When he pulled my pinky toe into his mouth, my breathing stopped. That felt some kind of good. "Could be."

"Is that right?"

"It is."

His fingers moved higher, rubbing my thighs. Wetness collected in my panties. I bent my knee and shifted a leg behind his back. Jare kissed my knee, my thigh, tongue trailing toward my center.

"Baby, Lucky is still awake." I wanted him badly, but I didn't want Lucky walking in on us. You know kids have that interrupt-parent-sex radar and Lucky wasn't ready for the birds-and-bees talk just yet.

"That means you will have to be *real* quiet, now doesn't it?"

Jare moved my panties to the side and dipped his head. His tongue flicked up and down my wet outer lips. Thick fingers spread me wide before sliding inside. I bit my bottom lip, stifling the moan trying to push outward.

"Have you been a bad girl while Daddy was away?"

"N—no," I wheezed out. Sparks shot from my lips as he lapped me long and deep. His beard scratched my inner thighs, made me jerk as his head rotated.

"Sure?" He pulled my panties down my legs. His tongue replaced his fingers; diddled my clit. My back arched off the couch under his wet assault. Tingles traveled up and down my spine; goose bumps rose on my arms and legs. I felt moisture crawling between my ass cheeks.

"P—pro-mise."

I wanted to yell as his stiff muscle stoked my hot center. My toes curled as a finger slid back and forth across my anal entrance, teasing circles that ended at my opening. I watched as he sucked on his finger, then returned it to its previous position on my ass. My thighs opened wider as a finger slid inside slowly. Back and forth gently, methodically in me; the sensations made my clit blossom.

"Good."

My bones almost snapped as his tongue followed the path of his fingers. He rotated and lapped, sucked and stabbed me deep. Gawddam! A low roaring began in my ears when his tongue slid between my holes, his fingers taking up the slack. I bucked on his face, tried to push him away; I wanted him to release me, wanted him to stay. Jare held me tight, refused me any wiggle-away room.

Aw shit, now!

My hands did a frenzied dance on his head, his neck, his back. He allowed me no relief from his focused passion. I squeezed and pinched my tight nipples. Pulled them free and sucked on my own throbbing bud.

Sweat broke out on my forehead as Jare picked up the pace. The sensations rushing through me had me gasping, grabbing air, pressing him deeper into me. I needed him to take me over the edge, extinguish the fire raging inside.

When he closed his mouth over my clit and sucked, tingles rocketed up my spine, forced me to buck against his mouth for all I was worth. I was a wild woman as I humped against his wet mouth, ready to release my juice to his waiting lips.

He bit my clit at precisely the right moment. The roaring became a booming cannon as all sensation triangulated and my pussy sprayed and sprayed honey across his face and lapping lips.

"Mommy?"

Uh oh. Lucky's voice was close. My mind was hazy, floating, full of sexual ideas, not capable of handling kid stuff at this moment. "I can't deal with this right now, Jare," I whispered.

Jare lifted his head from my pussy, simultaneously pulling my skirt down over my naked pubis. I spotted my panties just as Lucky reached the back of the couch.

"Hey, big guy. What's wrong?"

I slid the errant panties beneath me just as Lucky walked

around the couch, stopping between Jare's legs. "Hey Daddy. I can't get my Power Rangers movie to work." His face scrunched, he tilted his head; stared at Jare. "Daddy, why is your face wet?"

Oh, this is gonna be good. I covered my grin with my hand.

"Well . . . sometimes I act like you. I get a little messy when I'm drinking something I really enjoy." Jare glanced at me over Lucky's head, winked.

"Like me and vanilla milkshakes?"

"Something like that only . . . *sweeter. Much* sweeter." He licked his lips slowly, eyes shuttered in desire; it made me want to arch my back and throw my legs wide again. Mercifully, he focused back on Lucky. "Hey, why don't you let me wash my face, then I'll get that movie started."

"All right!" Lucky trotted off to his room.

Jare leaned over, kissed me, my essence all over his tongue and lips. He then ground his wet face on my cheek.

"Jare! You're getting juice all over me!"

He smiled. "Is it as good to you as it was to me?" His tongue stretched out to tangle with mine again. I pulled him close, plundered his mouth.

"Dad-dy!" Lucky yelled from the back of the house.

"Let me go see what he needs . . . then I'll be back." He wiggled his eyebrows.

"You do that." Cunnilingus was foreplay; Jare's thick pole would seal the deal.

Hot hands trailed down my chest, a finger teased my clit before he lifted off the couch to attend to Lucky. I sighed as I watched his broad back turn the corner.

You know, I think I love that man.

8

"Babe." A gentle hand shook my shoulder.

I opened my eyes and Jare was inches from my face. I ran my hand up the side of his cheek. "Hey, you."

"Looks like we're running late."

The clock read seven thirty. Definitely late. I grinned. "I know why, too." We'd had another marathon session of lovemaking last night. I stretched and yawned. Jare sat beside me, staring intently.

"Berze, I don't know what we are doing differently . . . but I love it." A hand ran over the curve of my butt.

"Me, too." I covered the hand, shifted it to my thigh then higher still to my vee.

Jare stopped my hand, shook his head. "Baby, you're gonna make me later than I'm already gonna be if you keep that up."

"You think?"

"This . . . I *know*." He lifted off the bed, pecked me on the lips. "You want to go out to dinner tonight?"

Alrighty now! The Plan was working.

"I'd love to go out to dinner with my husband."

"Six?"

"We'll be ready." I couldn't resist pulling him to me by his tie and slamming my mouth over his again.

"Umph, ump, ump. You keep teasing me and you're gonna have me doing this presentation with a boner."

I giggled at that. "We wouldn't want to give the guys anything *more* to talk about, now would we?"

"We surely don't." He kissed me again. "See you this afternoon."

"Hey." I reached in the bedside table drawer, extracted an envelope, and stuffed it into his jacket pocket.

His hands reached for the pocket. "What's this?"

I stopped the hand before it could retrieve the envelope. "Just read it before the presentation, okay? Not a moment before. Promise?"

"Promise. See you later."

" 'Bye." Frieda and Eduardo weren't the only ones who could write a hot love note.

It's amazing how switching things up could spice up your sex life. Since I'd ambushed him with that outfit, we'd been at each other like monkeys on moonshine. I was past satisfied and from the whistling he'd been doing after our morning "sessions," I'd have to say he was pretty satisfied, too.

Despite how great the sex was, I already knew firsthand it was difficult to sustain great bootylicious lovemaking for extended periods of time. Work, Lucky, family issues—life eventually intruded and disrupted, as it always did. But . . . I planned to drag every delicious drop of cum out of Jare before this ride ended.

I placed some gloss on my lips and checked my hair again before rousing Lucky. Just as I expected, he was grumpy and slow to get dressed and then gave me fits as he took his time choosing between Frosted Flakes and Apple Jacks. I tell you, getting him to the sitter's and me to work at a reasonable time was a feat in itself.

Finally, I pulled into the office parking lot, hoping today would be a slow, yet productive one. After all, I had a dinner date with my husband and I didn't need anything to mess that up.

My assistant, Sheila, had the "look" on her face as I rounded the corner. I knew that whatever would be coming out of her mouth wouldn't be good. And it wasn't.

"Morning, Berze. Mr. Hamilton just phoned. His paralegal is out and he requested that you help him today. He said he's working the industrial toxin case and he really needs the extra assistance."

Bummer with a capital B-U-M. Mr. Hamilton was the one partner no one wanted to work with. He was hyperactive, always running on full throttle, and didn't understand that the rest of the world was on idle most of the time. I'd bet half my check his paralegal was worked and harassed to the point of exhaustion and called in to get some relief. Besides I had my own briefs to research and type up.

"Great." I twisted my lips and nodded my head. "Sheila—"

"I know. Keep typing up our cases and I'll phone you if there are any new developments," Sheila finished with a capable smile.

"Right. Let me grab some coffee. I'm sure I'll need it."

And I needed it by the gallons. By the time lunch rolled around, I felt frazzled from all the multitasking I'd been doing—copying briefs, correcting errors, answering questions Sheila had concerning my other cases, checking and rechecking facts, running back and forth to the law library for more references so I could check and recheck additional facts. Thank God I'd worn flats because today was definitely not a stiletto day.

I was happy to put the final touches on the document at four o'clock. I ran the pages off and dropped the entire stack on

Mr. Hamilton's desk. Then I began arranging his paralegal's desk and left her notes to bring her up to speed when she returned the next day. God help me if she stayed out any longer.

Just as I slid my coat on and shut down the computer, what I'd feared most would happen did.

"Mrs. Stillman? You still out there?"

I wanted to tiptoe out the door, act like I didn't hear him, but my professional integrity wouldn't allow me to. "Yes, I'm here. Did you need something else?" I walked to the doorway, hoping whatever he needed would be quick and mundane.

"There seems to be some pages missing. Did you print out everything?"

Damn. I'd had to correct pages here and there, so there was a possibility I skipped a page or two in the running off. "I thought I did. What are you missing?"

"The information on *Havertown vs. Petroleum Steel.*" He fanned the paper, then pointed. "See here is where we began the information," he laid another page flat, "but here we jump to the next subject. I'm missing the pages that should be in here."

I had just enough time to pick up Lucky and get us showered and dressed before Jare arrived. "Let me see." I pulled the pages to me, eyes darting quickly through them, hoping I could spot if the pages were just misnumbered and out of whack. Dread settled into the pit of my stomach as I realized the missing info just wasn't there. "You're right. Let me run the entire document off again."

A grunt was his answer.

I powered up the computer, silently cussing as it took its time booting up. I clicked open the file, scanned it to make sure the information was included, before I hit the PRINT button. The document was one hundred and thirteen pages. My estimate was fifteen minutes tops. It would be tight, but I could still beat Jare home and have time to shower and dress.

Twenty minutes, a printer cartridge change, and sixty sheets in, I was revising that time. It actually took another twenty-three minutes since I checked and rechecked that everything was present before I handed it over to Mr. Hamilton. I crossed my fingers behind my back as he scanned through the document.

Without lifting his head, he stated, "Just leave the computer on. I'll grab anything else I need."

I skipped replying, grabbed my purse, and jogged to the elevator.

My heart sank as I saw Jare's car already in the drive when Lucky and I pulled up. I'd hoped to be primped and glowing when he saw me. Instead, I was frazzled and a bit unraveled.

Jare met us halfway to the door, scooped Lucky up, and gave me a big kiss. Not the welcome I'd expected at all, but I wasn't about to kick the gift horse in the mouth.

"Hey, babe. I knew something must have come up since you guys weren't here when I got home." He kissed me again and grinned like we'd won the lottery.

I pushed back my hair. "Yeah, it did. You're mighty happy. Did the presentation go good?" His smiling infected me.

"I thought I had everything all together . . . until I read your note." He lifted his eyebrows. "And you're wrong. You're not the luckiest woman in the world. *I'm* the luckiest man to have met and married you." He pulled me closer, lips closed over mine.

"Mommy, Daddy, enough with the yucky stuff," Lucky whined.

"Son, believe me, you only think it's yucky now. Later, you'll be trying to get all the kisses you can." Jare winked for emphasis.

"Uh uh." Lucky wrinkled his nose. "If a girl tries to kiss me, I'm gonna bop her in the head, then tell her mommy."

"That's right, baby. Nobody gets Mama's sugar but Mama."
I kissed his cheek and tickled him.

"Let's get ready to go out to dinner. I can't speak for any-body else, but I could eat a whole cow right about now." Jare's stomach grumbled, punctuating this thought. "Oh, my mom called. She has the other kids tonight and wants Lucky to stay over."

"Whoop! Whoop! I'm staying with Granny Panny!" Lucky wiggled about, clapping his hands.

I hesitated before answering. My mother, Golda, was the "good" granny, the one who followed my instructions down to the letter and wouldn't let Lucky eat everything and stay up too late. Jare's mother, Panela, on the other hand, was the "bad" grandmother. She ignored everything I said, balling up my notes about Lucky in front of me. She'd frankly stated that since she'd had four kids and Lucky was her tenth grandchild, she already knew what to do. Lucky pretty much stayed up as long as he wanted and ate every treat available.

"Well—"

"Please, please, Mommy!" Lucky grabbed me around the neck, kissed my lips. There was definitely something about the feel and smell of your own baby that caused unfair influence on your decisions. As I looked at Lucky's yearning face, I had to admit, I wasn't immune by a long shot. I finally nodded.

"Guess that's a yes." Jare grabbed me around the waist, pro-pelling us forward. "I love you, baby."

Yes indeed, I am blessed.

9

I let the warm water sluice over my tired neck and back. Jare was waiting for his mother, so I'd jumped in the shower, not wanting to delay our dinner any longer than necessary.

"*Woke up this morr-ning,*" Jare opened the shower door, a big smile on his face as he butchered Justin Timberlake's song. "*feeling kinda horr-ney.*"

I shook my hips to his warbly falsetto. "Is that right?"

"Feel that." He rubbed his lengthening cock against my soapy leg, "*Now let me go deep, deep, deep, deep, deeeeepppp,*" pulled the towel from my hands, licked my lower lip.

I closed my hand around the growing shaft, pumped it a few good times. Jare moaned and pushed himself forward.

"Practice what you preach, now hear?" I loved it when Barry White said it, so why not me too?

"*There ain't nothing wrong with a little bit of bump and grind.*" He pushed his pelvis into mine, grinding in slow circles.

"Oh no, you didn't use R. Kelly."

"Hey, the man might have his problems, but he sure enough has that sex thing down. Let me show you." His finger slid between my pubic hairs, parting my labial lips. His mouth claimed a nipple, nipped and licked at the sensitized berry. "This can be the beginning of a Twelve Play if you let it."

"True that." I wheezed out as he reclaimed my throbbing tits.

"So what do you say, Mama?" His tongue trailed down between my breasts, teeth bit me lightly on my belly, wetness in my navel. "Daddy wants you to *give it to me baby*."

I squinted. "Damn, I'm sexing a Rick James impersonator."

"Call me whatever and whoever you wanna."

His teeth pulled at my hairs, tongue slid between my lower lips, circled my clit. Sparks flew outward; chills ran up and down my spine. My fingers closed around each side of his face, pulled him closer into my snatch; his tongue diddled my stiff bud. Damn, I was feeling light-headed as sensations rolled through my body. I threw a leg over his shoulder, made my pussy totally and thoroughly available.

"That's it, Mama. Show Daddy you love what he does for you."

Damn I do. I undulated on his face; my toes curled as his tongue stabbed inside me, made my legs feel like jelly, made my pussy juice run from the sides of his mouth, mix with the shower spray.

Fingers gently sidled next to his probing tongue, spread me wider. I felt myself sliding in the soapy stall, tried to stop it, but with one leg across his shoulder, I had no real purchase. Jare didn't push me back up. Indeed, he kept his mouth glued to me through each soapy inch I descended. When I was finally on the floor of the shower, he turned off the water that was spraying directly into my face.

I pushed wet hair from my cheeks and wiped the water from my eyes. When my vision cleared, Jare was leaning forward, inches from me. With pussy juice dripping from his chin, he whispered, "Let me take you *there*." My heart double timed;

my breathing sped up four notches. He looked so earnest, so sexy. At this very moment, I'd snatch my kidney out with my fingers and give it to him if he needed it.

My voice escaped me; I could do nothing but nod. Jare pushed my legs high and opened me wide. He sat back, stared at my pussy, licked his lips. "God, you're beautiful."

My pussy lifted from the floor in response. Jare dove in, literally. His tongue flipped, flicked, pushed, probed, diddled, lapped; had my nails digging trenches in the ceramic tiles. My toes curled as he deep tongued me; my heart rate kicked into maximum gear when a finger was inserted in my ass. I was so close to coming, I felt faint. I pressed his head to me tighter.

Jare pulled back. "Uh, uh, uh. I'm not ready for you to come yet." He sat on his haunches, slid forward until his cock was positioned for entry. Each hand grabbed a thigh tight. He rubbed his cock over and over my pussy door.

God, I needed him in me now! I shifted my pelvis around, tried to slide him into my hungry pussy. Jare took his time teasing me, back and forth, insert the head an inch, pull out. I gnashed my teeth, nails etching deeper grooves in the ceramic floor at this slow, sensual assault. My fingers roamed all over his chest, his head, cupped his sac.

My pussy was slicker than an oil rig when he finally pushed my lips aside. I gasped as he stopped just as the head was completely in. I moved my hips, wanting to feel all of him immediately.

"Hungry for me, are you?" He held my thighs firmly as he pushed inside another inch.

"Yes!" My hands slid off slick shoulders as I tried to push farther onto his swollen cock.

Another excruciating inch. Nails scratched at his back, teeth bit his upper arms and shoulders as pleasure suffused me. I was wild with lust. I whimpered in frustration.

Jare pulled back, rolled me onto my stomach. I lifted to my

knees, ready to feel all of him deep inside. He surged into me. My pussy curved to his dick, wall clutching, gripping, and dripping. His belly smacked against my ass as he pistoned into me. I lifted my ass higher, pumped harder. He straddled me, balls slapping my clit, rode me hard. Hands tangled into my hair, pulled backward—beast fucking.

When each hand closed around a nipple and pulled, my clit began firing like an AK-47. I clenched him hard as delicious tingles spread throughout my body.

"Damn! Damn!" His hips pumped once, twice before hot jism poured into me and dripped onto the floor.

Sated. Dinner not even a blip in our mental waves.

10

"And the winner of our How Sexy Are You Challenge is Mrs. Jennings!" Cheryl, the hostess of the bridal shower gushed.

I looked over at my mother and shook my head. Sixty years old and she beat all the younger women in the Sexy Challenge. She was all smiles, patting her gray-streaked hair and giggling like a young girl. Cheryl was rummaging around in the bag, looking for her prize. I'd long ago given up. I'd failed the Sexy Challenge, made average on the Good Wife test, but passed the Does Your Lingerie Turn Your Man On? questionnaire with flying colors . . . but behind my mother. Batting almost one and my mother wins three out of the three.

Cheryl finally pulled the box free. I covered my mouth as I saw the photo on the outside of the package. It couldn't be! But it was. My mother had won a vibrator. And not just any vibrator. It was a Rabbit Deluxe, a model I'd salivated over but refused to order because I knew I couldn't hide it from Jare like the small bullet.

"Thank you, baby," she said and winked as she accepted the prize. "It's just what I needed. Another Thunder Down Yonder!" The room exploded in laughter as my face turned a darker shade of red.

What are you turning red for? You're very sexual. Where do you think it came from? The stork?

I had to smile at that thought. Like the saying goes, "Children don't take after strangers." Guess we were alike in more ways than I'd ever previously imagined.

"So Mrs. Jennings, do you have any lasting words of wisdom for us?" Beverly, the bride, asked innocently.

I held my breath as my mother paused and thought. She was full of surprises—she'd gleefully informed us my dad would love her in the blue G-string panties she'd won and they'd try out the fur-wrapped handcuffs this weekend. TMI in my opinion—so no telling what she would say next. "Well, baby, the secret to a good marriage, and I've been married for forty years now," she gave us the eye and held up her wedding band for emphasis, "is simple: The same thing it took to hook him is the same thing you'll have to do to keep him."

"All right!"

"I heard that!"

"Wait a minute, now let me finish." She waved her arms around to quiet the room. "So if you were hanging from the chandelier and screwing him every which way but holy," the room exploded in laughter, "then you got to remain down and dirty in the bedroom. If you don't, they feel like you did a bait-and-switch on them. And that's when their eyes start roving around."

"But Mrs. Jennings, some men's eyes rove around even when you giving them all the sex they want."

"True. But before you say 'I do' you got to know what you working with. You've got to figure out if the man you want to give your everything to is just a 'looker' or a 'partaker after looking.'"

"How are we supposed to do that?" Pam, the bride's sister, asked. "I'm just saying, when you're in love, it's hard to believe that the man that's telling you all that sweet stuff could be lying through his teeth."

"That's also true. But you've got to use that old female intuition. There's a reason women have it. Unfortunately, many of us ladies suppress it, but it will do its job every time and let you know when something is fishy with your man. You just have to heed the warnings."

"You know, it's pretty hard to get rid of the man you love just based on some intuition feelings." Cheryl's face was frowned as she spoke. "I mean, talk about looking crazy to your man. If I came at him with some 'My gut tells me you are cheating' he'll laugh me out of the house."

"They all will. But when you find out later that old Lady Intuition wasn't lying, who's laughing then?" My mother stood as she said this. "Now, I'm just an old woman who's been happily married for four decades and I'm gonna tell you *my* secret once again. Repeat it with me now: *The same thing it took to get your baby hooked is the same thing it takes to keep him.*"

The room clapped loudly as we all finished reciting. "Now I don't know about you young women, but I got to get home to fix my man some dinner." She had a death grip on the dildo package as she picked up her purse. "Y'all have a great evening and Beverly, I'll be at the wedding bright and early."

"Yes, ma'am."

Everyone exchanged hugs and kisses before we left.

Seated in the car, I had to ask. "Where did you hear that saying, Mama?" It was true, I just wanted to know who'd told her and why she hadn't shared it with me earlier.

"What? The hooked thing?" I nodded. "Girl, that's been around since women have been getting with men. I heard it from your grandmother who heard it from her mother who most likely heard it from her mother. Baby, men are simple creatures. Feed them, sex them, and let them think they are in control, and you can get anything you want from them."

She definitely wasn't lying, but I wanted to mess with her anyway. "Is that so?"

"Baby . . . just ask your daddy."

I had to laugh at that.

10 February 1868
Berkinshire, England

Eduardo,

I know my writing appears weak. It is. There is no easy way to tell you, so I'll just say it. My worst fears have been realized. I have lost our babe.

I developed a chill, then a persistent hacking cough, which quickly turned into a fever. The babe slipped from my body before anyone could do anything. I know your anguished tears are mixing with mine as I write this. Truly, if I could have prevented it, I would have.

There is some good news in the midst of our despair. Dr. Hought did say that I was recovering well and there is no reason why we could not try again.

Come home soon. I'm ready to begin anew.

Loving you always,
Frieda

15 March 1868
Madrid, Spain

Frieda,

I curse this blasted military! I am so far away when you need me most. Know that you are my love, my world, my universe. I will give you so many babies that the patter of feet will drive you insane.

Rest. 1 am on my way to you. Expect me to arrive the end of March.
Loving you,
Eduardo

Tears flowed down my face. The ache of loss tempered by love. And the love between these two . . . timeless, indeed. I felt it flowing from the fragile paper in my hands.

If Jare were gone tomorrow, would you have achieved the love you wanted with him? Or will you curse the time sitting on the sidelines, waiting for him to make a move?

Where did that thought come from? But it was a question that I needed to answer. Indeed, it had been long overdue for answering.

I finally sat down, got naked with myself. As I looked back over my life, I had to admit an ugly reality: It always seemed like I was *waiting* on someone else to give me love. I was always the one head over heels quickly and they took their time, didn't appreciate me like I'd wanted. I didn't complain, instead sat by patiently until they *got* me. I guess the reality was I didn't step up and lead my life. I was being led at their pace.

Not anymore.

I looked back at the letters. That was all the impetus I needed to stick with my plan.

11

It was time to Flip the Script. Time to switch things up, do something out of the norm for us. My solution: playacting. Specifically, dressing up like a French maid, ass cheeks peeping out and all. Since I was already downtown, I stopped at a strip mall after dropping my mother off. I'd seen the exact French maid outfit I wanted as well as some sexy shoes, a fierce pair of stilettos, from Georgette's.

I browsed the windows of the other shops I passed. I oohed at the silk table linens and admired an antique gown that wasn't nearly as nice as my own, but close. A framed photo caught my eyes in one shop window. There were the usual portraits, but this one photo had a man and woman unclad and embracing, laying on a fur rug, looking into each other's eyes. You could feel the love radiating from the picture. No one was there in their world but those two.

"I'm running a special on that particular photo series," a deep voice said behind me.

I lifted my head, turned to look at the owner of the bass

vocal cords. A dreadlocked, around-forty male smiled, then leaned against the window beside me. "Really?"

"Yes. I call it my Rejuvenation Series."

"Rejuvenation Series. Catchy. What, exactly, are they rejuvenating?"

"Are you married?" I nodded. "Then you know how it is. Things get a bit stale after a few years, so taking sexy photos together seems to get the juices flowing again, if you know what I mean." He wiggled his eyebrows.

Was he inside my mind? "I think I get the picture."

"Ahuh. I do mostly married couples, but sometimes there will be a single couple that wants to spice things up—to have that nude hanging above the bed or on their fireplace mantle to remind them of their commitment."

The idea was intriguing, to say the least. I hesitated before asking, "Can I see some other couples you've done?"

"Sure. Follow me. I'm Samuel, by the way." He lifted from the plate glass, held his hand out.

"Berze." He clasped my cool hand between his warm, large ones. I expected the perfunctory handshake, but he surprised me when he turned my hand over, lifted it to his mouth, and kissed the back.

A frisson of excitement slide up my spine. *Chivalry is* not *dead!*

This was further confirmed as he gallantly opened the door and ushered me inside. The shop smell was a lovely mixture of citrus and flowers infusing each other. Photos were everywhere—hanging on the walls, propped against the counter and chairs and sitting on the one loveseat. There were a myriad of posers and poses—babies, weddings, showers, family portraits.

"Yes, I do them all."

I turned to see Samuel holding a large portfolio. "I see."

"Here." He moved a portrait to the side and laid the port-folio on the counter. He took his time opening the clasp and spreading the leather book wide.

As I gazed at the first photo, all I could say was, "Wow. That's some kind of sexy." In the photo, a woman and man were in-tertwined, his head nestling against her chocolate breasts, her arms and legs wrapped around his golden body. Her head was thrown back, hair caught in a midair whip; like she was in ec-stasy. I could imagine him having just suckled her berries, talk-ing dirty about what he'd do next.

My pussy began to throb; my own nipples became pebbles.

"I have more."

He turned the page. The next photo was done through a fog-coated glass door. The shot showed the couple standing be-neath a showerhead, her mouth on his nipples, the water bead-ing up on her brow, his hand cupping her large bottom, fingers grasping, as water sluiced over them.

That brought back memories of me and Jare in the shower the other afternoon. I felt myself growing warmer, pussy throb-bing harder, nipples pushing and lifting; making themselves ob-vious. I shifted position as I fanned at my face, crossed my legs, clenched on my pussy.

"Getting hot, huh?" Samuel chuckled as I reddened, embar-rassed he had recognized the overt signs I was trying to hide. "It's okay. I get that reaction all the time when folks view this album."

"I can imagine."

"Let me show you my favorite." I held my breath as he turned a few more pages. If they were anything like the ones I'd just viewed, I might just cream right there. "Check this one out."

My breathing stopped. In this photo, the man and woman were facing each other, her legs splayed and intertwined over his, his wide and welcoming her within his thighs. Both of their heads were thrown back, her nipples peaking toward the sky, tongue sticking from her mouth; his teeth were clenched. Her leg shielded a direct view of his penis and her vagina, but from the positioning of the hands, I definitely would say they were mutually masturbating each other.

My clit blossomed; my knees buckled. I caught myself on the counter.

"Whoa. You okay?" Samuel stared into my face, a smirk just under the skin.

"Yeah. Just got light-headed for a moment." I shook my head, fanned at the heat suffusing my skin.

He chuckled. "I understand. Seeing love like that—like what we all crave up close and personal—does something to a person."

That photo was everything I wanted in my marriage—love, tenderness, closeness, acceptance. I suddenly felt emotional; my eyes began to burn. Maybe it was his tight summation of relationships; maybe it was my yearning to have a need met. Either way, a stray tear coasted the rim of my lids and slid from my eye. I refused to meet his gaze, instead rummaged around in my purse for a tissue. Finding a crumpled one, I dabbed at my eyes. "Yeah, it does."

He closed the portfolio, leaned his elbow on the counter. I felt his direct stare but still didn't look at him. He finally spoke. "So . . . you interested?"

This type of thing would be so out of the ordinary, so unique . . . and would go with my plan perfectly. I plunged ahead. "I am."

"Well then, let's see how good of a rate we can negotiate." He winked, smiled, and rubbed his fingers together, mimicking the money slang gesture. I had to laugh at his antics.

We spent the next ten minutes deciding on a dollar figure. It was steep, but, then again, I was shooting the moon, betting the payoff would be worth it. Samuel escorted me to the door once I'd made the appointment and paid a hefty deposit.

"Next Tuesday, six thirty."

"We'll be here." I turned to leave.

"Oh, Berze," I stopped, looked backward, "think about what positions you'd like."

I figured there were standard positions or he'd give me a sheet of positions and I'd pick them out at random. "You don't have a list or a guide or something?"

He shook his head. "Everyone is different. But if you could call me with some ideas, I'll work something out. Believe that."

"Deal. 'Bye now."

" 'Bye."

Positions. I didn't want some soft and sickly-sweet photos. I wanted something that let the true me shine through. Definitely something animalistic, since I believed the rougher it was, the better the sex all around. Of course it all depended upon Jare—

I gulped, suddenly brought back to reality. I forgot about the stilettos since I had one major dilemma: I had to actually *convince* Mr. Straitlaced Jare to get the portraits done.

"You did what?" Irritation was an understatement. "Berze, woman, have you lost your mind?" Eyes were wide, disbelieving.

Yep, over you eight years ago. "No, Jare. We need to do this. It's something neither of us has ever contemplated—"

"Doggone right. Naked pictures. We are *not* porno stars." He yanked his shirt from his pants, undid the buttons, fingers spastic, yanking.

He'd just arrived from work, so perhaps my timing wasn't the best, but I'd begun, so I planned to continue. I let out a long sigh. "Jare, this is not porno. It's erotic pictures taken between a husband and wife. You and me. Us."

His head tilted, hands stilled. "Have you been looking at porn on the Net?"

This struck a nerve. I couldn't stop the peevishness in my voice. "No, I haven't, but I am old enough if I wanted to." I sighed. "Again, this isn't porn. This is you and me taking classy, naked, erotic photos."

He snorted as he stepped out of his shoes. "Shoot, if we wanted some naked pictures, I could just pull out the old digital camera and fire away." His hands flailed the air, punctuated his irritation. "And, for clarification purposes here, just who is going to be shooting these photos?"

"The owner of the shop. His name is Samuel."

He stopped moving; eyes became narrowed slits. That was a very poor sign. "Samuel."

I kept my voice neutral as I spoke. "Yes, his name is Samuel and he is the owner and photographer. A seasoned professional, judging by the portfolio I saw."

"Ahuh." Arms crossed his chest. "Samuel what? And you met him where again?"

"I didn't ask for his last name and I met him when I was browsing the shop windows on my way to Georgette's to buy a pair of sexy stilettos."

He looked around the room, eyes searching for a shopping bag. "Stilettos." He rubbed his chin; a smile played on his lips. "You know I like you in stilettos. Why don't you put them on and model them for Daddy?"

He was good at switching the topic, but not today. The point was moot anyway. There were no stilettos. "I didn't actually *buy* them since I got sidetracked with the photos."

The smile left; an eyebrow arched. "No stilettos since you met this dude who was what? Just standing outside his shop flashing naked pictures at passing pedestrians?"

"Of course not." I rolled my eyes heavenward. I hated when he got flippant with me. "You are really being dramatic for no reason." His other eyebrow arched in response. "Look, this is how it was. I was on my way to Georgette's to buy some stilettos I'd seen earlier. As I was walking down the sidewalk, I was browsing. I stopped because there was a photo on display that caught my eye. A photo of a couple entwined. While I was *innocently* standing there, Samuel came out and asked if I'd like to know more about those types of photos."

"And you said?"

"Yes." Jare threw his hands into the air and shook his head. "Look, the photo intrigued me; I went inside for a closer look. The way you're acting, I feel like you're insinuating something is going on between me and this guy."

His head swiveled back to me. "I wasn't, but since it's been put out in the open, is there?"

"Stop." My lips pursed. Hell, I was trying to drive his ass wild, not some dude I'd just met.

"No *you* stop." He placed a knee on the bed, leaned forward. "You do realize you are asking me to let a guy, a real live got-a-cock-of-his-own dude, take a photo of my naked wife, right?"

"He's a professional. He sees naked women all the time."

He shook his head. "Not my wife, he doesn't."

Once again, we were getting nowhere fast. "Jare." I scooted closer to him on the bed, wrapped my arms around his stiff body. Jare turned to sit beside me. I caught his face in my hands. "You promised to keep an open mind about new things," I whispered. "I understand your hesitancy about another man seeing me nude, but know I love only you. I want only . . . *you.*"

Jare remained silent, eyes darting all over my face. *Push your point home, girl!* I slid my hands up and down his chest. Blew on the side of his neck. "We need to give this a try. I think it would be good for us. And, once we're finished, just think of how horny we'll be." My teeth captured an earlobe, nibbled.

"Really? Convince me."

My tongue dipped inside his stiff cartilage, probed his canal. His breathing increased. I lifted, sat behind him. I pressed my pelvis firmly into his hips, began a slow grind on his buttocks. "I see it as a twofer. We express our exhibitionist side during the photo shoot and afterward," I licked the back of his neck, "we express our purely sexual side at home." I pinched his nipple, then pulled the hard flesh.

"Go on." His hand rubbed my calf, over the knee, and up my thigh.

"All that pent-up sexual tension . . . we ought to be on fire for each other." My hands slid downward over his belly, the front of his pants. His pole was just beginning to stiffen. I massaged him slowly through the fabric.

"Not sounding half bad."

"Oh, it won't be bad at all. In fact, I believe it will be way better that either of us imagined." I unbuckled his pants, unzipped his fly, pulled his rod free.

"Better?"

I stroked his swelling head. "In fact, I'm sure I'll do something for you we've never done before." His rod jumped in my hand.

"Be careful, baby. You're playing with fire here."

"You come with the fire stick and I'll provide the moisture." I wasn't afraid to talk shit since I was more than sure about him. He *was* the poster child for vanilla sex. So whatever I did outside of our normal sexual triad—missionary, ride him cowgirl, then hit it from the back—was something we'd never done before.

I leaned back, pulled the bottle of massage oil from the nightstand. I squirted a small amount into my hand. "In fact, why don't we start now?" I covered the head of his cock with my oil-saturated hand.

He jerked. "Damn, girl, what is that?"

"You like?" I stroked up and down the length of his pole.

"It's getting hot." I smiled as his fingers bunched and released his pants over his knees. He cock was now a steel rod.

"Just wait." I rotated my slick hand over the head, felt him blossom beneath it. I took my time, pulling at the corona, pressing firmly to the base, palming his balls. My pussy leaked; I felt moisture oozing from between my lips. I lifted my knees, pulled myself closer, pressed my clit deeper into his ass.

I put my other hand into play. I worked his rod, hands moving in opposite directions as they twisted and stroked. Jare's breathing was heavy and ragged. I was definitely getting to him.

"Oh, baby, this is good. *Damn* good," he whispered.

I know. I do it on the regular.

"I—I never thought it'd b—be like this."

I smiled as he began to thrust into my waiting hand. I bit the back of his shoulder; rubbed my cheek into the sweat sliding down his face, humped his ass lightly. His thrusting increased; I felt the heat of the friction in my palms. He was close. Real close.

Now is the time.

"So . . . that's a yes?" I murmured against his ear.

"O—oh yeah, baby. We can d—do *anything* you'd like."

That's my baby.

I increased my pace. His thrusts sped up. I clamped down at the base with one hand, caressed his sac with the other hand. Gave long rubs up and down his shaft as I undulated my pussy on his ass. My panties slid around, the fabric rough, stimulating my clit. I was close, too. I chocked his head with my fisted hand, knowing all that pressure on his sensitive tip should do the trick. And it did.

"Damn! Damn! Daaaammmmmmmnnnnnn!"

Liquid coated my fingers as he came. Blood rushed to my face, my nipples, my clit. I bit into his shirt as my pussy gushed and gushed and gushed. Mission accomplished.

12

1 June 1868
Her Majesty's Royal Navy
London, England

Mrs. Eduardo Smythe,
    It is with great regret that I inform you that your husband, Eduardo Smythe, was aboard the <u>HMS Chastity</u> on 20 March 1868 when they encountered a hurricane. No sign of the ship has been found. We have assumed that all lives perished. We are saddened, as are you, by the loss.
    Our condolences,
    Admiral James Thankard

"No!"
I'd been flitting about, excited about the photo shoot later this afternoon. I'd pulled out a letter in boredom. I'd expected another sexy letter, reading about making more babies, not this. My heart ached fiercely as I reread the letter. All that love they shared and this happened.

Tomorrow isn't promised to anyone.

That's true . . . but that just meant I had to make the most of today. I straightened my spine, refolded the letter, and placed it in the chest, determined that tonight was going to be one hell of a night no matter what.

A bell tinkled as we entered Samuel's photo shop. Jare was nervous. His knee jumped and light sweat was apparent on his forehead as we stood inside.

"Relax. I'm sure we'll have a great time." I offered him a tissue.

He patted across his brow. "I'm trying." He looked at me and smiled. "You know you hoodwinked and bamboozled me, don't you?"

"Who me?" I feigned innocence, then laughed. "You can't say I don't try to keep the old home fires burning now, can you?"

He laughed along with me. "I surely can't."

A door opened and Samuel's head came into view. "That's what I like to see—my clients happy." He walked over. "Hello again, Berze." He held out his hand to Jare. "I'm Samuel, the owner."

Jare shook his hand. "Jare. You've already met my wife, Berze."

"Of course." He nodded at me and I returned the favor. He then glanced at his watch. "You guys are a bit early. Couldn't wait, huh?" He chuckled. I couldn't.

"Actually, I think Jare is still a bit tense, but I think if you showed him the photo album I saw the other day, he'll get a better idea of what we will be doing."

"Sure. Follow me. I need to finish up with the clients I have, but I'll grab it for you guys." He walked over and turned the Open sign to Closed.

We trailed behind Samuel to the counter. He lifted the same

leather book onto the top and spread it open, "Enjoy. I'll be back for you shortly."

Even though I'd seen the photos and knew what to expect, seeing them again still made me warm. I knew they were having the same effect on Jare when he said, "Dog, this is amazing."

"I know." I rubbed circles in his lower back as he turned page after page in silence. The shower scene photo made him pull me closer. As I leaned into him, I felt a brush of stiffness against my thigh. My nipples peaked, my pussy leaked.

I brushed Jare's cheek with my lips. "Has this given you any ideas about what positions you'd like us to portray?"

"Some."

Lead your man, girl.

"Baby, I'd like something that pushes the envelope; something that lets our crazy, sexy love shine through." I nibbled on his earlobe.

"Like what? Simulated 69?"

I nipped the tender flesh. "That's a start, but I also want something animalistic; you pulling my hair, cupping my breasts as you seem to take me from behind. You know, beast fucking." I rubbed my ass across his hardness.

"Damn, Berze. You *have* been thinking about this!"

"Why not? We do want these to be as sexy as possible, right?"

A creaking sound made me look around. My eyes were drawn toward the door Samuel had entered. Light drifted through and I realized the door was open. I grabbed Jare's arm and pointed.

"Hey, the door is open. Let's see what the other couple is doing." I grabbed his hand. Jare resisted.

"I'm not sure that's a good idea."

I refused to allow him to be a stick-in-the-mud today. "What could it hurt? It's not like we opened the door or anything. It opened to us, invited us to see." I knew my logic was flawed, but dammit, I wanted to know what was going on.

I could see the war going on in Jare's mind, but he finally relaxed and let me pull him along. We slowly peeked around the
edge of the door like two bad kids spying on their parents. The
room was well lit, with furniture made out of wedges in the center, and we could clearly see all the action.

"That's it. Go with your flow," Samuel instructed in a low
voice while Maxwell sang in the background.

The chestnut body of a woman was folded over a triangular
cushion, her wide ripe ass pointed straight at us. Her partner
stood in front of her, his eyes closed as his hips slowly thrust
rhythmically forward and backward. Though I couldn't see
over the cushion, either they were doing a great simulation of
fellatio or she was actually giving him head.

"That's sexy as hell," Samuel urged as his camera clicked.

The man's hand rubbed down the dark back, grasped the ass
in both hands and pulled forward before he gyrated each cheek.
I gasped as the pink of her pussy came into view.

"Shit!" Jare whispered against my hair. I guessed he'd seen it
also. Jare began rubbing my ass. I leaned into him, turned on
like hell. I undulated against Jare with movements ancient as
time; felt his return movements match my own.

The man's fingers parted her, dipped a long digit into the
pinkness. The woman spread her legs, lifted her ass, as she
pushed her body forward. He leaned over, hips still moving
rhythmically, cupped her pelvis and lifted her slightly.

"That is so hot," Samuel urged them on.

Jare's hands rubbed upward, covered a breast. His lips pressed
against my neck, his breath floating over my chest. I nuzzled
my head in the crook of his shoulder, pushed my chest out as
fingers pulled at my nipples through the fabric. My dress was
lifted as a hand crawled up my thigh and slid between my legs.

Another finger slid into the woman's pussy beside the first.
The man spat between the woman's ass cheeks. I watched as the
saliva slowly rolled over her anus. His fingers pulled from her

vagina and he sucked on his thumb before reinserting them back into her waiting hole. The thumb rubbed around and around the anus.

My body jerked as hot fingers brushed over my tingling clit. I gasped as Jare parted my own hairs, marinated his fingers in juice as he opened my lips, let a stiff finger push inside. Jare began to pump. I growled low in my throat, squeezed my thighs around his hand, needing the roughness.

"You like that, huh?"

I responded by clenching him tighter. Jare grabbed a handful of hair, pulled backward as his fingers increased their pressure and speed.

I watched, eyes glazed, as the man wormed his finger inside her high hole. The woman bucked, ass gyrated into the air. The man's hips sped up; the back of the woman's head lifted into view on each push.

Jare diddled my clit, fisted my breasts, bit the tender flesh on the back of my neck. His cock was pressed into my ass, my body wedged in the corner of the door, unable to get any respite from this sexual experience. Not that I wanted to. His cock was rock hard, egging me on.

I closed my eyes as he slicked his fingers, rubbed them back on my clit. I smelled my juices as they poured over his roaming fingers. Damn, he was nearly as good as I was. I felt my lips engorging, knew I was close. I spread my legs; his cock pressed me deeper into the wall. His fingers sped up, sensed I was about to fall over the edge of the cliff.

Jare plucked my clit like a banjo, sending sparks radiating up and down my body, made me jerk; made me bite my lip to not cry out. I couldn't help myself. This shit was just too damn good. I rotated my pussy around his fingers, gasping, clawing at the wall.

He turned me; fabric-covered iron cock drove into my clit as I came hard. I opened my mouth to scream my pleasure; Jare captured my scream with his own mouth. I rode the wave, our tongues intertwined and battling.

I was covered in sweat and heaving against his chest.

"You like that shit, huh?"

Jare never talked dirty. His voice was husky, different. That was a good sign. But I could only moan and nod in response. His fingers flicked across my sensitive clit and I jumped. "Don't touch it, baby. I can't take it right now," I managed to eke out.

Jare chuckled but gave me my downtime.

The door opened suddenly. Samuel stopped, arms full of linens, surprised, I imagine, to see us standing just outside the door. I knew my pussy scent was in the air and it was confirmed as he smiled at us and winked with knowing eyes. "If you guys are ready, let me grab some new sheets and I'll show you where to change."

"We are." Jare sounded confident. Vanilla man had vanished.

Samuel dumped his load behind the counter, grabbed up another armful, and motioned for us to follow him. He led us to a door near us and said, "Change into the robes. When you are ready, I'll be." He winked again.

There were robes hanging in a closet. We each selected one and removed our clothes. Naked, I saw Jare's cock was still at attention, throbbing in the air. "Hey, let's try to not get carried away, okay?" I reminded him. "Later, we'll work him over."

Jare gave me a noncommittal shrug. "I'll do what I can, but this is some shit he's not used to, so I can't promise he'll behave. Look at him now." His cock bobbed in rhythm to his heartbeat, precum glistening on the head.

I kneeled down and let the cock brush across my cheeks, let my breath blow as I spoke directly to the flesh-covered steel rod. "Need me to lick you now, huh?" The cock lifted higher in response. I gyrated my hips as I slid to my knees, let my tongue circle my lips, getting them ready, leaned in—

A knock on the door. "You guys ready?" Samuel called.

"Y—yeah!" Jare managed to wheeze out through clenched teeth.

"Any time then."

"Poor baby," I spoke to the now-dripping cock. "Hold that thought until later."

"Berze, girl, you about to make me lose my mind." Sweat beaded Jare's forehead.

I shrugged noncommittally this time. "Hey, the man says he needs us now." I gave him a What Can I Do? look and put my hand on the doorknob. "You coming?"

Jare righted his robe and followed me out the door.

"Well, the rules are very simple: There are no rules," Samuel stated. "Whatever position you'd like me to photograph you in, I'll do. I use a digital camera, so no negatives or need to outsource to get the photos developed. I'll print them here. I'll also sign a confidentiality agreement stating these photos will never be released and in fact will be destroyed after you collect them unless you agree to have one in my album." He opened a folder and pulled out a sheet of paper.

I nodded, feeling better. The last thing I wanted was to see our photos popping up on the Web. All three of us signed the agreement quickly.

"Let's start with something simple." Samuel motioned us in front of a blue screen with white sheets spread on the floor. "For this pose, Jare, I want you to stand behind Berze, one arm covering her breasts, one hand covering her pelvis. Berze, you wrap your arms backward around his hips, while you guys kiss. Sounds simple, but the results will be spectacular," he assured us. "Any questions?" We both shook our heads. "Then let's get you out of those robes and allow you to let your sexuality flow."

The way he'd explained everything made us both feel easy.

We dropped the robes with no hesitation. With Samuel coaxing us, we moved into position.

"Jare, move your arm lower so that her nipples are covered." Jare shifted according to the directions. "Now spread your lower hand, so that as much of her bush as possible is hidden." Jare's hand spread across my pelvis as I positioned my hands on his hips.

"That looks great!" Samuel's camera began clicking. Jare's lips came down to meet mine; his cock awakened and pushed into my butt. "Adore" by Prince began playing. My hips began rocking to the slow sinuous beat as our tongues tangoed with each other. My hands clenched his cheeks, spreading and pushing them closed. His cock stiffened, poked. I gasped as Jare let a finger flick over my clit. Shit! He was not playing fair!

But I heard nothing as blood pulsed in my ears; my uninhibited ass gyrated over an iron cock; a finger strummed major nerves. His hand began rotating around in my bush. My pussy was revved, manufacturing juice. I knew we were getting carried away but couldn't stop; didn't want to stop.

"Excuse me!" We broke apart, surprised to see Samuel fanning himself with a church fan. "I think I have enough of that pose. Ready for another?" If we weren't, from the sweat sprouting on his forehead, he sure was ready for us to be.

"Let's try this lying-down position. Jare, you're laying on your side, facing the camera. Berze, you're in front shielding his privates. Your legs are intertwined and, Jare, your arm will drape across her waist."

We nodded and began positioning ourselves. I waited until Samuel was satisfied nothing essential was visible before I made my move. Two can play the tease game. Since I was also lying on my side, I used my free hand to wrap my fingers around the head of Jare's cock. He inhaled quickly. I smiled at him as my fingers rubbed his shaft long and firmly. He swelled, head mushroomed as I stroked and swirled around it.

I stared into his glazed eyes. "I need you in me," I whispered.

"Baby, if you don't stop, I'm gonna shoot off right here."

Cum began to leak. I rubbed the lubrication around and around his head. "Stop what?" I teased. "You know you want me to do this to you."

Jare took rapid, tight breaths. "Baby—shit, that feels good—but if you keep it up, I'm gonna pop."

Samuel mercifully saved him. "That's a wrap. How about a shower scene?"

I rolled over and sat up, shielding Jare's hardness from view. "That's the simulated fellatio, right?"

"Simulated, real, it's up to you." Samuel's smirk was back.

"Cool." I looked at an uncomfortable looking Jare. "You like the idea?"

"You're playing with a damn volcano that's gonna explode all over you," he murmured.

I turned smoky no-room-for-no eyes to him. "At least water will be nearby." I lifted, held out a hand that brooked no refusal. Jare covered his erection and took my outstretched hand.

We strode hand in hand over to the shower stall. The head was outfitted with a spa attachment, so the water flow was light. I regulated the water temperature, then stepped inside. I wet my head fully, already knowing what I planned to do. Samuel began his instructions.

I interrupted him. "I've got this," I assured him. I crooked a finger at Jare. I placed Jare so that he was facing the camera. His cock already knew I wasn't about to simulate shit. This was probably as close to being an exhibitionist as I would get with this husband, so I planned to wrap my wet lips all around him. It bobbed in anticipation.

As the water sluiced down Jare's neck and chest, I pulled his head to me for a kiss. I tongued him like this was our last time before kissing down his chest, his belly, and kneeling before him.

I looked over my shoulder at Samuel. "Everything covered?" He nodded and gave me a thumbs-up. My hands pressed into Jare's waist; my chin slipped up the side of the thick shaft. Then, my lips covered his head. Jare's head rolled around on the shower glass, face scrunched, teeth clenched, as I pulled in his pole millimeter by millimeter. My tongue swirled, nails scratched his thighs as I sucked his cock further in my mouth. I gagged when he touched the back, but I didn't care. More slicking for the licking.

The spray wet my face; his hands tangled in my wet hair, guided my motions. I sucked harder than I ever had in my life. I twisted my head, stroked his sac; refused to allow his iron rod to even feel the room air. My head bobbed with gusto. Time was short and this was now or never.

My fingers circled his base, stroked rapidly as I drove him deeper down my throat. The depth did him in.

"Fuck! Fuck! Fuck!" His hands grasped, pulled like hell at my hair. I felt his cock well come to life and began pumping. I swallowed and swallowed as the salty sweet fluid filled my mouth to the brim; my pussy released its juices onto the shower floor.

The water flowed, cooling us. When we finally opened our eyes, Samuel was nowhere to be seen.

"Think we ran him off?" I asked.

"Naw, he's probably in the bathroom jerking off, wishing he'd gotten what I just did." Jare chuckled before pulling me into his arms. He brushed wet strands from my face and kissed my hair. "Berze, you amaze me. This . . . this was an experience I'll treasure forever."

I leaned back and searched his face. Was he finally thawing? "You really mean that?"

"Bank it."

We turned as a door opened. Samuel walked out, drying his hands on a paper towel. I covered a smile, wondering if he had indeed been jacking off. "Wow, that was some session, wasn't it?"

"It was a wild ride, I've got to give you that," Jare answered, then shook his head. "Naw, that shit was just downright awesome."

"Love is like that, you know." Straight. No chaser.

"That it is."

"Well, you guys can get dressed and I'll clean up here."

"When will the photos be ready?"

"Friday good for you?"

"I'll be here to get them myself," Jare spoke up.

There ain't nothing in the world like a man finally getting with a plan.

13

I was bushed. The high I'd been on since the photo shoot was finally worn down from the drudgery of work. Today had been a particularly busy one. It seemed that every major case we had would be tried in the coming week and brief on top of brief had to be prepared, ripped apart, rewritten, and prepared again. My fingers ached from the typing and stapling, my calves burned from walking up and down the ladder to grab another reference book, and my back groaned from the reaching, lifting, and carrying. All I needed was Calgon to take me away.

I knew Jare had already picked up Lucky, so I wasn't surprised to see his car in the driveway. I loved my baby, but I fiercely hoped if he wanted park time, his daddy had already taken him. Otherwise, I would be the one needing a stroller.

As I opened the door, the sound of "You Are So Beautiful" floated into the air. My stomach grumbled as good smells infused my nose. What the heck? I paused, definitely not expecting this.

Jare rounded the corner wearing sweatpants and a T-shirt, a rose clenched in his teeth, a smile on his lips. He walked over to me slowly, held up his chin. I took the offered rose. He pulled me into his arms, hands skimming over my waist, lips capturing mine.

"My mom has Lucky," he answered before I asked. His feet began moving and he pulled me into his slow dance. I let him lead me around as James Ingram's song finished. I then wanted some answers.

"What's going on here? You got the contract?" Since it was apparent we were celebrating, I figured that had to be it.

"This isn't about the contract." He stepped back, held my chin. "Berze, I'm one lucky fool."

"You're no fool."

"Yes, I am." He nodded slowly. "I read all the letters in the trunk."

"You did?" This was a surprise.

"That Eduardo and Frieda managed to find that 'uncommon love' we all want."

"Yeah, they did."

"Did you cry when you read about Frieda losing the baby?" I nodded. "And Eduardo getting lost at sea . . . baby, I teared up myself. I didn't see it coming. I thought they'd live to get old and gray together, raise a bunch of kids . . . but that's how life is. You think you've got it all planned and Bam! monkey wrench."

"Big-time monkey wrench."

"It made me look at myself. I mean, I sat down and really evaluated the man in the mirror. And I realized I've got this wonderful woman that wants only me and I refuse to do the things she needs to please her because I selfishly wanted to stay in *my own* comfort zone, control the situation . . . the masturbation and toys among other things."

"Jare—"

"Shhh. Let me finish." I stayed quiet. "Berze, I realized *you* are the best part of *me*. Hell, without you, there is no me." I felt the meltdown starting in my legs. "You asked me for something simple: to try to make us all we could be." He gave a little snort. "The male in me heard but dismissed it. You know us. As long as we get fed and have regular sex when we want it, we're good. Not once giving thought to how we're shortchanging our partner.

"But baby, you *showed* me how good we could be. How we could push the limits within *us*. That photo shoot? Yes, I was reluctant at first. What man isn't when he's stepping outside his comfort zone into a zone someone else created and controls?" He smiled again. "Stupid, since we want our partner to believe in us, follow us blindly, but when the shoe is put on our foot, we try to act like it's not the same." He shook his head. "But baby, that was the bomb! I would have never ever come up with that idea. But you did."

"We needed it," I whispered. I loved him with every breath I had, but I couldn't live without the passion I needed in my world.

"We did. I may not tell you how much you mean to me often enough, but I heard this song today that put it best: I need you bad as a heartbeat; bad as the air I breathe. Baby, I can't imagine living my life without you in it. You . . . are . . . me."

Tears slid down my face unchecked. He brushed them aside. "Baby, whatever you need, I want to be there to provide it. Whatever your heart desires, I want to be your Santa Claus and give it to you. Whatever you want to try, your boy is down for it. You name it, I'll move hell, high water, the devil, and the army to get it for you." He pulled me into a hug. "Baby, I'm crazy about you and for you. Please don't ever leave me. I'll go insane," he pleaded into my hair.

I couldn't stop the tears if I wanted to. Yes, I'd plotted and planned, hoped and prayed, and doggoneit if everything I wanted hadn't come to pass. I felt . . . full. Jare's eyes were shiny with tears. Seeing them, the faucet opened wide and we cried together.

Tears mingled with kisses.

Kisses were followed by rubs and hugs.

Rubbing and hugging led to grasping, biting, and licking.

The bites and licks made my pussy slick, his dick like an iron pipe.

I wanted more Jare. My hand tugged at his waistband. I was shocked when instead, he brushed my hands aside. "Just wait." My mouth dropped open as he picked me up and carried me upstairs.

He lay me on the bed, picked up the remote, and hit the stereo. Prince's "I Would Die 4 U" boomed out of the speakers. Jare began gyrating on the first note. I sat back, not sure what was about to happen but ready for him to brang it on!

Jare pulled his shirt over his head, twirled it around, and threw it at me. I caught it in midair. He turned his back, began pulling at the waistband of his pants. I was surprised to see his naked butt as he slid them down his legs.

Jare jumped around, and my eyes became marbles as I took in the black pouch G-string he was wearing. He was already hard, so his cock was straining at the material. My pussy leaked.

U! I would die 4 U!

He shook his hips, made his cock pop against his thighs. I clapped my hands as he rolled his lower body in beat to the music.

"Work it out, baby! Work it out!" I screamed.

He then pulled at the G-string, teased me with a show of his thatch before covering back up.

"Take it off!"

Jare winked, then pulled his cock out of the thin material, waved it at me.

"Yeah, baby!" I was on my knees, scrambling to the bottom of the bed, wanting to get my lollipop.

He pulled it close, then back just as I was near enough to taste, teasing me unmercifully. I couldn't take it anymore. When he turned around, I bear hugged him, one hand on his cock, the other spanking his ass.

"Those are some sad girlie slaps," he taunted me.

I put my back into it . . . well, as much as I could focus anyway, because precum had dripped from his cock and over my hands, slicking things up . . . and I took advantage, squeezing and rubbing his thick shaft.

"Oh, you trying to make me pop early, are you?"

Jare twisted around, grabbed me around the waist, and sat me on the bed. He rummaged around in the nightstand, coming up with the silver bullet he'd taken from me weeks earlier.

"Let's do this together."

My pussy *vroom, vroomed*!

Jare lay beside me and claimed my lips again. He tied my tongue in knots before pulling my blouse over my head. His fingers traced the patterns on my bra. "I love your tits." He could never tell me that enough. My horniness shot up to the stratosphere.

I pulled my breasts free, palmed them, held them out for him to suckle. I sighed deep as his hot lips latched on, sucked me like I was producing milk. His tongue traced beneath my breasts, to my belly. I felt his warm breath on my pube.

Jare shifted his body so that his cock was closer. "These are the rules, Berze: no mouths. Hands, or, in this case, toys only."

Damn. Just when I was about to stuff my mouth full. But I was game. "Cool."

The bottle of lube was passed around. I slicked both hands, knowing two hands were better than one when masturbating a man. I watched Jare lube up the bullet lightly. Then it was on!

I fisted, pulled, rubbed, and stroked Jare's cock. The bullet hummed over, beside and around my sensitized flesh, teasing me terribly. I moaned and jerked as the bullet was slid onto my clit. It felt like electric jolts passing through my lower body. That didn't make me let up on Jare's cock, though. I swirled my fist over the head, pushed at the frenulum tissue, massaged his balls. He thrust forward into my waiting hands.

Jare fucked me with the bullet. My hips lifted to meet each push of the vibrating toy. My walls sucked the metal shell, greedily pulled at the sensations-emanating machine.

"Damn!"

Jare surged into my palms, his hands pistoning the bullet into my sopping pussy. I ringed and vised his cock. He pushed fingers in beside the bullet and stroked. I felt that shit down to my core. My body began to shake, my heart raced.

We both screamed as we managed to hit "the spot." Jare creamed all over my hands and I shot a load of juice a few inches into the air.

I was damp and sticky as he moved to lay beside me. He cuddled me. "I never knew it could be like this."

"Oh baby, this is just the beginning."

"The beginning?"

"You'd be amazed at the toys they make now."

"And I guess you plan to try them all out?"

This was new territory so I couldn't be greedy . . . yet. "Only with you to help me, baby. Only with you."

Jare thought a moment. "It's doable."

"You have no idea."

We hugged, chuckled, and loved into the evening.

I was cleaning out the bottom of the chest. The wedding dress and corsets had fetched a pretty penny on eBay, well above my expectations. I had made enough for us to have a second honeymoon in Cabo San Lucas.

A piece of paper I hadn't seen before was wedged into the

side of the trunk. I gingerly teased it out. I spread it open and realized it was a letter I'd missed.

1 May 1870
Los Angeles, CA
United States of America

My dearest Frieda,
*   I know this letter is a shock to you. Most likely I have been declared dead, however, that is not the case. I was one of the fortunate five that was rescued after a few weeks floating on the ocean. I can't say if we floated to shore, but I woke one day in a hut with women taking care of me. It was unfortunate that the natives did not speak our language and we had no idea of where we were. I suspect the Guam Islands. We did attempt to travel inland in hopes of meeting with assistance, but the jungles made that impossible. Two of us were lost, swallowed up in a pit and quicksand.*
*   Finally, a boat traveled to the island for trade and I was able to beg passage from the captain to wherever he was going. It was to Los Angeles, California, in the United States.*
*   Frieda, I am not the man I was. In fact, I am in pitiful shape. I have lost a great deal of hair, teeth, and weight and from the mirror, resemble a stranger to myself. But know that despite my outward appearance, my heart beats strong with love for you. I hope you can accept that.*
*   It was thoughts of you that kept me pressing forward, looking for a way out. I don't care for my heart to beat unless it's next to yours. I don't care to breathe air if I can't share it with you. I don't care to live, if dying will*

*have us meet again sooner. I only hope my prayers have
been answered and you have not remarried.*

*I am on my way to you. I shall arrive by the end of the
month.*

Loving you into eternity,
Eduardo

Folded inside the letter was a newspaper clipping:

5 August 1870. Society News.

**It was a night of celebrating love as Capt. Eduardo
Smythe renewed his vows with his wife, Frieda.**

**Eduardo, as you all know, was missing for a few years,
lost somewhere on a remote island and declared for
dead. His return has been something straight from a
fairy tale. Indeed, the love they obviously share makes
those not in love green with envy. Good luck to them
both.**

I screamed! Frieda got her Eduardo back. I ran downstairs
to find Jare. "He came back!" I shouted into his startled face.

"Slow down. What happened?"

"Eduardo didn't die at sea! He was rescued on some obscure
islands until a boat came that took him to Los Angeles. Here.
Read it." I thrust the letter into his hands.

Jare read the letter and a smile broke onto his face. "Damn,
that's amazing."

"Isn't it?"

"What's more amazing is that he said something similar to
what I said. Need you bad like a heartbeat, bad like the air I
breathe."

"Wow. Guess we've got that 'uncommon love' thing going
on too, huh?"

"Looks that way."

Jare stood, took my hand. "Have I showed you how much I love you today?"

My pussy sputtered to life. "No, I can't say that you have."

He claimed my lips. "Bed, table, or floor?"

I pursed my lips, thought a moment before replying, "All three?"

Jare burst out laughing. "Woman, you *are* too much."

"Just for you, baby. Just for you."

We then began a dance old as time . . . together.

Captive

Kimberly Kaye Terry

1

_____

"Hell no, we won't go, hell no, we won't go, hell no—"

Tessa lightly touched her friend Peaches' shoulder to get her attention.

"Peaches, it's not that kind of party, sweetie. This is a peaceful demonstration."

"Oh shoot, girl, my bad!" Peaches lowered her voice dramatically and glanced around at the other demonstrators gathered around the steps of the National Mall. "This is my first protest. I guess I kinda got carried away," she admitted with a sheepish grin.

"No! I *love* your enthusiasm. Just for this one, we need to keep it as calm as possible," Tessa replied and gave her friend a reassuring smile.

"Girl, now you know, that might be kinda hard for me. Peaches don't really *do* calm." She pursed her full, crimson tinted lips into a moue.

"Well, how about low key?" Tessa asked, biting back a smile.

"Hmmm. I *guess* I can do that . . . for a minute!" Peaches

replied and both women laughed. "I don't want to embarrass you. Seriously. You know I can get carried away a bit."

"A *bit*?" Tessa asked, arching a brow.

"Okay, okay. More often than not," she admitted and again they laughed. "For you, I'll try and rein in the shine," Peaches replied while smoothing her long, sculpted nails over her perfectly coiffed, mahogany-tinted upswept hair.

"Always the diva."

Tessa shook her head, yet her smile remained in place. Peaches had really made her laugh and it felt good. It had been a while since she'd even felt like smiling about anything.

"Is there any other way to be?" Peaches asked and winked.

Tessa had been friends with Peaches for most of her life and knew that behind the mask of a glamour girl, the woman had a heart of gold. Growing up, Peaches had often been the only child of her own age that her father "allowed" her to associate with. Peaches' father had worked for Tessa's father as his personal chef, and the two girls had grown up as close as sisters from the time they were in diapers.

Although their lives had taken different turns, moving them miles apart from one another, Tessa going away to go to college in Atlanta and then law school at Harvard, and Peaches going to a top culinary school in Italy, one Tessa's father had helped to finance, the two women had kept their friendship strong. Tessa had recently moved back home after several needed years away from her father, and the two had picked up their friendship as though they'd never been apart.

"I wouldn't want you any other way." Tessa gave her friend a quick hug. After exchanging a few more words with her she moved away, making her way toward the makeshift bleachers she'd had put in place in front of the crowd of demonstrators.

As she walked, she glanced around at the other protestors, pleased with the large turnout. After the last demonstration,

Tessa hadn't been so sure she'd have very many of her supporters there.

She glanced toward the bevy of DC police, most with protective, bulletproof shields placed in front of them, some on horseback, shields in place on their bodies as well as on the horses. She sighed.

Several of her regular demonstrators, ones that had been steadfast supporters in her campaign to get KhemCom to own up to their culpability in potentially harming the health of many in a small farming community in Nebraska, had informed her that they'd received threatening, anonymous messages.

Messages that escalated to overt threats after their last protest, making Tessa unsure of what to expect in the way of support for today's protest.

Tessa wouldn't have blamed any of them if they had been afraid and hadn't showed. She herself had received similar threats.

She shuddered, remembering the latest "message" she'd had delivered to her.

She'd opened her front door of her apartment and had found a beautiful bouquet of red roses leaning against the wall near her door. There'd been no carrier with a form to sign for them, just the beautiful flowers.

Wondering who'd sent her such beautiful flowers, particularly since she was currently single and definitely *not* looking, she'd picked them up and taken them inside. After placing them on her counter, she'd noticed the note. After opening the note, a chill ran through her.

We would hate for Jessica not to receive the care she needs to fully recover.

The note was an exact duplicate of one Lauren Woodridge told Tessa that she'd received at the hospital a week prior. The note had been tucked inside an innocent-looking, bright arrangement of helium balloons for her daughter, who was in intensive care, and Lauren had been afraid, unsure what the subtle threat meant.

As Tessa thought of the little girl in the hospital, hooked up to lifesaving devices, her resolve strengthened. Scare tactics wouldn't deter her from trying to help Jessica and her mother receive justice for what had happened to the little girl. What *could* happen to anyone in the small community.

Jessica had simply been the first one to fall ill, directly, Tessa knew, because of the barely legal practices of the industrial company, KhemCom, whose facility was located just miles outside the small town.

Forcing the memory of the helpless little girl to the side, Tessa plastered what she hoped was a confident smile on her face as she approached the makeshift podium.

If all went well, they'd get the attention from the media, attention that would force those greedy, slimy bastards to own up to what they were doing and end their secret dumping into the community's main water source, she thought grimly.

A sizzle of awareness suddenly arced over her. Tessa *knew* she was being watched. And not just by the benevolent eyes of the supporting crowd.

Her eyes darted around, the feeling of being watched growing with each second. She felt vulnerable—and, if she were honest with herself, afraid.

She swallowed the fear and tapped the microphone to make sure it was connected.

"Thank you all for coming in support of the efforts of Planet Now," she began, relieved when her voice came out crisp and clear, strong. If there was a slight hitch in her voice, indicating her extreme nervousness, she was sure not many picked up on it.

She began to speak, outlining the reasons for their demonstration, and why the continued abuses of KhemCom couldn't continue. "I had the pleasure of meeting with, Jessica Holt," she began and stopped, clearing her throat. This time the emotion that flooded her had nothing to do with fear, but of the poignant memory of the first time she visited the child at St. Augustine Children's hospital, as her mother sat at her daughter's bedside, holding the little girl's frail hand as she fought for her life.

"Studies have shown a very strong direct link with this small town's increase in children's asthma and respiratory problems, and the contaminants that are being systematically dumped into this community's own backyard. No more."

There were murmurs of approval from the crowd as she continued.

"This new standard of exempting thousands of tons of hazardous wastes produced at hundreds of refineries all in the name of greed *has* to stop!"

Tessa warmed up to her subject, ignoring the increasing feelings of danger. She held up a hand. After the applauding and cheering of the supporters died down, she continued to speak.

"With a sweep of a congressional pen this stuff is no longer deemed harmful if it's converted into gas and burned. But," she said, clenching her raised hand into a fist, and raising her forefinger to make a point. "Make no mistake, these wastes *are still toxic*! Not only are they killing our fish and marine life, but they're also harming our children."

Tessa held up a photo of Jessica as she lay in the hospital bed, her pretty face obscured by a mask with tubes connecting her to a breathing device. Despite it all, a brave smile graced the little girl's pale face behind the mask.

"And companies like KhemCom are the ones directly responsible. They *must* be held accountable," she finished grimly.

Suddenly, Tessa felt a sharp pinprick of awareness, followed by an even more distinct feeling of being watched.

The hand that held the child's photo began to tremble. She

squinted her eyes and ran a glance over the crowd, knowing instinctively she was somehow in danger.

Yet she stubbornly forced aside her fear.

Tessa pressed on, readying herself to say more when she caught, in her peripheral vision, a flash of someone moving swiftly toward her.

In what felt like slow motion the next series of events unfolded.

A loud, masculine voice shouted, "Move!" and a large body tackled her just as she heard a whizzing sound. She grabbed her shoulder, crying out in pain, stunned when she realized someone had shot her.

The man, one whose face she hadn't been able to see clearly, rolled with her to the soft grass, landing on top of her and covering her body.

Before the darkness of unconsciousness enveloped her, she distantly heard someone scream, "Oh God, Tessa has been shot!"

Seconds later Tessa fainted.

2

"You went too far this time, Tessa!"

"*I* went too far?!"

"Yes!" Senator Evan Waters rasped. The strong grooves bracketing his generous mouth deepened as he stared at his daughter in anger . . . and disapproval.

More than anything, Tessa picked up on his disapproval.

"Dad, you're overreacting! The bullet only grazed me," Tessa replied in a tired voice. She grimaced, unable to hold back the hiss of pain after she shifted in the narrow hospital bed and a shot of pain radiated from her bandaged shoulder across her chest.

When her father heard her gasp he strode toward the bed, penning her with a stern look.

"Do you even *hear* what you're saying? Good God, Tessa, those words shouldn't even be coming out of your mouth! 'I only got grazed by a bullet!' " He shook his head. "Do you even *hear* how ridiculous that sounds?"

"I—"

Before she could speak, her father cut in. "And why do you *have* to do this? Why you? Why do you have to be involved?" He asked the question and began to pace the room. Not allowing her a chance to answer, he continued, "I have come to realize you aren't going to make any meaningful use of your law degree. A law degree from Harvard, the most prestigious university in the entire damn United States."

His glance raked over her. She flinched from the disappointment she saw reflected in his dark gaze. He turned away.

"I think you're not interested in taking your career seriously. Why squander your training on these do-gooder causes? To go after KhemCom is just plain lunacy and beyond ridiculous!"

Tessa wished her father would accept her, love her, for who she was, and not who *he* wanted her to be. She squared her shoulders. "Ridiculous, Dad? How you even shape your lips to say something like that is beyond ridiculous to me! You know KhemCom is responsible for all those kids being sick. They're responsible for Jessica nearly dying. You know they're illegally—"

"There is *nothing* illegal about what they're doing! They are adhering to EPA standards—"

"Yeah, standards the EPA put into place for conglomerates like KhemCom to continue to grease their greedy-assed palms and get by with the bare minimum of regulation! They don't give one goddamn—"

"Watch your mouth, young lady." Her father shot her a warning look.

Incredulously, Tessa stared at her father. She took a deep breath, and briefly closed her eyes, again desperately wishing she and her father could find some common ground. The pain of his disappointment in her cut deeply.

"You make it sound as though I'm doing this *to* look ridiculous! I'm not! I'm doing this because the public needs to know the truth! You can hide your head in the sand as long as you want, Dad. It won't change the facts," she said grimly.

"Like I said, they're not doing anything illegal, Tessa! Why don't you just let this go, baby?" Her father turned insistent eyes toward her. Tessa saw the pleading gleam in his eyes as well as a look of desperation that she didn't understand.

"Dad, it doesn't make what they're doing morally right just because it's legal. Barely legal," she said, her voice lowered. Her father simply stared at her, a worried frown on his face.

"You know, you keep asking me why I do what I do. So why are you defending these slimeballs? What do you have in all of this?"

Before her father could turn away, Tessa saw a dark flush redden his dusky-colored cheeks. A deep, unsettling feeling gripped in her stomach.

"Dad?" she questioned, her voice hesitant.

He kept his back turned away from her. His hands were clasped behind him as he stared out of the hospital window in the corner of her room.

It was a long time before he spoke again.

Tessa leaned back against the thin hospital pillows and listened as her father listed the many reasons why she was a damn fool for even getting caught up in her current situation. As he ranted on, she closed her eyes and tuned him completely out. What was the use anyway?

He never had listened to her. What had made her think for one minute he would start today? He shouldn't be arguing with her, not for a second.

Had an unknown someone not knocked her to the side seconds before the bullet that grazed her shoulder hit, it would have made its intended target and blown her heart away.

Tessa shied away from the implications of it all, not ready to think about the bullet that could have ended her life, or her father's reaction.

". . . and that is exactly why, since you refuse to listen to me, and stop all this ridiculous *Tree-hugging-save-the-environment* nonsense, I've had to take matters into my own hands."

At this, Tessa's eyes flew open. "What are you talking about?" she asked, a different kind of sinking feeling settling in her gut.

The kind that told her she was not going to like what came out of her father's mouth next.

She was right.

"You heard me. And to that end, I've brought in someone to watch over you."

"Watch over me?" Tessa's voice rose in direct proportion to her heartbeat's increase.

When her father turned away and avoided her eyes, her uneasy heart thumped even harder against her chest.

"Yes. I've secured a bodyguard for you. Someone I can trust. Someone who'll not only protect you, but will also let me know if . . . *when* . . . you get yourself into situations you can't handle."

Tessa fought back stinging tears and ground her teeth together until her jaw ached. As usual, her father was treating her like a child.

"And just what makes you think I'll let some *bodyguard* watch over me? Come into my life and disrupt it?"

"Because you know you need me. That's why." The answer didn't come from her father. Tessa turned her head swiftly toward the door.

Before her father could answer, the door to her hospital room had quietly opened and both she and her father stared at the man who filled the doorway.

He stared over at them both, nodding his head toward her father, before turning his deep gray eyes toward Tessa, with a lift to one of his thick brows.

He kept his gaze on Tessa as he strode into the room. His

tall, hard body seemed to dwarf the room and its occupants, Tessa thought with a shudder.

Tessa felt like she'd been hit by another bullet.

Stars flashed before her opened eyes and her throat grew dry. Her heart plummeted to her stomach as she stared at six feet plus of gorgeous man standing in the doorway of her hospital room, his gaze locked with hers.

She could look at nothing and no one but him. Everything around her faded from her existence at that moment.

Barring small changes in his appearance, he looked the same as he had the last time she'd seen him.

His dark, wavy hair was neatly drawn back from his broad forehead in a low ponytail that ended at the end of his neck. His concession to respectability, Tessa thought with an inner, painful laugh.

He was wearing a dark gray T-shirt, the color identical to his eye color, eyes fringed by dark, dense lashes. His skin was the tone of rich, decadent coffee with a healthy dose of sweet cream, features chiseled to perfection, with an aristocratic nose, full lips, and a squared chin sculpted as though by a master's hand.

He wore a closely cut beard and mustache that did nothing to hide his full, sensual lips, the beard cut low so that the strong cleft in his chin was easily discernible.

She ran her gaze down his body.

Her eyes drank in his masculine beauty, starting with the hard lines of his densely packed musclar chest.

He wore his gray T-shirt untucked, the hem brushing a pair of faded old Levi's that were wrapped around a pair of thighs so thick the rough denim did nothing to hide their massive beauty.

He stared at her, his thick dark brows drawn together in a frown, nearly meeting in the middle. A burning, intense look she could feel clear across the room.

Tessa felt sweat trickle down her face, trailing a path down the valley between her breasts.

His solemn gaze followed the path.

She gripped the edges of the thin hospital sheet and pulled it to her chin in an instinctual act of self-preservation.

Gideon Myrie.

The man her father thought would protect her.

The same man who, seven years ago, had been the one to nearly destroy her.

Gideon's eyes drank in the sight of Tessa like a man lost in the Sahara searching for water. The cheesy mental analogy made him wince, but damn if it wasn't true.

He forced his gaze away from her.

After a brief nod of acknowledgment toward Senator Waters, he turned his attention back to the small woman who lay on the narrow hospital bed staring at him. His hungry eyes went over her beautiful—and angry—face.

Her large, dark brown eyes widened as she stared at him, while the bottom edge of her wide, lush lips quivered a little.

Nothing much had changed from the last time he'd seen her close up, over seven years ago. Especially those eyes. They gave her the appearance of a virginal innocent, completely at odds with the woman he knew her to be.

His gaze traveled down the short bridge of her nose and zeroed in on her lips. Her mouth was a perfectly shaped bow, like a present ready to be opened, he thought. He remembered a time when he'd been the first man to sample what her decadent lips promised.

Instead of the standard-issue hospital gown that showed a patient's entire backside, ass included, to the world, Tessa's small frame was wrapped in a scarlet red, silk gown with narrow straps, the deep red striking against her chocolate brown skin.

Although half of her body was covered by the sheet she was snuggled under—which she'd brought all the way up to her chin in fact, once he entered the room—Gideon already knew what the sheet hid from view.

LaTessa Price-Waters had a body built for sin seven years ago.

Seven years later, just looking at her sweet self, even hidden beneath a thin hospital sheet and white throw, made his dick thump in excitement and his balls swell in anticipation of getting next to her. He almost forgot the reason he was back in her life.

To no avail, he willed his unruly cock to calm down and kept his face neutral.

Now was not the time to take a trip down memory lane. Now was not the time to remember what it was like to be inside her, making love to her until they both lay sweaty and exhausted, unable to move.

Shit.

He'd come here at the senator's urging, hired to protect her before she got herself killed. Not that he'd needed the senator's say-so. Gideon had decided long before Senator Waters contacted him that it was time he came back into Tessa's life.

With or without her controlling father's approval.

The fact that Waters had been the one to contact him and ask Gideon to actually *protect* his daughter, well, that was an irony that hadn't escaped Gideon's attention.

He quelled his gut reaction to seeing her looking vulnerable and hurt. Her pretty dark skin was ashen, and the dark circles underscoring her eyes too obvious.

His first inclination was to pick her up and haul her out of the hospital and hide her from those wanting to harm her. He took note of the soft bandage that wrapped around her shoulder beneath her armpit and the small bandage placed above one of her finely arched brows.

She'd come damn close to being killed. Had he not tackled her to the ground seconds before the bullet hit, it might have hit its intended target: her heart. Tessa would have been stone cold dead, instead of lying in the hospital bed, staring at him as though she was seeing a ghost.

"Gideon! So glad you're here. Maybe you can talk sense into my daughter. God knows, she's not listening to me!" Senator Waters exclaimed, seeming relieved that Gideon had interrupted what looked to have been yet another heated argument between father and daughter.

Despite her surprise and obvious displeasure at seeing him, she shot her father an incredulous look, Gideon noticed. The senator flushed under her penetrating stare. Nothing had changed between father and daughter, either.

No doubt Tessa wondered at the gall of her father, bringing Gideon back into her life. Particularly since her father had been instrumental in removing Gideon in the first place.

"I don't know what's going on here, but whatever it is, you can forget about it! I don't need a bodyguard . . . protector . . . or whatever! I'm perfectly capable of taking care of myself."

"Why don't I leave you two to get reacquainted?" Senator Waters said to Tessa, ignoring her indignation.

After delivering an absent kiss on her furrowed brow, he quickly shook hands with Gideon and moved toward the door.

"What? Dad! I don't think so! Wait—" Tessa cried out, left talking to the swinging door. Senator Waters had moved with admirable speed out of the room, giving his daughter no time to react to his leaving.

Smart man.

Tessa stared after her father, pulling her bottom rim of her lip between her teeth, the frown still firmly in place. She then turned toward Gideon.

Like a recalcitrant child, she crossed her arms fiercely and glared at him.

Unlike the child he likened her to, her ample breasts were pushed up when she crossed her arms beneath them, and the upper, plump part swelled above her gown. He tore his gaze away and, mimicking her, crossed his arms over his chest too. He leaned against the wall near her bed and waited.

He didn't have to wait long.

"What the hell are you doing here, Gideon?" she asked angrily, barely getting the words out between her tense lips.

"You've been quite the, uh, philanthropist over the last few years, I hear," he said, purposely goading her, sliding his gaze lazily over her as she lay under the covers on the hospital bed.

He pushed away from the wall and walked closer to the bed. In a second or two he was so close to her, the heat from her body felt like a caress.

Unable to stop himself, he reached out a hand and stroked her soft cheek.

Her eyes stayed glued to his, her lips parted a little. Her soft breaths escaped as he allowed his finger to stroke down the line of her long neck, stopping before he reached the wound.

His eyes left hers and he stared down at the bandages. Then he lightly stroked his fingers over the white sheet wrapping around her shoulder and partially covering the swell of one of her breasts.

"God . . . you could have been killed, Tessa," he murmured, inhaling a deep breath.

"Would it have mattered to you, Gideon, if I had?" she asked, a hitch in her voice. There was a wealth of emotion in the depths of her dark eyes, from pain to anger, before she closed her expression down.

But before that, just for a second, he caught the look of longing that flashed in her pretty dark eyes.

Her mouth tightened and she snatched the sheet higher up to her chin with one hand, staring at him malevolently.

If looks could kill, he was a dead man standing, Gideon thought with unease.

"Of course it would matter, Tessa," was his only reply.

She glanced around the room, as though the answer could be found there. The need to get away from him was paramount.

"It's been a long time," she said with a shrug.

"Time has nothing to do with it. I've never stopped thinking of you," he said, looking deeply at her, as though trying to read something that was no longer there.

Something she refused to admit *was* there, despite the mocking inner laugh that reverberated in her head, calling her all kinds of a liar.

She moved restlessly in the bed, the crisp sheets suddenly hot and itchy on her now hypersensitive skin.

"How—" she stopped and cleared her throat. "Why—did my father get you involved?" She watched with wary eyes as he stood and began to walk around the room, as though looking for something.

When he stopped and turned back to face her, there was a look in his eyes that instantly made her heart skip a beat.

"He knew I was the only one you'd listen to," he replied, crossing his thick arms over his broad chest. "I was the only one who could make you behave."

Tessa felt a sudden desire to throw the brown pitcher filled with lukewarm water on the nightstand near her bed at his mockingly handsome face.

"I don't need you or anyone else to *make me behave.*" Tessa said in a clipped voice. "I've grown up, Gideon, in case you haven't noticed." She squelched the desire to stick her tongue out at him, feeling all of ten years old as he stood staring down at her, his face set in stern lines.

His gaze rolled over her, and despite the sheet, she felt naked; exposed, as his gaze seemed to center on her covered breasts.

"I noticed," he replied.

Defiantly she shook her head. "Well, whatever you and my father think you're going to do, it's not going to work."

"I guarantee you won't be continuing with this Tessa. You will stop." He gave her a slight smile, but his canine teeth showed, sending images through her mind of the Big Bad Wolf seconds before he devoured Little Red Riding Hood.

She shot him back what she hoped was a confident, uncaring smile. "Make me."

"It'll be my pleasure."

This time his smile sent shivers of fear mixed with an involuntary shudder throughout her body.

3

"Let me check everything out first." Gideon turned toward her, after cutting the engine of his SUV.

He opened his palm, silently indicating he wanted her to give him her keys. Noting the determined expression on his handsome face, Tessa sighed and fished her keys from her purse and handed them over.

"Stay here," he said, pinning her with a look, his thick brows drawn together.

"I don't need you to—" Before Tessa could finish the automatic protest, he'd opened the door to his SUV, eased his long legs out, and was striding toward the front door of her condo.

Tessa leaned back and blew out an irritated breath as she watched his long legs quickly eat up the short distance.

Watching him walk was like watching a panther in the jungle: way wild. He was all man. And he wasn't the type to take his responsibilities lightly.

She knew only too well that since he'd given his word to her father to "protect" her, there was nothing she could do to try and get rid of him.

She had so many questions. She leaned back against the leather headrest.

Why had he come back? When he left she thought she'd never see him again. "God, why me?" she murmured out loud, staring out the car window watching as lights began to flicker on in each room of her garden level apartment.

It would take him a while. Gideon was nothing if not thorough in everything he did.

Thoughts, unbidden, came to her mind of the last time they'd been together. It was right after they'd made love. And just like everything else, he'd been . . . thorough.

She'd lain there beside him in his bed, her body completely satiated, boneless, satisfied sexually, but mentally a mess, thinking of what she had to tell him.

"Gideon, I have something to—" Tessa began, only to stop.

When he turned to face her, his sexy gaze low and drowsy after making love, she lost her nerve.

"I have wonderful news, baby," he'd said at the same time. Realizing that she'd spoken first, he laughed low, "You go."

She smiled in relief. He was giving her a reprieve.

"No, you go. Mine can wait."

He reached a hand and stroked a soft caress over her hair. She automatically leaned into his touch. "I think your father is coming around."

The mention of her father had the opposite effect of Gideon's sweet touch. Her body tensed, instantly.

"You spoke with my dad?" she asked. "He told you?" She rose from the bed and faced him, the sheet falling off her body, exposing her breasts.

"Told me what?" he asked, a frown settling across his thick brows.

"Never mind. What are *you* talking about?"

"Your father asked me this morning if I'd be interested in

setting up the new resort he's opening in Jamaica. He told me he'd give me free rein, I'd have autonomy to make a lot of the decisions," he continued, oblivious to the look of relief that flashed across Tessa's expressive face.

He turned toward her and lifted her up to lay on top of him, straddling him.

"Gideon!" She laughed, despite the anxiety she felt clawing in her chest.

He laughed with her. "Don't you know what this means, baby?"

She smiled lightly. "No, why don't you tell me?"

"It means what I said—your father is finally coming around. No more sneaking to see you, no more feeling as though I'm not good enough. I can prove to your father I'm more than an ex-military grunt. If he can trust me to do something this big, he'll trust that I can take care of his daughter!"

She cringed and Gideon, always in tune with her, picked up on it.

"Damn, baby, I didn't mean it like that. I just—" He stopped and pulled her down on top of him, and kissed her.

His comment sent a short, jabbing pain to her heart.

"It's okay. It's true. Daddy always put business first. He has to," she said, after he'd released her lips. She forced a smile.

Gideon cupped her face. "Baby, I just meant—"

Tessa placed her finger over his lips. "Ssh. I know." He closed his eyes and kissed her finger. "It's okay," she murmured and kissed him gently.

"I think your father's seeing the light. We can finally be together, really together."

He filled her in on what her father had proposed—that Gideon be the point man in overseeing his new resort in Jamaica. The job would be a yearlong project, and he was leaving within a matter of days.

"What? A year long?"

"Baby, this is a big deal. I'm moving up to another level. It takes that long to set up a new resort. I'm not just over security—I'm over the setup, overseeing the entire execution. I'm doing this for us," he explained, his voice soft.

"What do you mean you're leaving next week?" she exclaimed, zeroing in on that aspect. "I don't have enough time to get everything in order to leave that soon, Gideon! God, this is so soon. I have to call Peaches, let her know what's going on." She stopped and laughed. "Before I do, I guess there are other pressing things to do. Like calling the school, getting someone to take over my lease, telling—"

When she saw an odd look cross his face she stopped again. "What is it?" she asked.

He rose from the bed and drew his shirt over his head and stepped into his jeans without putting on his boxers. He turned and faced her.

"Baby . . . you're not going," he said softly, regret in his eyes.

Tessa stared at him open-mouthed, feeling as though someone had kicked her in the gut. Before he'd told her all that she had been about to tell him of her news.

Our news, she thought, laying her hand in an unconscious gesture of protection over her belly.

"Everything looks to be in order. Or in as much order as it can be, considering—" Gideon stopped speaking mid-sentence.

Tessa had obviously been lost in thought and hadn't heard him open the car door. She jumped when he spoke.

The look in her eyes held a faraway expression of pain etched harshly in their dark depths, before she closed down emotionally, just as she had in the hospital.

He wondered what thoughts he'd interrupted. From the look on her face, he would bet money they weren't pleasant ones. He'd also lay odds she was thinking about him.

Giving him a tight smile, she allowed him to help her out of his SUV and, after grabbing her bag from the back of his vehicle, escort her to her door.

Gideon opened the door and allowed her to precede him into her apartment, closing and locking the door behind them.

Tessa walked briskly inside and just as she went into her living room, turned around and said over her shoulder, "Come inside. I'm going to put my things away in my bedroom. I'll be out. Make yourself at home." She then vanished behind a corner that Gideon knew led to her bedroom on the first floor. Without waiting for him to reply, she swiftly left.

She wasn't going to make this easy.

As he waited for her, he walked around her living room, taking it in at a more leisurely pace, this time no longer looking for potential danger but for clues to tell him who she was today, the woman she'd grown into.

He walked over to the white marble fireplace and ran his glance over the delicately framed photos that sat on the mantel.

He picked up one of her and her father, obviously taken at a fund-raiser of some sort. The senator was turned out sharply, wearing a tuxedo that fit his tall lean frame as though custom-made for him. Which, Gideon knew, it more than likely had been.

Tessa was immaculately dressed in a beautiful, long, formal gown, the pearl color complementing her deep brown skin. The smiles they gave the camera were posed ones, those smiles that came with ease to the rich and famous, that showed all of their gleaming, professionally whitened teeth.

Ones that were as fake as they were well-practiced.

Gideon stared closer at the photo, his gaze going to Tessa and Tessa alone, paying close attention. She had the most beautifully soulful eyes he'd ever seen.

A direct reflection of her emotions. No matter what facade she put on, Gideon had always been able to tell what she was feeling by looking into her eyes. In the photo, despite the bright smile, he saw her misery.

He also noticed the faint shadows that underscored them despite her flawless makeup.

"That was taken a few years ago. After Dad won reelection."

"You two look happy," Gideon said, smoothly placing the photo back on the mantel and facing Tessa.

"Dad was happy," she replied.

"You must have been proud of him."

"It was a tight race," she said, her lips lifting in a small smile, yet he noted the adroit way she avoided his direct question.

"Would you like something to eat or drink?" she asked, walking toward the kitchen.

He walked closer to her and leaned against one of the tall columns, studying her as she removed an old-fashioned kettle from a cupboard.

"I'm making tea. Would you like some?" she asked, staring up at him.

"Always the good hostess," he murmured, walking closer and removing the kettle from her hand. "Why don't you go and sit down? I'll do this for you."

When she looked as though she was going to protest, he gently guided her to the mahogany table in the kitchen and, keeping his hand beneath her elbow, helped her to sit.

"I'm not an invalid, Gideon. I can manage," she said, but he noted the way she leaned against the chair back, obviously glad to be off her feet.

After filling the kettle with water, he turned to her. "Stop fussing. Just rest a little. You could have been killed, Tessa," he said.

"I know," she whispered. Before she could turn away, he caught the glimmer of tears in her dark eyes.

Gideon placed the kettle on the counter and walked over to her. He hunched down and turned her to face him.

"Why do you do it, Tessa?"

"What?" she asked, refusing to meet his eyes. "Try and protect those who need it?"

"Yes. At the risk of hurting yourself. This hasn't been the first time, Tessa," he said grimly.

"How do you know—?"

"I know a lot about what you've been up to, since—"

"Since you left me?" There was a sharp bite in her tone. Gideon sighed.

"I wasn't the one who ended it, Tessa, you did," he reminded her.

"*I* ended it? Are you serious, Gideon? God, please tell me you're kidding me!" she said with so much vehemence, Gideon stepped away from her. "*You* were the one who left me!"

"Yes, I left! But I did it to help *us*. I left so that we could be together!"

Her face twisted when she made the reply and Gideon felt as though he was caught in some weird dimension of confusion.

"I came back for you. You wanted nothing to do with me when I came back. Just like the scared little girl you always were, you allowed Daddy to convince you I wasn't good enough for you," he bit out angrily.

"You are a piece of work, Gideon!" Tessa angrily stood from the chair and moved to turn away. Before she could take more than a few steps away, Gideon forced her to turn back and face him.

"You told me you loved me. When I came back, I found you—" he stopped himself short. "You no longer wanted me," he said instead. "So much for all that love you seemed to have."

Tessa stared at Gideon, feeling old angers and past hurts surfacing. She didn't feel like going down that road. Not today when she was feeling vulnerable and afraid. She knew what he thought when he'd come home and found her in another man's arms. But it hadn't been what he thought. She and Michael had been friends since college. He had been consoling her, nothing more.

Not that she'd wanted to tell Gideon the reason Michael was consoling her. Not after what he'd done to her, months and months of no returned calls, not even an e-mail. She'd heard exactly nothing from him. She hadn't even known he was coming to see her when he walked into her apartment and found her, Michael's arms wrapped around her as they lay in her bed—

Gideon pulled her close, staring down at her with that intense expression of his. "Tell me you loved me, Tessa. Tell me that asshole didn't mean anything to you," he demanded, his brows drawn fiercely together, his warm breath blowing against her face.

"Yes! I loved you! Okay, I said it, are you happy? But that was in the past. There was nothing I wouldn't do for you. I gave you my heart . . . my virginity. I would have given you my soul had you asked for it!" Tessa's chest heaved with her exertion as she tried to pull away from his grasp.

He refused to allow her to move away, his expression set.

Tessa exerted more force this time and pulled away from him. Both were breathing harshly. "I damn near did. When I lost the—"

"What?" His thick brows nearly met in the middle as he stared at her. "Lost what?" he asked and grabbed her by the arm and moved her around.

"Ouch!" She hissed in pain when he pulled her around to face him, underestimating his own strength. Her hurt shoulder bumped against his hard chest.

As soon as he realized he'd inadvertently caused her pain, he dropped his hand away. Tessa wanted to laugh outright at the look of horror that crossed his face.

"Tessa, I'm sorry!" he said, a look of concern etched on his face, which turned into one of determination.

"What are you doing? Put me down!" she cried out in surprise when he scooped her up in his arms and strode with her the short distance to her bedroom. He gently set her down on the bed.

"You need to really rest. You're in pain. The rest of this can wait."

"Gideon—"

He fluffed the pillows around her and positioned her so that she lay in the middle of the bed as he sat beside her.

"Just go, Gideon! I don't need your help. Just leave," she mumbled.

"You need help. Quit being so damn stubborn, woman!" With that, he carefully unbuttoned her silk blouse and peeled it away, easing her arms out of it. She was left with only a silky tee beneath it. His eyes left hers and traveled down, resting at the crests of her breasts that pushed against the camisole.

"Let me take care of you," he said, his eyes coming back to meet hers.

The simple request was her undoing. And the way he said it.

Had he demanded, tried to bend her to his will, she could have easily told him to march his ass straight to hell. Instead, she gave a short nod of assent and at his insistent nudging, leaned back on the thick pillows propped against her headboard.

He moved his gaze away from hers, then lifted her hips and eased the skirt from them, and placed it at the foot of the bed.

Tessa felt heat flood her face when his gaze traveled over her half-clothed body.

He pressed her down onto the comforter and she breathed a sigh of relief when his attention turned to her bandaged shoulder. He ran his fingers lightly over the area before looking back into her eyes.

"Stay here. I'll be right back," he murmured. He rose from the bed and walked toward her adjoining bathroom. Tessa heard a faucet turn on. Moments later he returned with a small white face towel in one hand and the paper bag she'd been given in the other and sat back down.

Before being discharged from the hospital, her nurse had replaced the more cumbersome bandage that wrapped around her shoulder with a smaller, four-by-four white gauze and surgical tape, and supplied her with more of everything to replace as needed. As the nurse had been changing the bandage, Tessa had looked away.

Gideon placed the warm, wet towel over the bandaged area. He caught her questioning look and said, "Won't hurt this way. It'll make it easier to remove."

She never considered herself particularly squeamish, but she was strangely reluctant to look at her wound. When he peeled away the bandage, she turned her head and bit her bottom lip.

"Are you in pain?"

She shook her head no, without replying. Quickly he removed the bandage and in seconds had replaced it. Once that was done, he placed two fingers beneath her chin, making her turn and look at him.

"Why, Tessa?"

"What—what do you mean?"

"Why do you put yourself in danger like this?"

"Does it matter?"

"If it didn't, I wouldn't ask."

"Someone has to do it. Why not me?" she replied and shrugged, feigning disinterest. "I'm not putting anyone at risk, just me."

"But why, Tessa?" he asked.

Tessa tried to turn away, uncomfortable with the intent way he was looking at her. He wouldn't let her.

"Do you have so little regard for your own life that you'll keep putting yourself in danger like this? Don't you know how those who love you would feel if anything happened to you?"

4

The moment stretched out.

Keeping his eyes on hers, Gideon leaned down and placed his open mouth over the soft silk of her camisole and kissed her breast through the tank, leaving a hot wet spot after he withdrew his lips. The sensual roughness of his low beard caught against the silk of her top for a second.

Tessa's eyes drifted shut. When she offered no resistance, he carefully pushed her shirt up, exposing her to his hungry gaze.

He leaned down and took her nipple deep into his mouth and she moaned. He sucked her entire nipple and the flat disk of areole deep inside, massaging the other heavy globe with one hand.

When he finally withdrew from her breast, his tongue trailed a path across her skin before it reached the other breast. He mouthed her, lightly scraping his teeth over the underside of her breast, before flattening his tongue and lapping her areole.

"Hmmm . . ." Tessa exhaled a long breath. Instead of pushing him away, she drew him closer, tunneling her fingers into the drawn-back hair at the back of his head.

When she didn't stop him, he smiled against her breast and trailed his tongue up her body before he reached her mouth. He gave her small, light kisses, nibbling the corner of her sweetly bowed lips. His tongue licked them sensually, moving back and forth, silently demanding that she open for him.

With a groan, Tessa did. She moaned when his hot, slick tongue invaded her mouth.

He knew she was as hungry for him as he was for her. Her fingers loosened the band that held his hair in place and she pulled him even closer as the kiss deepened, their tongues meeting in a clash, each seeking out the sweetness of the other.

Gideon pulled her tongue out and latched on to it, sucking it, stroking it, forcing her head back against the pillows as his demands grew.

He placed a hand on her hip and pulled her close, never breaking contact with her mouth. In the position he placed them, he was able to pull her snugly against him, her injured side positioned so that there was no strain.

Nothing had changed, Gideon thought as he made love to Tessa's mouth. Her mouth was just as sweet, so damn hot. In all the years, he'd never been with a woman who could make him forget what it was like to surge into her heat. No woman could compare to her. Just one kiss and it all came back to him: the intensity, the incredible feeling of lying next to her, of being inside her . . .

He'd fooled around since Tessa, sure, but no one had made a dent in his heart or erased the memory of what it had been like to be inside *this* woman. There was no one who got to him like she did.

No one who mattered like she did. Despite their past.

He broke the kiss.

"Damn!"

"What?" Tessa cried out.

He didn't answer, remembering how good it had been with her. Their bodies had always been in perfect harmony. Sex between them had been off-the-charts *hot*. He shoved the thought to the side that he felt anything besides lust for her. Seven years was a long damn time

He ran a steamy glance over her.

He doubted she felt anything for him that wasn't purely sexual. But, no matter what her other personal feelings were, Gideon knew lust was one. Hell yes. The look in her eyes told him. The way she sized him up, the way her mouth opened, breaths coming out in short, hollow gasps. The way she devoured him with her big eyes . . .

He'd never forgotten what she tasted like, how sweet her cream felt on his tongue. And he would never forget how much she meant to him, how she was the only woman he'd ever—he shook his head.

Sex. That's all he wanted. That's all he *needed* from her.

What he craved.

He lay her on her back and shoved her legs up, spreading her wide. His eyes on hers, he lifted her hips and removed her panties in one smooth gesture. She offered no protest to what he was doing, simply watched him, her eyes lowered, half hooded. Once he'd removed her panties he stared at the tight thatch of curls guarding her sweet pussy from him.

"Wha—what is it?" she asked, and Gideon turned his gaze away, reluctantly stopping himself from staring like a man possessed.

Her eyes widened and uncertainty crept into her gaze. His mouth stretched in a grin, pleased for some reason by the look of apprehension on her beautiful face.

"Gideon?" she asked, a hitch in her voice. Her tongue snaked out and swiped across her bow-shaped lips.

She'd invaded his dreams for seven years. Her touch, her scent . . .

He leaned down and inhaled her.

He shut his eyes when her unique fragrance wafted over him. Engulfing him. Marking him.

"Fuck!" With a growl, he spread her legs even farther apart, placed his hands beneath the plump round spheres of her ass.

"Gideon?" On her lips his name was a breathless plea.

When he spread her legs farther apart, completely exposing her to his heated stare, Tessa's heart raced, thudding hard against her chest. When his dark head went down between her legs, and he rubbed his face back and forth over the springy curls surrounding her femininity, a whimper escaped her lips.

The eroticism of the moment slammed into her, overwhelming her.

"Gideon—" she said again, when he said nothing.

Two fingers spread the lips of her vagina. She inhaled a swift breath of expectation.

She was rewarded when his warm breath blew over her mound, and his tongue, his hot, slick tongue, stroked against the inner flesh of her vaginal lips.

"Gideon, I can't—" She broke off when his long tongue went deep into her core. And pulled out.

"God, I've missed your sweetness," she heard him murmur. She didn't know if he'd even heard her token protest, his attention was ultra focused. She hoped that if he had, he would ignore her plea.

She desperately needed him to continue what he started.

He made hungry sounds as he continued to eat her, suckling her, dragging her clit out from where it nestled deep inside her hood. Like a man possessed he devoured her, got his tongue deep into the well of her pussy and ate her cream. Savored it.

One hand left her thigh and traveled up her body, grabbing as much of one of her heavy breasts as he could, thumbing her tight, engorged nipple.

She released a breathy moan of delight when he continued to explore her with his tongue, and eased two fingers deep inside her body. Her natural lubrication coated his fingers, allowing him to easily glide in and out of her clenching sheath while his expert tongue teased at her clit.

Feeling an orgasm begin to unfurl, she twisted her body. Reaching down, she pulled Gideon closer and ground against his face, completely giving in to the sensations. Violent shudders racked her body as pleasure that bordered on pain in its intensity washed over her.

"Yes! God, yes, Gideon!" Tessa bit her bottom lip until she felt the taste of blood pepper her tongue, the pain only adding to the sweet pleasure of her release.

Long moments later, once her orgasm eased, she lay back limp and exhausted, her heart still thudding erratically against her chest.

As her pulse slowly returned to normal and the stars receded from her eyes, she slowly opened her eyes.

It was several minutes before unwelcome reality crashed down on her, and ended her euphoria.

Gideon was the one. The only man who'd ever brought her to such screaming climaxes. The only man to ever complete her. His lovemaking was just like him: devastating.

"This doesn't change anything, Gideon. I don't need you to protect me. You have to go."

Gideon rose from the bed and stared down at Tessa. The utterly sensual look of a woman well satisfied was still stamped on her features, even as she was rejecting him again.

He bit back the angry retort and schooled his features into a mask of indifference. Walking over to where she lay against the pillows, he bent down to her, kissing her, transferring the flavor of her own essence into her open mouth.

"Make me." Her mouth became a comical perfect O as he gave her a final kiss before leaving the bedroom.

5

Gideon pulled to a smooth halt behind Tessa's Mercedes and cut the engine of his Range Rover. He calmly waited for her to ease her legs out of the car and hand her keys over to the waiting young man she paid to park it, before he followed suit.

He jumped out of the car and tossed the kid his keys, something he'd been doing over the past week. With a grin he took Gideon's keys and pocketed them, before sliding his long, gangly body behind the wheel of Tessa's car.

Gideon noted the irritated look Tessa threw over her shoulder at him before she turned around and, at a fast clip, walked toward the entry of her office building.

Staying several feet away from her, he nonetheless didn't try and hide the fact that he was following her. To do so was pointless. Over the last few days they'd had the same routine: he waited for her outside her apartment until she exited, then followed her as she drove thirty minutes to her downtown law offices.

After she'd told him in no uncertain terms she didn't want or need his protection, he wasn't surprised.

Even if he *had* been able to convince her to allow him to guard her per her father's request, while finding out who'd tried to hurt her, he knew going after her sexually hadn't helped.

But damn, it had been too long since he'd made love to her. Why had he thought he'd be able to get that close to her and not sample the goods? His mind told him that his memories of what it had once been like between them weren't for real . . . no, he couldn't blame her.

No way in hell was he leaving. He'd expected her to react in the way she had, despite the senator's belief that Gideon could bend easily her to his will.

No, Gideon knew Tessa a hell of a lot better than her father did. He'd been prepared. Before coming back to the area, he'd secured an apartment in the complex she lived in.

No sooner had he moved into his temporary digs than he'd phoned her father.

"Well, how did it go?" Evan Waters had asked without pre-amble. "Did you manage to convince my stubborn daughter to leave KhemCom alone? I don't need this latest fiasco of hers to be endlessly rehashed in the media. Reelection is in November. I don't have to tell you how badly she's fucking things up for me. Many of my constituents work for or do business with KhemCom, one way or another. "

Gideon felt a tic pulse in the corner of his temple. Nothing had changed about the man. Instead of asking how his only child was doing, the distinguished senator's first move had been to ask if Gideon had been able to make his daughter stop making him look bad.

"*Fiasco?*" Gideon asked, kicking off his boots and striding over to the kitchen. "Don't you want to know how she's doing, sir?" he asked, keeping his voice mild.

There was a pause before the senator quickly assured him, "Of course I do."

Opening the refrigerator door, Gideon pulled out a bottle of beer and popped the top. After taking a long swig, he answered, "It's going the way I expected."

The senator laughed. "I translate that to mean she wanted nothing to do with your ass," he replied, condescension in his voice. "So what in hell are you going to do about it? I expect you to get her in line. God knows I've tried. She refuses to listen to anything I say," he finished in disgust.

"Get her in line?" He threw Evan Waters's words back at him. "Look, Waters, I didn't come here to '*get her in line.*' I'm here to help protect your daughter from getting harmed or killed. Nothing more, nothing less."

"Is that all, Gideon?" There was a significant pause.

Gideon could see him in his mind's eye, looking at Gideon as though he wasn't worthy enough to lick the bottom of his boots. Yeah, that look. Something else he'd never forgotten.

It had taken his dumb ass longer than necessary, as in seven years, to wise up and realize that was the *only* way Senator Evan Waters would ever see him.

"I'm repaying a debt long overdue," Gideon finally replied.

"That's what I wanted to hear," Evan Waters said smugly. Gideon allowed him to think the debt he was repaying was owed to the senator.

"Now, tell me your strategy," he asked, his tone jovial, as though they were two friends discussing a friendly game of pickup basketball.

Gideon quelled the urge to tell Waters what he could do with his plan. Instead he listened as the senator told him what *he* wanted to do.

"You've got to get close to Tessa. If anyone can do it, you can," he said, reconfirming Gideon's belief that Senator Evan Waters cared about no one but himself.

Correction, Gideon thought. The only things the Senator cared about were his money, his image, *and* himself.

"Turn on the charm. I'm sure you know how, boy. Do whatever it takes to make her stop."

"I've never been your *boy*, senator," Gideon interrupted. "Just get that straight, now," he finished, without raising his voice. It was enough to make the other man pause before continuing arrogantly.

"Don't be so touchy," he said, infusing bogus warmth into his voice that didn't fool Gideon by a long shot. The bastard was about as warm as a coiled python. "Then you're going to convince her to step away from this," Waters continued. "She'll do it for you. She might be angry now, but she's never stopped having that embarrassing crush on you."

Gideon listened in disbelief as the senator continued his spiel, speaking about his only child as though she was nothing more than a nuisance. A nuisance that needed to be taken care of. Which was the only reason he'd contacted Gideon.

Seven years ago, he wouldn't let Gideon within ten feet of Tessa if he could help it, had done everything in his power to keep the two of them apart. Now, he was all but selling his own daughter to him, in an all-out effort to keep her away from KhemCom.

There was something seriously wrong with that picture, and although Gideon listened as Waters went on to outline in precise detail the way he wanted Tessa *handled*, he had other plans in mind.

"I need to have this taken care of before Saturday." Waters wound it up, reminding Gideon of the small, private party he was planning at his residence, one that he didn't want Tessa to know anything about. "And I don't want Tessa there. Keep her busy. I'm sure you know how."

Well, Waters, that's not how it's going to go down, Gideon thought, plopping onto the sofa and taking a healthy drink of his beer, while clicking the remote at the television.

No fear, he thought as he listened to the senator drone on. He'd make sure Tessa stopped before she got hurt. But it wouldn't be the way her father had planned. Gideon had plans all his own. A smile of anticipation spread across his full lips.

Now, as he stood in the doorway to her office, he heard her utter a mild curse and quietly opened the door. He shamelessly listened in on her conversation. She had her back to him as she spoke on the phone.

He listened to her talking to her best friend—Peaches—and smiled. Although he couldn't hear what was said on the other end, he heard Tessa's response. Obviously agitated, she made a sweeping gesture and hit the glass of liquid near her, overturning it.

She jumped up and bent down to pick up the spilled glass, and the hem of her skirt rose slightly.

Gideon was able to get a nice visual of her pretty round buttocks and a hint of lacy panties. She stood with the glass in her hand and spun around, her gaze meeting his.

She nearly stumbled as she stared at him, one hand holding the glass, the other holding a phone to her ear. She stopped speaking in mid-sentence, her large eyes widening as she stared at him.

"I don't know, Peaches. It's not as easy as that," Tessa sighed into the phone, her eyes narrowing as she stared at her computer monitor, reading the latest e-mail from Lauren, the mother of Jessica Holmes.

"Damn," she whispered as she reread the contents.

In the e-mail, Lauren mentioned that she'd tried calling Tessa, but had been unable to reach her. She also stated that she no longer was interested in pursuing the lawsuit against Khem-Com.

She'd received a visit from one of their lawyers, along with the CEO of the company, and the men had informed her of the company's desire to not only continue to pay for her daughter's medical care, but also to give her, a single mother, all the time off she needed—full pay plus a bonus—to care for her daughter until she was fully recovered.

Although one part of Tessa vehemently protested the company's buying her silence, Tessa knew it had been an uphill battle for Lauren to fight the company with limited resources. She also knew the funds Lauren had in savings were slowly dwindling away.

"What is it?" Peaches asked.

In the background, Tessa could hear the active sounds of a bustling kitchen, as Peaches worked. "Hey, don't you drop my crawfish, doggone it! That shipment cost me an arm and a leg!" Peaches' voice boomed, speaking to one of her employees, her attention obviously divided between her conversation with Tessa and running her kitchen.

"Nothing you can do anything about, girl. Nothing I can do anything about either," Tessa muttered, more to herself than her friend.

"How's everything with Gideon? He still sniffing after you like a dog after his favorite bone?"

The question took Tessa by surprise, eliciting a reluctant chuckle from her. "Well, I wouldn't have put it like that," she laughed. "But, if you're asking if he's still 'guarding' me, the answer to that would be yes. Unfortunately."

"Come on now, girl, this is me you talking to, Boo. Y'all haven't done any more . . . uh, you know . . . horizontal shuffling, have you?"

"We didn't quite get down like *that*, Peaches!" She'd told Peaches what happened after Gideon had taken her home a week ago, and had promptly wished she'd kept *that* piece of information to herself. But, at the time, she'd been so confused, she needed someone to talk to. "Besides, that was a mistake. It definitely won't be happening again," Tessa said, firmly.

"Umm, hmmm," Peaches replied, noncommittal.

"It's been a long time. Both for us, as well as me. I just got caught up, that's all," she answered and snapped her mouth shut, hearing in her own voice a need to convince someone other than herself.

"Tessa, don't you still have *some* feelings for him? I mean, you once called him the love of your life." Peaches' voice was soft and hesitant.

Tessa blew out a disgusted sigh. There was no hiding the truth, from her friend or herself.

"Yes, I suppose there are some residual feelings. Kind of . . ." she let the sentence dangle.

"*Residual?* Kind of? You either do or you don't. That's like saying you're kind of pregnant. I mean, really, Tessa, if—" Peaches stopped as soon as she heard Tessa's indrawn breath.

"Sorry, Tessa. Girl, you know I didn't mean anything by that."

"It's okay. I know you didn't. Besides, it was a long time ago."

Both women were silent before Peaches spoke, "So, what's going on with you now? I mean . . . are you two back together?"

"God, no! I told you! It was just something that happened." In her agitation, Tessa fumbled for her glass of organic juice sitting beside her, knocking it over. The glass tumbled to the floor. Again?

She jumped up and yanked several tissues out of a box to wipe up the mess. "Look, I'll have to chat with you later."

She was about to hang up the phone when a sound let her know that she wasn't alone in her office. She glanced up to see Gideon's large body filling her doorway.

"Uh, Peaches, I *really* have to go. Someone just walked in," she said, staring at Gideon as she blindly hung the phone up in relief, ignoring Peaches' indignant demands that she finish telling her what was going on with her and Gideon.

Her unknowingly hungry gaze slid over him. His hair was pulled back in the familiar low ponytail, perfectly groomed, yet an aura of untamed, raw sexuality surrounded him.

"The receptionist told me I could come in," he said, his eyes lazily roaming over her.

His eyes followed the path of her tongue as it darted out to wet her lips. One side of his generous mouth lifted in a small smile, one that let her know *he* knew that his presence had affected her.

Memories of their sexual encounter less than a week ago flashed in Tess's mind.

Since that night she hadn't seen him, had refused to allow him to stay with her as he wanted. Yet, for the last week she hadn't been able to shake him or their lovemaking out of her mind.

Despite her telling him she didn't need a protector, each day as she'd left her apartment and drove out of the garage to the condo, she'd glance into the rearview mirror of her sporty Mercedes coupe and see his Range Rover pull out and follow her.

Her first reaction was to confront him and demand that he leave her alone, but she'd resisted the urge. Instead she'd done her best to ignore him.

That had worked about as well as her trying to ignore their heated, erotic exchange.

She'd woken up, night after night, her hand buried deep inside her own crotch, sweat pouring down her face, a throbbing need insidiously crawling through her body, to finish what she'd started with Gideon.

"I hope that was okay." It was more a statement than a request, as he didn't bother waiting for a reply. It took her a moment to realize what he was referring to. Not that it mattered. Instead of waiting for her assent, he strode into her office.

Tessa leaned back in her chair and sized him up.

She hoped her casual manner projected an air of nonchalant boredom. Hoped that he couldn't somehow see the thoughts racing through her mind, thoughts of him. That he didn't know that she was trying mighty hard not to notice how damn good he looked wearing a pair of loose-fitting dark jeans and fitted knit shirt and black boots. Clothes that on any other man wouldn't be all that remarkable.

But on him, they looked as though they were custom-made for his hard body.

She hoped he didn't notice that as *soon* as he'd walked into her office, her body had gone into straight cat mode. Everything in her reacted to his presence. Like some damn heroine in a romance novel, her body responded just by being near him.

Tessa blew out a disgusted breath, ashamed of herself for her uncontrollable thoughts.

When his smile deepened, his sexy eyes darting to her breasts and her traitorous nipples, she folded her arms across her chest and glared at him.

"Nice office," he murmured, looking elsewhere.

She tensed as he walked around. He picked up a framed photo of her and her father before placing it down and idly glancing at the others before moving on.

He strolled around her office, looking at her things as though he had a right to, occasionally stopping again to inspect other photos, not saying a word.

The longer he casually studied her stuff, the more anxious she grew, the tension in the room becoming palpable. At least it was to her. Gideon acted like it was nothing new for him to waltz back into a woman's life after seven years as though he'd just been with her the day before.

He tapped a finger against one of her framed articles. "I remember hearing about this case. I didn't know that you were involved." He turned to face her; the genuine interest reflected in his eyes eased her nerves somewhat.

She walked over to where he stood and peered around him to see the article he was referring to.

She smiled, remembering the case. "Yes, because of Planet Now we were able to help that family get some closure." A class action suit had been brought against a major manufacturer of children's toys when the paint had been found to contain lead.

"Arguing about acceptable levels of toxicity—well, there aren't any. But that's business as usual for big corporations. Do what you can get away with," she said with resignation.

He cocked a brow.

"And do it somewhere you can hide by outsourcing for cheap labor. They profit by sending the work overseas for manufacturing. Costs less than half what they'd have to pay American workers," she answered his unasked questions.

"Most of the time not even that," he commented before placing the framed article down.

She looked at him in surprise.

His wide mouth lifted in a humorless smile. "You forget. I've lived in a lot of places."

She saw a shadow pass over his expression and reached out to lay a consoling hand on his arm.

"No, I hadn't forgotten, Gideon."

The moment stretched out, memories clouding her mind of the times they would lie in bed after making love and he would tell her about the places he'd lived, sometimes invaded, when he'd been in the military.

She remembered once, although he hadn't been able to go into detail about a mission, not able to share everything because of security reasons, he'd told her things that made her heart cry out. Not only for the people in the poor countries who lived the way they had, but for the young soldier he'd been, seeing so much poverty and destruction and forced to carry out his mission nonetheless, unable to help those in need.

He covered her hand with his. Bringing her hand away from his arm, he brought it up to his mouth and with his eyes on hers, gently kissed her palm.

"Oh God, Gideon . . . what are you doing to me?" she asked, a distinct tremble in her voice.

With a groan, he pulled her pliant body closer. He stared down at her and laughed roughly.

"No . . . what have you done to *me*, Tessa? I've never been able to get you out of my mind. No matter where I've gone, who I've been with."

"No!" Tears burned her eyes and her nostrils flared with emotion. "I don't want to hear where you've been. And not who you've been with," she cried, trying to pull away.

He wouldn't allow her to. "No," he said, his face set, his expression filled with anger. She didn't know if the anger was directed at her or himself.

"Don't walk away from me. You've tried that for the last time, Tessa."

He slanted his mouth over hers. Tessa expected a hard, rough kiss. Instead, his lips teased her, slyly played with hers, beguiling her to open for him.

With a whimper of need she surrendered to his silent demand, leaning into the kiss. He gently opened her lips with his, licking sensually.

Hungry for him, she opened her mouth wider, and pressed her tongue inside his warm mouth.

He grabbed her by the bottom and pulled her tight against him, the kiss growing more heated as their lips and tongues met in a hot exchange of carnal sensation. She moaned against his mouth, rubbing her body against his, glorying in the feel of his thickness grinding into her lower body.

He got his fingers into her hair, upsetting her careful updo. Pins popped and flew everywhere. But Tessa didn't care.

The urgency, the slick, hot urgency of their kiss, obliterated all thought from her mind. To hell with propriety.

His hands went to the buttons on her shirt, deftly undoing them. Once opened, he pulled the ends apart and unhooked her bra. With a groan, he leaned down, capturing one of her nipples in his mouth, suckling.

"Gideon . . ." she whispered, gripping the back of his head. Her hands left his hair and traveled down the front of his shirt. Tugging his shirt aside, she ran her fingers up his torso, restlessly trailing over his rock-hard abs, trailing over his small, tight, tawny-colored nipples.

With his mouth fastened on her breast, one hand went to her skirt, impatiently unbuttoning the buttons before easing his hand inside the waistband. He slipped a hand inside her panties and cupped her warm, wet mound. One finger separated the lips of her moist folds, gently fingering her clit, eliciting a groan of pleasure from her.

He snatched his mouth away from her breast, his breathing labored, looking down. "Tessa . . ."

A loud knock stopped him. Tessa turned toward her door. She glanced at the clock mounted on the wall, her lust-fogged brain registering the time.

"Oh hell. I have a meeting."

She shoved away from him and ran her hands through her hair, knowing she looked a hot mess, her eyes frantically going back to Gideon's.

He pushed her behind him. "I'll take care of this. Go get yourself together," he said and walked quickly to the door.

Tessa ran to the small adjoining bathroom and turned around, glancing at him over her shoulder. He nodded, and once he was sure she was inside, she heard him open the door.

Closing the door behind her, she leaned against it, closing

her eyes. She heard his deep voice as he spoke to her assistant on the other side, and pushed away from the door, walking over to the chipped oval mirror that hung over the sink.

She ran shaky hands over her hair. Taking a deep breath, she grabbed the small bag on the wicker shelf above the toilet and went to work repairing the damage to her appearance.

She glanced at herself one last time in the mirror. Although she'd fixed herself, and reapplied her makeup, her lips were still puffy from Gideon's kisses. She licked the full bottom one and blew out a breath of air.

"Lord . . . what am I *doing*?" she questioned herself before turning away, knowing her reflection held no answer, and leaving.

6

When Tessa emerged from the bathroom, minutes later, she glanced toward Gideon and quickly averted her face, but not before he got a good look at her. What they'd been doing had to show. Had to.

"Your receptionist says the meeting was canceled. She said she'd let you know when they wanted to reschedule."

She nodded her head and walked toward her desk her eyes keeping from making contact with his. Avoiding him, and the meaning of what they'd done. She began to fiddle with scattered paperwork, stacking and restacking items.

He wasn't going to let her.

Gideon walked toward her. Although she kept her eyes averted, Gideon caught the fine tremor of her fingers. The sheaf of paper she had a death grip on shook too. He stopped several feet away to give her the room she obviously needed.

"Have dinner with me tonight."

At that, her eyes flew toward his, her expressive face showing her inner conflict.

He held up his hands, a tentative smile on his mouth. "I promise to keep my hands to myself."

"It's not you I'm worried about," she mumbled. As soon as she said the words, her deep brown skin flushed and she glanced away. "Uh, I have a lot of work to do. I can't—"

"Look Tessa, this tension, this whatever, isn't going to go away. Don't you think it's time we really talked? Don't you think it's time we talked about . . . us?" he asked and waited.

She stared at him, biting her lip in indecision.

"I swear, I won't push you. I just want some answers. I want to know what happened seven years ago. Why you left me."

Emotion flared in her dark eyes and she looked away. She didn't speak, and he didn't push. He wanted her to come to him of her own free will, without any coercion from him.

She turned to face him, and gave him a short nod of acceptance. That filled him with more elation than it should have.

Tonight, he would find out why the woman he loved seven years ago had been in bed with another man.

7

"Please, allow me," Gideon said and pulled back Tessa's chair for her.

"Thank you," she murmured. After she sat down, she felt his warm fingers touch the nape of her neck in a faint caress that could have been accidental. Goose bumps rose along her back and down her arms. She drew the dark wrap closer around her bare back.

Yet she knew it wasn't. Nothing he ever did was accidental, she thought, glancing at him from beneath her lowered lashes as he sat down.

The man was lethal.

At the time she'd accepted his dinner invitation, she'd thought being out in public with him was preferable to being alone. When it was just him and her, the man had her forgetting her own name and engaging in the type of necking sessions she'd done as a teen. But she was a grown woman. Too old to allow lust to control her. A restaurant was just safer.

Although now, she wasn't so sure.

"I'll leave you with the menu, sir, ma'am," the hostess said, although her eyes got stuck on Gideon. "Your server will be with you shortly," she said. "I recommend the halibut. It's particularly fresh tonight. I'm sure you would appreciate something *fresh*, sir." She smiled at him, licking her crimson red lips, one hand throwing her shoulder-length blond hair over her shoulder. "But if you need *anything* before he arrives, just call me," she said and had the audacity to wink at him. She then placed Tessa's menu on the table and handed Gideon his.

The lingering look she threw Gideon's way said that *anything* applied only to him. And she wasn't just talking about what was on the menu.

Irritated, Tessa picked up her menu, snapped it open, and blindly scanned the entrées.

Over the edge of her menu, she watched as the openly flirtatious hostess gave Gideon one final look from her big, baby-blue eyes, eyes that Tessa had the sudden urge to poke out. The hostess turned and walked away, swinging her hips in an exaggerated swish.

Tessa turned to Gideon, sure he would be watching the woman's obvious display, and was surprised to find his eyes on hers.

She flushed.

"Have I told you how beautiful you look tonight?" he asked, looking her over like *she* was a delicious item on the menu. The over-the-top behavior of the hostess slipped from her mind as though the woman had never been there.

"Yes, but, a second time is always nice," she replied with a smile, some of her irritation and tension melting away.

"Second time around is often better, I heard," he replied, a slight smile on his full, beautiful lips.

She'd not been sure what to wear for this date. Indecision had almost made her late as she'd gone through everything in her considerable wardrobe, discarding one thing after another, littering her closet floor until she finally settled on the simple bare-backed little black dress.

After donning it, she'd gone to her jewelry box, searching for the perfect accessory.

She picked up the one necklace she hadn't worn in almost ten years. Her fingers caressed the center stone, her birthstone surrounded by tiny diamonds suspended on a fragile white gold chain. It had been a gift from Gideon on her twenty-first birthday.

The minute he'd seen her, he'd looked at it and smiled. She'd shyly met his eyes and a bittersweet moment of nostalgia passed between them.

She fingered the charm lying against her neck as her eyes remained locked with his. "So they say."

Gideon leaned across the table and stroked the rough pad of his thumb down her face. Then he touched the necklace. Tessa's eyes lit up, before she caught herself and subtly moved away from his touch. His hands dropped, yet his subtle smile remained in place.

At that moment, the waiter appeared and asked if they were ready to order. Wetting her lips with the tip of her tongue, Tessa returned her gaze to her menu.

"May I?" he asked, referring to ordering her food for her. Tessa shrugged and allowed him to select.

Peaches had raved about the haute cuisine at this new French restaurant, and she'd had plans to go with her friend, so when Gideon asked which restaurant she wanted to go to, she'd chosen this one.

She sneaked a peek at him as he ordered for them in impeccable French, his accent flawless as far as she could tell.

French was one of several languages Gideon spoke fluently. During his tenure in the army, although he liked to say he was only a grunt, he had been much more than that. He'd been in Special Forces, and part of an operation where knowing multiple languages was necessary, as they would have to seamlessly blend into various countries.

With his beautiful café au lait coloring, aristocratic features, and dark wavy hair, he could easily be one of many nationalities.

She watched as he lifted his wine goblet and allowed the waiter to pour a small amount inside. After swirling the contents in the glass he lifted it to his mouth and drank, the strong column of his throat working the liquid down. At his nod, the waiter first filled Tessa's glass and then his.

"I knew my training would come in handy one day," he said, turning to give her his full attention after the waiter left.

"I don't think I remember you speaking French before," she murmured after taking a sip of her wine, the smooth flavor delicate on her tongue. "I didn't know you spoke it so well," she said, placing the goblet on the cream-colored tablecloth.

"There's a lot about me you don't know, Tessa," he replied.

Tessa opened her mouth to make some flippant reply, and promptly closed it.

Although she and Gideon shared a lot of history, she knew that what he said was true. Seven years ago she'd known him intimately. Or as much as Gideon allowed anyone to really know him.

Yet now there was a definite, different strength to him, or maybe it was simply that he'd fully come into the man he was meant to be.

His aura of toughness had always been there, but now it was magnified, making her feel slightly on edge around him.

The changes in him, although subtle, were intriguing. Especially that all-male confidence. Tessa found him more exciting now that he was more mature.

At that moment, the waiter brought two bowls of soup and a pretty basket of hot rolls. After setting the rolls in the center of the table, the waiter placed the steaming bowls of soup in front of them.

"Hmmm, this smells delicious," Tessa said, peering into the creamy bowl of soup.

Gideon smiled. "I heard they make a great oyster bisque." He watched her as she picked up a spoon. One spoonful of the creamy soup in her mouth and her eyes closed. A smile flirted around her lips as she swallowed.

"Delicious," she murmured.

"I remember you once said you could never find an oyster soup as good as the one in that Creole restaurant in New Orleans you visited."

"I can't believe you remember that," she said, reaching across and lifting a dinner roll from the basket.

"I don't think I've forgotten one thing about you, Tessa."

Tessa was at a loss for words. That he remembered something so trivial amazed her. "All right," she replied simply.

They exchanged small talk as they finished the soup until the waiter brought their entrées. An eager smile broke across Tessa's face. She had no idea what he'd ordered, French not being one of the languages she studied in college, despite her love for French cuisine. Braised halibut. One of her favorites.

"You definitely know the way to a woman's heart."

"By any means necessary," he said, laughing lightly, a dimple flashing endearingly in one of his cheeks.

She smoothed her hair, suppressing a grin, and picked up her knife and fork.

"Do you do any work outside of Planet Now?" he asked, several minutes after they both began to eat.

"Planet Now is my full-time job. It takes up all of my time," she answered, after swallowing.

"Your clients are able to pay you for your services?" he asked.

She chewed thoughtfully before answering. "Well, for many, we do pro bono work, but there are some big settlements. Our percentage is determined from the get-go if we win the case. However, we never take on a client expecting that. We're truly nonprofit. We do get generous donations, donations which allow us to continue doing what we do."

"Not enough to get rich from," he replied.

Tessa laughed. "No, definitely not that. But I didn't go into law for that reason. I went into the field to help those who needed a voice."

"You don't see that type of devotion very much. At least, not from any of the lawyers I know."

"Yeah, as a profession, the sharks out there give us all a bad rap," she laughed. "But it doesn't hurt that I have a trust fund to fall back on. Because of that, I'm able to devote myself full time to Planet Now. I'm the only one at the organization who is."

She saw his genuine interest, yet she felt strangely uncomfortable under his admiring gaze.

"What about you?"

One of his thick brows rose. "What about me?"

"After you . . . left. What did you do? Where did you go after you left?"

She saw the considering way he observed her and stiffened, knowing what he was thinking. When he took a careful sip of his wine, his eyes trained on hers over the rim of the goblet, she felt her face flush and turned away.

"After I left, I went into business for myself," he finally answered, breaking some of the tension.

"Doing what?" she asked, truly interested in what his life had been like.

"I decided to go into real estate and eventually bought a resort in the Bahamas—a small one—more like a small hotel," he added, when her eyes widened. "But it was a start. If nothing else, your father taught me the value of thinking big and investing my money. It was enough to buy my first resort." He continued. "It was run down, I fixed it up, hard work and all that," he said, negligently, yet she saw the pride in his eyes and felt an answering pride for him. "After a couple of years, I was able to use my profits to build it up, and I bought another one," he finished.

"I knew you would be successful."

"Well, like I said, I learned from the best. I recently bought a second one. This one in the Cayman Islands. It's where I spend most of my time. You'd love it there," he said. "Beautiful palms, deepwater fishing, warm weather year-round. A perfect getaway. A perfect place to live," he answered.

Tessa felt his intense gaze and shifted in her seat, uncomfortable.

"What happened to us?" he asked.

The question came out of the blue, as startling as it was direct. She'd just taken a drink of the wine when he asked. She coughed, her eyes beginning to water.

Gideon jumped up and was at her side within seconds. "Are you okay?" he asked, running a large hand soothingly over her back. Once she'd gotten her embarrassing coughing spasms under control she wiped her mouth and nodded.

"I'm fine, must have gone down the wrong path," she said, looking everywhere but at him.

He stood there, unmoving. "Are you sure?" The concern in his eyes pierced directly to her heart. "Yes, yes. I'm fine," she answered in a low voice.

Hesitantly he returned to his chair. After long moments, she cleared her throat.

Moving her food around her plate, lost in her thoughts, she began to speak.

"After you left, when I didn't hear from you for so long—"

"Didn't hear from me? I e-mailed you, called you. You were the one who didn't respond, Tessa," he said.

She glanced at him, noting the straight line his mouth had settled into. "At first, no. You're right. I was upset. You left and didn't take me, no matter how I begged you." She stopped and took a breath.

"That was for you, baby. I wanted you to finish school. I needed to wrap my brain around the big responsibility your father had entrusted me with. But most of all I wanted you to finish school. I didn't want to be the one to prevent you from realizing your dream."

"It wasn't my dream, Gideon. My dream was to be with you."

The disconnect between them was sudden and sharp. Their waiter returned, refilling their glasses.

When he left, Gideon spoke. "I wanted you with me just as badly. But I didn't want you, later on, to resent me. Your father was right."

Confused, she turned toward him. "Why would I resent you? I was an adult! I knew my own mind. And what do you mean, my father was right?"

"I called once and spoke with him. He told me to give you time. I did. I waited another month. When I called, I spoke with your father. Told him I was coming back to see you. When I did . . ."

Her eyes darted to his when he stopped speaking. "You came back?" Bewildered, she reached across the table, grasping his hand. He stared down at her hand, his face set in angry lines.

When he said nothing more, she shook his hand, her gut churning, feeling as though she was missing something important.

"You'd obviously moved on," he said, and carefully withdrew his hand from hers.

"Gideon . . ."

"Let's drop it for now."

Her eyes darted over his face, searching for something, anything, that would clue her in to what he was obviously leaving out.

The rest of the dinner they ate in uneasy silence, finishing the meal. Tessa turned as the band began to play. When the female member of the band began to sing one of her favorite songs, a smile spread across her face, despite the mood at the table.

As Tessa closed her eyes, happy to just listen while the woman sang, Gideon was struck anew by her beauty. She had reason to fall into a reverie. A nostalgic smile tugged at the corners of his mouth as well.

The song playing was the one that Tessa had deemed "their song" long ago. The memories of dancing to it with her on the day before he left, brought a thousand sweet yet painful memories to mind. He wondered if she remembered.

"Would you like to dance?" he asked, clearing his throat.

Her eyes flew open and with a hesitant smile, she nodded.

He guided her to the dance floor and wrapped both arms around her small waist. When she raised her arms around his neck, he brought her closer.

Immediately she pushed away but just slightly. The memories of the two of them together, locked in each other's arms as they danced to the song so long ago, was playing hell with her heart.

But Gideon wasn't going to allow her to keep him at a distance.

And really, she didn't want him to.

He pulled her even closer, so that no space was between them, and she could feel the hard length of him pressed hotly against her, his heat pulsating, burnishing her through the thin gauzy material of the dress she wore.

They danced as though the seven years that'd separated them had never happened. Easily she fell into his pattern, their bodies moving in a sensual way that was so smooth it felt orchestrated. He guided her body expertly, swaying with her, their bodies blending, merging together almost as one.

No words were exchanged as they swayed to the music, each lost in thought.

The feel of Tessa's sweet curves molding against his body was heaven and hell for Gideon.

In the years of their separation, he'd never forgotten what it felt like to hold her. Dance with her. Make love to her.

He took a deep breath.

He'd never forgotten her smell, either. Unique. Spicy. Alluring. And elusive. Just like her.

As they danced, he felt his erection swell. Another inevitable thing. He couldn't be within two feet of her and *not* get a hard-on, no matter how angry he was with her, he thought, an inward laugh shaking him.

She looked up at him in question.

"Nothing . . . it's nice to dance with you. I think I missed that most of all."

Her large eyes stared up at him, as she nipped her lip. He swallowed a groan, the simple gesture unbearably erotic to him, particularly in the heightened state of arousal holding him hostage. He barely resisted the urge to cover her lips with his.

She must have sensed his primal need to take her. Her eyes widened, and she inhaled a deep breath before releasing her lip.

She smiled hesitantly at him. "I missed it, too," she replied in a low, sexy voice.

With a groan he pulled her back and continued moving with

her, yet eased her away from his growing—painfully so—erection, hoping she hadn't felt the hardness of it against her mound.

Tessa hadn't missed the hot thickness of his cock pressing against her lower belly and felt a keen sense of disappointment when he'd subtly moved her body away.

She knew he wanted her. And damn if she didn't want him just as badly. She didn't want to dwell in their painful past, didn't want to think about the pain, anger and sadness. Not tonight.

Their curtailed lovemaking in her office earlier hadn't been enough. Neither had it been enough when he'd made love to her after bringing her home from the hospital.

At the time she wouldn't admit to herself how much she still needed him, how desperate she was to feel him sliding deep into her, loving her in ways no one else had ever been able to, touching her in ways—

"Let's go home," his deep voice interrupted her thoughts.

She glanced up at him, and read the sensual intent glowing in his eyes. She nodded and allowed him to escort her off the dance floor.

After collecting her wrap and purse, and paying the bill, they left the restaurant. His arm was wrapped around her waist.

A knot of tension, the same knot she'd had throughout the meal, began to loosen. Pure passion took over, zinging through her body.

When he tightened his hold on her, she willingly leaned her body into his embrace and walked out into the cool night air, fear, longing, and wild anticipation running through her.

8

"I had a wonderful time," she said softly, when he turned to face her after unlocking her apartment door. "I, uh—" The sentence was cut off when he slanted his mouth over hers, devouring the rest of her words.

With a grateful moan, Tessa sank into the kiss, wrapping her arms around his neck and pulling herself tight against him.

Gideon pressed her into the door, his kisses demanding, urgent as his hand roamed over her body, sliding over her. He pulled away and she whimpered in protest, only to hear him release a deep-throated, rough chuckle and pick her up.

Once she was secure in his arms, he brought his lips back down to hers, reestablishing their kiss. Striding determinedly through the darkened apartment, their mouths never lost contact. The kiss heated, escalated, his tongue tangling lustfully with hers. One part of Tessa's mind marveled at his ability to walk straight and kiss her senseless at the same time. Surreal but fabulous.

He strode through the dark apartment with her body held high in his arms, not stopping until they reached her bedroom.

He kicked the door open and walked inside, and allowed her to slide down from his arms.

"Oh God, baby," he said huskily, finally releasing her lips. "Damn, I need you." Her breath caught when she heard the distinct tremble in his deep voice. He divested himself of his clothing, kicking off his shoes before pulling off his suit jacket and ripping the ends of his shirt from his slacks and pulling it over his head. Seconds later he had unzipped his slacks and taken them off too, allowing his clothes to fall to the floor near her bed.

She had mere seconds to admire the broad width of his shoulders, the jet black hair silky against his thick chest muscles, feathering down the length of his tight, six-pack abdomen, where it disappeared into a vee into his dark boxers, before he lowered them as well.

When his cock jutted forth, his beautiful, long, thick cock . . . Tessa swallowed. Hard.

She drank in the sight of *serious* fun, and before she knew it, she reached out her hand, as though to touch it.

"Come here," he said in a low voice. Before she could take a hesitant step toward him, he was on her.

He lifted the hem of her dress and slid it up over her body, leaving her wearing nothing more than her delicate bra and scrap of panties, both of which barely covered her body, along with her high heels. She began to bend, as though to remove her shoes, and he stopped her.

"No, leave them on," he demanded, his voice rough. "I like the way you look, halfway naked wearing stilettos." The hot gleam in his intent gaze sent chills over her body.

Her body instantly reacted to both his look and the hot piece of manhood hanging so enticingly between his thick thighs.

Her pussy hollowed, pulsed; and her nipples grew hard, pressing against the flimsy bra.

Suddenly feeling shy, she forced her gaze away and placed her hands over the tops of her breasts in self-preservation.

"Please don't hide from me." The plea was made in a hoarse voice.

He gently moved her hands away from her breasts. With his eyes on hers, he deftly unhooked the front closure of her bra, allowing her full breasts to tumble free.

"Oh yes," he moaned, his nostrils flaring. He leaned down and pulled her extended nipple deep into his hot, hungry mouth.

"Take it," Tessa breathed the words, grasping his shoulders.

She threw her head back and closed her eyes as he suckled her breast, the greedy lapping sounds increasing her urgency to feel him deep inside her. When he finally let go, dragging his mouth slowly away, Tessa's body was on fire.

He lifted her, placed her on the bed, and lay down next to her.

"I want to take my time with you. I plan to savor every moment," he said, the lustful promise darkening his eyes. "Is that okay with you?" One side of his full mouth hitched in a sexy smile, and all Tessa could manage was a weak nod of her head.

"But first we have to get rid of these," he said, one big hand brushing over the silk of her panties. "Lift your hips," he said in a deep, *let me do you* voice. Cream eased from her vagina.

She shook her head, marveling that a simple demand could turn her on so much. She lay back against the pillows and lifted her hips. He hooked his fingers into the band at the top and slowly slipped the panties down, past her hips.

He took his time with her. Just as he promised.

Keeping his eyes trained on hers, he drew the panties away from her body, and every inch of the way he stopped and kissed her, starting at her mound.

He blew a hot breath across the trimmed hair covering her mons.

Her body arched sharply away from the bed when his tongue

darted out and swiped a lascivious caress between the slick folds of her vagina. She felt the silky short hair of his beard caress her inner thigh as he slid the panties down farther.

When he reached her knees, he lifted them so that her feet were planted on the bed. Pushing the panties past them, he turned his head and licked the underside of each knee with a slick swirl of his tongue. Tessa's eyes fluttered shut as she squeezed her thighs together.

"So sensitive there. You always were," he murmured against her thigh and she felt his smile.

Her eyes flew open and met his. Her lips curved into a purely feminine smile.

No other man had ever done to her what he could do.

No other man had ever taken the time to find out what *did* it for her.

And never had she'd ever been interested enough in his replacements to school them.

He continued stripping her panties down her body until he reached her feet. Lifting them, he pulled the panties from her body. Totally.

"I've always loved your toes," he said, and she watched as he lifted one and brought it close to his face. "So pretty. Delicate," he said. With a slight grin on his face he said, "Sweet. Just like the rest of you," and proceeded to swipe the underside of her big toe with the flat of his tongue.

"God, Gideon," she laughed shakily. Damn, the man even turned her on doing that. Then all thought flew from her head as he pulled her toe into his mouth and sucked. Hard.

One hand traveled swiftly up her thighs until he reached the juncture of her upper legs. He slipped his middle finger past her moistened lips and pressed into her deeply.

While he suckled her toe, his finger pressed in and out of her creaming pussy, playing havoc with her self-control. She bit her lip and placed her hands on either side of her body.

"Yes," she said, breathlessly, her body undulating against his talented fingers and tongue. Her body caught instant fire and incredibly, she felt an orgasm begin to unfurl.

He released his hold on her foot and she gritted her teeth when he pulled his finger out, protesting, whimpering.

"Sssh," he said, climbing on top of her and kissing her mouth.

"I want—I need—"she said, her speech halting.

"I know what you need baby," he said with a dark smile. He leaned over the side of the bed and quickly withdrew a gold-foiled package from his jacket and turned to face her.

Despite the arousal and need to feel him deep inside her, she gave him a quizzical look.

He smiled an endearing smile, and placed two fingers over his chest. "Be prepared—scout's motto."

Tessa bit back a need to laugh as he swiftly sheathed his erection. She watched in fascination as he began to roll the condom on. She stilled him. "Can I?" she asked, wanting to feel his cock in her hand.

"Next time, baby . . . now I need to get at that pretty pussy," he said. She gave a breathless laugh when he pressed her back against the pillows.

With his big body covering hers, he placed his hands on either side of her legs, to spread her wide, the knob of his dick pressing against her slick, wanting core.

"I can't wait, I'm sorry, Tessa," he said, his face set, too aroused to stop.

When she felt him begin to push inside her, her eyes fluttered closed, and she felt a fine sheen of sweat begin to trickle down her face.

"No . . . it's okay, I—" she cut off with a harsh cry when he began to press more of his turgid cock inside her tight channel. "Oh God, Gideon, I forgot how big you get," she gasped, her eyes flying open to gaze at him, frantically pushing her hands against his shoulders, trying to stop him from giving her any more of himself.

"I know, baby, I know," he panted. His jaw tightened, and he startled her when he barked out a rusty-sounding laugh. "But, you saying things like that isn't going to help." He moved his hips, embedding even more of himself inside her. Her eyes widened more when she felt him grow even bigger inside her.

"I'll go slow. I promise," he said, cupping each side of her face, the look in his eyes intense, yet filled with an emotion Tessa didn't want to even try to identify. "Just hold on to me, okay? I'll take care of you, baby. I always have. I always will," he promised and leaned down to kiss her.

His words, his consideration, the feel of him sheathed in her, was what she needed. She nodded her head, giving him permission to continue.

She screamed in a mixture of pain and pleasure when he grasped her hips and shoved into her, deep, so deep, her body sank heavily into the mattress and her head tapped against her headboard.

He captured her cry and began to stroke into her. His thrusts were slow, careful, yet she still felt as though he was filling every crevice within her body. He pushed his tongue deep inside her mouth, demanding entrance while he continued to shaft her in hot glides.

He broke the kiss and pulled his upper body away to gaze down at her.

"God, I missed this." He leaned down and captured a breast, opening his mouth wide to put as much of the heavy orb deep into his mouth as he could, licking and scraping his teeth over her areola, pulling on her nipple deeply. Tessa felt a gush of her own liquid heat escape past his cock and trickle down her leg, the cream easing the constriction so that the pain of his penetration eased.

She felt his smile against her breast as he increased his depth and speed of stroke, going into her with faster thrusts.

"Ummm, Gideon . . . oh God." Tessa panted the words, nearly overwhelmed with his loving.

Keeping his mouth on her breasts, alternating from one to the other, he lifted her legs by the knees, forcing them wider apart. His thrusts became more forceful, so hot and hard they jostled her entire body, forcing the top of her head to tap in an increasing *thump, thump, thump* rhythm against the padded headboard. The friction of his hard body against hers, his thick cock shafting inside her and the way he had her body responding, was unlike anything she'd felt in a long time.

At least seven years, she thought, her breath catching when he shifted her body and rocked into her at a different angle.

He was in so deep she felt she was breathing him.

"Oh, yes, yes, yes," she cried, her head tossing back and forth, her body completely yielding to his wild loving, catching each hot, sweet thrust and giving back as good as she got.

She grasped the back of his head with both hands to pull him closer. Pulling out the band holding his hair in place, she tunneled her fingers through his silky strands, her hold on him tight.

Twisting her body, she moved with him, their moves in sychrony as they strained and thrust against each other, each striving not only to gain the ultimate pleasure, but to give as well.

Perfect.

As she felt her orgasm sweep through her, tears burned the back of Tessa's eyes.

He threw back his head, the corded muscles in his neck in stark relief as he grunted, his body jerking as he came inside her. He clenched each side of her hips, pinning her in place as he thrust two final times before they exploded in unison.

His body slumped down on top of hers for long seconds.

Tessa reached out a shaky hand to run her fingers through his hair, moist with sweat from their lovemaking.

He turned his head and kissed her hand, then moved away from her, settling her in front of his body, then reaching out for her.

"Tessa, I've been thinking."

Tessa stretched her body, feeling satiated and happy. Happier than she had in a long time.

"About?" She smiled when he feathered his fingers over the back of her hands, and laid a sweet kiss on the side of her neck.

"About you."

He tugged her around, so that she lay flat on her back, with him lying on his side, his body close to hers. "Your life. What you've been doing."

Tessa laughed humorlessly. "Besides getting shot at?"

He laughed softly. "Yeah, besides that."

"Do you really want to know, or are you asking because Daddy paid you to?" The minute she said it, she wished she could take back her words. The soft afterglow, the kind that was only achieved after fantastic lovemaking, evaporated and she felt his body tense against hers.

"I'm not here because of your daddy, Tessa," he said, tersely.

After long moments, Tessa spoke. "I'm sorry. Guess I'm still a little on edge."

When he didn't speak she pulled her lower lip into her mouth, worrying it back and forth with her teeth as she stared up into his fathomless eyes.

"Didn't I just take care of that?"

"Guess so."

One long finger traced the outline of her nose, down to her lips, softly outlining their fullness. Tessa's eyes fluttered shut against the sweet caress. She felt his body relax and smiled, gently.

"We-ell," she began, dragging the word out. "I helped start Planet Now, a few years ago," she said.

"I didn't know you were one of the founders," he said.

"I started with Baker and Chase," she said, mentioning one of the major law firms in the area. "Worked as an intern there, my last year of law school. Daddy got me an internship with them."

"Aw," he said, his tone careful, noncommittal.

"Yeah. Good old Dad. Nothing less than the best."

"He wants the best for you, that's all," he murmured.

"I got halfway there. After graduating they offered me a junior position with the firm." A half-smile tugged at her lips. "That lasted all of a year."

"What happened?"

She sighed. "Nothing, really. They were good to me, got me plum accounts, considering I was so wet behind the ears. But . . ." She stopped and blew out a tired breath.

"It wasn't for you?"

"No. Working as a corporate lawyer wasn't what I had in mind when I graduated from law school."

"No, that wouldn't be what I'd see you doing."

"Working to help big businesses make even more money was *definitely* not what did it for me. All I was doing was helping the rich get richer, and well . . . like I said, it wasn't what I envisioned."

"Was corporate law your specialty?"

She scrunched her nose. "Yes. And I loved working in the area, but like I said . . ."

"It wasn't what you envisioned." He finished for her and they both laughed softly, together.

"Daddy was furious when I quit. At first, before I quit, I began taking on pro bono work, exactly what I wanted. I was helping those who couldn't afford to help themselves."

When she stopped, he filled in, "And you found what you'd been looking for?"

"Yes. Something like that," she agreed. "I needed something

to fulfill me," she replied simply, a wealth of meaning in the simple words.

Although he couldn't know how losing the baby had affected her, catapulted her into growth as only that type of grief could do, she felt as though he and only he understood.

She felt him kiss the back of her head before he pulled her securely into his arms.

She felt her eyes close as she lay wrapped in Gideon's arms, content. She knew she needed to tell him about the baby, what happened, how she lost it and how her world changed. She knew he had a right to know all of that.

But, for the first time in a long time, just as she had when he made love to her, she felt complete. She didn't want to talk about the pain of losing their baby. She didn't really want to talk about the pain of their past.

For this one night, she just wanted to be a woman satisfied and laying in Gideon's arms.

The arms of the man she loved. The man she'd always love.

9

"Don't make a sound and you won't get hurt."

Tessa's eyes flew open when a low, deep voice spoke low in her ear. She opened her mouth to scream.

Her heart slammed against her chest when a large, callused palm slid over her mouth, effectively silencing her.

When he lay on top of her, his hard body blanketing hers, shoving her into the mattress, fear kicked in and she knew she had a finite amount of time to escape. If not . . .

She bucked against him, kicking with the back of her legs, trying to make connection with any part of his body she could reach, but he was too strong, his hard body too unyielding. For all of her thrashing around, she hadn't made the least impression on him. He hadn't even had to move. Simply pinning her beneath him was all it had took to make her struggles not mean a damn thing.

Breathing in desperate gasps of air, she stopped. She swallowed frustrated, angry tears and mentally reevaluated her situation.

"If I let you up, do you promise to be a good girl?" He

snarled the question, his even breaths against her temple sending shivers down her spine.

Anger surged over her as she realized she hadn't impressed him, despite the intensity of her one-sided struggle. She chewed the inside of her cheek and nodded her head.

Despite the nearly debilitating fear that threatened to overwhelm her, Tessa gritted her teeth in a surge of anger. "Good girl." She'd show his ass what a good girl she could be the minute he rose, she decided.

She nodded her head docilely, promising silently to be a *good girl.*

He slowly rose from covering her back, and released his hold on her a little.

His fault.

No sooner had he raised enough to allow her to breathe than she reared back and head-butted him.

With a muffled curse, he fell away from her.

Wanting to give him no time to recover, she swiftly rolled over to the side and jumped off the bed. She turned to glance over her shoulder just as she was inches away from the door.

Her fault.

In less time than it took for her to blink, he was on her.

Neither one of them wasted time speaking. No word did he say as he grabbed her by the waist and pulled her down. He secured her hands behind her back and moved down her body, securing her legs by the ankle with the same soft but unyielding bonds.

"What the hell is this? You don't know who you're messing with, assho—" Tessa began, sheer bravado forcing the words out despite the fear that engulfed her when he slapped duct tape over her mouth, effectively ending the torrent of cusses she was ready to let fly.

Once she was securely bound, he flipped her so that she lay on her stomach, her cheek on a pillow.

"Whatever you want, I don't have—"

"You have *exactly* what I want," the deep voice said, and moments later, Tessa felt big, hard hands run roughly down her sides, over her back, before lifting the hem of her short, silky nightgown. She felt the cool air from the air conditioner fan her bared buttocks.

"Now, be a good girl, and everything will be okay," he promised.

Her heart banged against her chest, and real fear set in this time. God, he planned to rape her! The thought energized her. No way in hell was she going to allow some asshole to rape her, not here, not now, not ever. At the same time she wondered where Gideon was while she struggled against the binding restraints.

When she felt his big, hard hands snatch the gown away from her body, and a slick tongue caress down the line of her back, she stopped fighting.

The minute his tongue licked her, the minute she felt the hard—familiar—hands slide over her naked skin, she realized who her *kidnapper* was.

She wasn't in danger. Her unknown assailant hadn't climbed in a window.

So he wanted to play games, did he.

"You won't get away with this, you asshole," she said, a freaky grin of anticipation splitting her lips.

"Oh no? And who's gonna stop me?" He breathed the words against her spine. Her body reacted and a shiver of delicious anticipation tickled her flesh.

It was *on.*

Renewing her struggles in earnest, she swiftly rotated her body, bent her arm and shoved back, elbowing him. She heard the satisfying thud of elbow connecting with hard, muscled abs, and she grinned wider.

She relished the moment too long.

With a wolfish laugh, he captured both of her hips, pulling her tight against him with big hands. She felt the corded length of his cock pressing against her ass and inhaled a deep breath.

She arched her body, struggling to raise her upper body, swiveled her head, trying to look at him.

Wordlessly, he turned her back around, forcing her to lay her upper body back down, her face pressed into the pillow with her ass in the air. She waited with bated breath as she felt the fat end of his shaft rub insidiously against the puckered hole of her anus.

"No . . ." she breathed the words into the pillow. In the dark room, bound as she was, she felt helpless yet aroused at the same time.

"You have no say in this," he murmured darkly and ran a warm, heavy hand over the globe of one of her buttocks. She felt his tongue lick the same path, trailing over her ass, lifting her higher, so that her behind stuck high in the air. His hands separated the globes, spreading both her ass and lips of her vagina wide.

Her heart struck a wild chord, beating out of control as she waited. God, she'd never done it this way. Fear mingled with lustful curiosity had her crazy hot; out of control.

When she felt the slick press of his tongue lick her perineum, the sensitive line of soft skin that separated her anus from her pussy, she moaned loudly. He slowly, slowly licked her pussy. She squirmed around his tongue, needing him to go faster, lick harder, but he continued his careful laps.

"Gideon . . ." she whispered his name, her body on fire from his careful ministrations.

He inserted one finger deep inside her while keeping his licks nice and slow, concentrating on the tip of her clitoris. He pressed his tongue in short stabs on the hot little nub as his finger rotated inside of her.

When he removed his finger and moved his mouth away

from her, her eyes flew open. He pulled her smack against his hips, and she waited as he rubbed his fingers over the rosette of her anus, and gently pressed a finger just barely inside.

She squirmed around the pressure, straining, and her body on fire. He leaned down and covered her back with his chest, angling his body so his finger remained deep inside her ass.

"Sssh, it'll be okay. I'll make sure it's good for you," he promised sensually. "As long as you promise to be a good girl. Okay?" He lifted the lobe of her ear into his mouth and bit down, scraping the lower end of her lobe between his teeth, before slowly releasing her.

She nodded her head, her breath escaping in short, shallow puffs of air.

He leaned away and slipped the tip of his finger out of her bottom, before plunging his cock deep inside her vagina.

She shut her eyes in a mixture of relief and surprising disappointment.

The disappointment didn't last long. He pressed deeply into her moist core, and began to ride her. In tight, controlled thrusts he slammed into her body, his shaft slipping in and out of her in strong, sure glides.

Her breathing increased and she swallowed. The sweat that dripped down her forehead trailed a slow path down her face and landed in the corner of her mouth. Her tongue swept out and licked the moisture away.

With her head bowed down low she accepted his harsh, demanding, driving cock. He reached a hand around and grabbed on to one of her breasts, cupping the hefty weight in his hand, thumbing a caress over her engorged nipple.

She cried out when his fingers slipped away from her breast to run down the line of her stomach, before burying between her moist folds. He gently tugged on her clit, twisting the thickened bud while his thrusts grew in strength. The harsher his thrusts, the harder she pushed back against him, her ass slapping against his groin in a steady rhythm, her body lunging forward with each heart-pounding stroke, until her orgasm unfurled.

Thumbing her clit, he angled his dick to the side of her, slightly rearranging her body so that he was digging into her from the side, tapping against her soft, spongy, hot inner spot.

"Oh, God . . . oh, God . . . yes, yes . . ." she began to chant, panting, her body beginning to quake.

He covered her back with his chest and bit down gently on her shoulder, keeping her in place when she began to undulate wildly beneath him.

"So good. This pussy is so damn good," he whispered the guttural words against her neck. "Are you ready to come, baby?"

She could only nod her head, logical thought and actual verbal communication completely beyond her at that point.

He laughed low, placed the heel of his hand above her pelvis, and pressed hard while stroking into her.

Tessa shut her eyes and screamed as she came, her entire body on fire, burning as the orgasm consumed her and her body slumped forward on the bed, with Gideon following her, still pumping inside.

She heard his shout of release and the hot feel of his cum splash against her womb seconds before she shut her eyes, a blissful smile of content on her mouth.

10

Tessa opened drowsy eyes to see Gideon peering down at her.
He stroked a hand down her face. "You know, that could
have gone a lot different, Tessa," he said softly, concern reflected in his eyes. "It could have been a lot rougher."

"Oh yeah?" She quirked a brow and smirked. Then promptly
winced when she stretched her body. "I don't think I could
have handled rougher, Gideon, although it does sound . . . intriguing," she replied with a saucy grin.

"No, baby, I'm serious. Those men after you aren't playing.
They're big boys, playing in a big boys' world. I don't want
you to get hurt."

Tessa sighed and pulled away from him. She sat up and
looked down at him. He stared somberly.

Rising from the bed, she ignored the aches in various parts
of her body, due to his rather . . . extreme . . . lovemaking, and
stood. Lifting her gown, she turned to him and simply lifted a
brow, dangling the garment in front of her, showing him the
shreds of what was left of one of her favorite gowns.

"You owe me," she mumbled. She walked over to the corner

of the room, picked up her silk robe, and wrapped it around her body.

"Glad you're taking me seriously," he said.

She turned to him. "Look, I know it's serious, this situation with KhemCom. I've got it under control."

He rose, crossing the room in seconds, his expression set, fierce. She was filled with fear for a moment, so angry and set were his features. He bore down on her and touched her shoulder, reminding her of her injury.

"Listen, the whole reason I got involved with this was to help out a single mother and her child. To help them see justice, that's all. Believe it or not, I don't actually like being threatened," she said and walked back over to where he sat on the side of the bed.

"You sure have a funny way of showing it."

She laughed without humor. "Actually, Planet Now is backing away from the project. For now," she added, when she saw the relief cross his face. "They *bought* Lauren's silence," she said and then filled him in on what had happened, what Lauren Woodridge had told her when she finally spoke with the woman. "So, for now, they're off the hook." Her anger was still there, despite the fact that there was some resolution.

"Can you really blame her?" Gideon asked.

When she didn't speak, he turned her to face him. "Hey, baby, you did your best. You've brought awareness to what they're doing. Maybe it'll be enough to get them to—"

"No! It won't be enough!" She spun around to face him, anger tightening her expression. "Don't you get it? Companies like this, big businesses like this, won't stop. They will do the bare minimum, in order to save money. They don't give a damn about what they're doing to the environment, to our children. If we let them, they'll run this world into the damn ground all in the name of money!" she said angrily. "That kind of thinking is why they keep getting away with bullshit like that!"

Gideon rose and walked toward her, turning her around to face him.

"I'm not discounting that. I'm not the enemy, Tessa. I just don't want you getting hurt, that's all I'm saying. Your welfare is the only thing that is important to me. Don't you know that by now? Damn, what do I have to do to convince you?" he asked, anger tightening his features as they faced off.

"I need to go to my apartment. I'll be back, later," he bit out, and turned sharply on his heel, leaving her gaping at him as he angrily slammed the door behind him.

11

"We need to talk."

Gideon spoke quietly, so that only Senator Waters could hear him. His approach had been silent and the man hadn't heard him.

His dark eyes frantic, the senator's head swiveled around, glancing over the small crowd before he turned back to Gideon.

"What are you doing here? Please don't tell me you brought LaTessa with you," Senator Waters hissed.

"No. Tessa is at home."

"At home?" Waters, despite the obvious anxiety he felt, raised a brow in question at Gideon's wording. When Gideon offered no further explanation, the senator went on. "Good, that is something I *definitely* don't need right now. Her coming here would completely ruin everything."

Gideon gave a nonreply in the form of a grunt.

"Follow me, we can go into another room to talk. Privately," Gideon said. The senator sputtered as Gideon gruffly took hold of his arm and all but dragged the man behind him.

After he'd stormed out of Tessa's apartment like some adolescent pissed off at the world, he'd gone to his apartment and cooled down.

He'd made a few calls, one in particular to an old army buddy who'd shared information he'd managed to dig up about Senator Waters. Information about whose pocket the senator was into, deeply. Something he'd already figured out.

What his buddy told him next had been new, that one of Waters's assistants had been responsible for the attempt on Tessa's life.

He'd then returned to Tessa's and quietly laid down behind her, turned her over on her back and mounted her. He'd caressed and loved her until they both were satiated.

After she'd fallen asleep he'd gotten up and dressed. She woke as he was leaving and he'd told her he'd return soon, telling her that he had work to finish. When she'd smiled and told him he could work at her place, he'd reluctantly lied, and made up the excuse that he needed to make a few calls to his managers.

She hadn't questioned him, and that alone made him feel guilty as hell, although he knew that the reason he'd lied had been to protect her.

"Why don't you meet me in my office? It's on the second floor, third door to your right. Make yourself at home, there's a full bar, fully stocked. I'll be up, shortly," the senator said, bringing his attention to the present.

"No. You come with me now, or I let everyone here know one of *your* staff tried to have your daughter killed, you son of a bitch!" Gideon said, grabbing hold of the Senator's arm.

The senator's dark face blanched. His skin looked ashy and old. He turned to the woman speaking to him and offered her a weak smile before allowing Gideon to "escort" him away.

12

Gideon walked quietly into the bedroom and stared down at the woman lying so peacefully on her side. He smiled down at her.

One of her hands lay outside the sheets, palm up, the gesture one of trust.

His jaw clenched. He hated to be the one to make her feel as though she couldn't trust him.

He'd allowed her father to come between them before, with his lies, manipulation, and half-truths.

He was damned if he'd allow him to continue to do that.

With a weary sigh he sat on the edge of the bed. He reached over and ran a thumb down the line of her soft cheek.

She smiled, eyes still closed, and leaned into his caress.

"I'm sorry, baby, I didn't mean to wake you," he said when her eyes fluttered open.

"It's okay," she replied sleepily. "What are you doing up . . . and dressed?" she asked, stifling a yawn by placing her hand over her mouth. "Sorry. I haven't had much sleep, I guess," she joked, the dimples in her cheeks flashing.

"Come back and join me?" she asked, reaching her hand out to run over his arm.

"Later. Now, I think we need to talk." He noted the flicker of wariness in her dark brown eyes. He felt as though he'd said that particular phrase more times than he could count over the last few hours, but he knew they were long overdue.

"This sounds ominous," she said, raising her body, the sheet falling down just below her breasts. He took pleasure in the fact that she didn't seem to notice, her attention solely on him.

"It is. It's about your father. I went to see him tonight."

"Tonight? When?" she asked, her glance running to her night table and the small clock radio. "God, I didn't know it was so late. I thought you had to go grab some things from your apartment."

"Your father had a private fund-raiser tonight," he said, without preamble.

"What do you mean, private? He always tells me about his fund-raisers. Usually demands that I'm there. Why not this time?"

Gideon was torn. The entire drive back to her apartment, he'd hadn't been sure how much he would tell Tessa about her father. He knew the two of them had always had a tumultuous relationship at best, yet, how in hell was he supposed to tell her how far her father was willing to go to ensure his position in the Senate? And that one of his own staff had been behind the attempt on her life? He ran a hand through his hair in frustration.

"What aren't you telling me?" Tessa sat up straighter in the bed. "Gideon, what is it?" Her voice, once low, deep from sleep, sharpened.

"Your father is involved with KhemCom. He's in their pocket, deep, baby," he said gently and stopped at the look of disbelief in her eyes. "They were the major contributor to his last campaign . . . and he's got a deal under the table with them for some new resort in Hawaii."

"No. I don't believe you!" she cried, and turned away, moving to get out of the bed.

Before she could move, he pulled her back around to face him. "Damn it, why would I lie to you? Don't you know that you're the only one I care about?" Her face was set in angry lines as she stared at him.

He pulled her into his arms. "If something were to happen to you, because of KhemCom, or your father . . ."

She pulled away from him, a question in her eyes. "What do you mean my father? He brought you here to protect me."

He schooled his features, careful that she didn't see the volatile anger he felt. No matter what, Tessa loved her father.

As he stared at her angry face, with his heart heavy, he told her what he had found out.

He left out how he'd nearly slammed the Senator's face into a wall after he confronted him with what he knew. It had only been because the Senator was Tessa's father that Gideon hadn't killed the son-of-a-bitch, blaming him for her brush with death. Instead, he'd allowed him to live, after he threatened to expose to all his beloved *constituents* what a greedy, self-absorbed, money-hungry asshole he really was.

"His assistant had the notes sent to the demonstrators, to you . . . to Lauren and her daughter. One of his men was behind it all, baby," he finished.

She'd quietly listened, her body still as death. Her face gradually lost its color.

When he finished she finally spoke.

"Get out. I never want to see you again. Get. Out."

Her face was devoid of all emotion; she looked at him as though he wasn't there.

"Baby . . ."

"Get out." She got up and left the bedroom, quietly shutting the bathroom door behind her. Although he didn't tell her that her father was the one behind her attack, the sick look on her face told him she'd figured it out herself.

"Fuck!" The expletive burst from his mouth as he slammed out of her apartment.

After Gideon stormed out, Tessa crumpled in the middle of the floor, covered her head with her arms, and cried.

She allowed the cleansing tears to freely flow, finally releasing the heartbreaking ache that had held her mind and spirit captive for so long, grieving for the history she and Gideon shared, and for the spark of life she carried for that short span of time. And finally, her tears of release were for what Gideon had told her about her father, things she didn't want to hear or believe. Yet she knew they were true.

13

Gideon stared at the enticing jiggle of Tessa's rounded buttocks as she vigorously attacked the walls of the shower. She
was scrubbing them as though her life depended on it.

"You can't get rid of me that easily," he said, leaning against
the door frame.

With a start, she turned to face him, rag in hand, her eyes
widening. He ran his gaze over her nude body, his shaft already
growing thick, hard, just from looking at her.

His cock stirred even more when her tongue came out and
swiped across the seam of her lips as she stared at him. Realizing she was nude, she hastily grabbed the towel placed over the
hook near the wall and wrapped it around her body, shielding
herself from his avid gaze. After knotting the ends, she faced
him again.

"You came back." A fine blush ran beneath her pretty brown
skin.

Although it had only been two weeks since he'd seen her
last, it felt as though it had been a lifetime.

His hungry gaze settled on the fine tremor he caught in her

lower lip. It was then he noticed her eyes were puffy, the whites stained red.

"Did you think I wouldn't?" he asked. He walked over to her and raised his thumb to her face and gently caressed her swollen lids, before he dropped his hand.

The question hung between them, unanswered.

"I didn't know." Her breasts strained against the towel as she drew in a deep breath.

She turned away and moved as though to shut off the streaming water from the showerhead. His hand stalled her.

"I left because you needed time alone."

With his hand covering hers, their touch set off a spark that seemed to sear his skin. Mark him.

He turned her around to face him fully. Unable to stand the look of question, uncertainty shining brightly in her dark eyes, Gideon drew his shirt over his hand, and swiftly divested himself of his clothing. He then brought her body close.

He leaned down and brushed her lips with his. His tongue danced with hers in a playful yet hot tango of dueling tongues and open-mouthed kisses.

"I suppose this means that you forgive me for kicking you out," she murmured against his lips once he released her mouth.

"Yeah, you could say that," he whispered back. "And this time I'm not letting you go," he finished.

She offered a tremulous smile and leaned on tiptoe to place her mouth over his.

With a groan, Gideon placed his hands beneath her buttocks and lifted her, wrapping her legs around his waist.

With his lips locked with hers, he turned with her, opened the door of the shower, and stepped inside. He was thankful the shower was large, easily accommodating his large frame.

With maneuvering room.

When he flipped her around and Tessa felt the cool, wet porcelain shower wall against her back, she moaned within his kiss.

Her body began to strum with pleasure. His big hands dug into the globes of her buttocks, massaging the orbs together while grinding his shaft against her mound. His kisses grew more heated, wet and sweet, just the way she liked them. The feel of his hard body pressing hers into the shower wall, his hands roaming her backside, and his raunchy kisses set her body on fire.

"I'm sorry, baby, I can't wait," he said.

He had her wide and spread, with the tip of his thick shaft pressing insistently at the lips of her vagina.

"Are you ready for me?" he asked, his voice coming out in harsh breaths that fanned her temple. When her cream trickled down her thigh, mingling with the pelting shower, she laughed breathlessly and nodded her head.

"Hold on, this won't be an easy ride," he promised. His dark promise excited Tessa and she opened her thighs even more to give him better access.

"Yes," she moaned when he began feeding her his dick in slick, hot, painfully slow increments.

She wrapped her arms around his wide shoulders and held on. She released mewling cries as he pressed himself inside until he was seated to the hilt. She felt like weeping, it felt so good to feel him housed deep inside her. Right where he belonged.

He slowly began to flex inside her, his strokes strong, deep. Deeper than she'd ever felt him.

He reached around and hoisted her higher so that her face was nearly level with his. As he stroked into her, he leaned down and captured her lips with his.

As his strokes picked up in speed, his kisses became wilder, his tongue plunging in and out of her mouth in direct orchestration with his shaft plunging in and out of her welcoming core. He kept a firm grip beneath her thighs as he steadily rocked into her.

"Oh, God, yes, yes . . ." she chanted over and over when he broke the kiss. He trailed kisses down the line of her throat, placing scattered caresses along her neck and collarbone, before laving the hollow of her throat with the flat of his tongue.

"I missed you," he said in a barely audible voice.

Tessa heard his voice break. She pushed the slick, wet strands of his hair away from his face so that she could see him.

"I missed you too, Gideon. I'm so sorry—for everything. I—"

He covered her mouth with his, silencing her apology. "Later. We have time for that later . . . now I need to feel you."

With that, there were no more words exchanged.

Gideon pressed into her in short, staccato plunges. The depth and strength of his strokes soon had Tessa tightly gripping his back, her short nails sinking deep into his flesh.

She wrapped her shaking legs tighter around his hips and held on as he rocked into her. She pressed hot kisses against his wet chest, laving his small nipples with her tongue, smiling as he groaned when she captured his nipple deep inside her mouth and pulled, hard.

She felt sharp tingles wash over her, her head fell to the side, and she cried out as her orgasm raced over her.

Yet he continued to thrust.

He stroked inside her clenching heat several more times, until, with a shout, he slammed his mouth over hers, ground into her, and delivered one final stroke that slammed them both into climax.

Tessa's head swam and her legs trembled as she released. Long moments passed before her heartbeat slowed.

Gideon placed a soft kiss on her mouth and slowly withdrew from her.

"Ummm," Tessa groaned, as he dragged his turgid cock past the swollen lips of her quivering vagina and completely withdrew from her body.

Once completely out of her, he turned her around so that the stinging sprays from the shower sluiced over her heated flesh, cooling her down.

He reached over and lifted the small towel from the rod and liberally applied her shower gel before turning to her.

He opened the towel and began to ease it over her back, working the soapy length over her entire backside.

She closed her eyes. "That feels good," she said, closing her eyes.

She heard him utter a small, deep laugh, and continued to rub the towel over her in deep, massaging circles.

"After you left, I spoke with my father," Tessa said.

There was a slight pause before he continued to wash her. "And?"

She sighed. "And . . . you were right. About all of it."

All he did was grunt, saying nothing. Tessa swallowed. "I'm sorry," she said, simply.

For long minutes he simply continued to wash her, and Tessa leaned her body into his embrace and closed her eyes. Although they had a lot to talk about, she hadn't felt this relaxed, this . . . at peace . . . in a long time.

After he washed her body, she turned to him. "Let me," she said, and looked into his eyes as she took the cloth. With a groan he allowed her to return the favor. She lathered the towel and began to run it through the silky hairs covering his chest.

She ran the towel down the midline of his body, stopping when she reached his groin. Gently she cupped his heavy sac, running the towel over the twin plump spheres. When he groaned, she smiled and looked up at him. His eyes were closed, the water spiking his inky black lashes that lay against the upper curve of his sculpted cheek bones.

She returned her attention to cleaning him, enjoying it as much as he was.

She wrapped the warm, wet towel around his dick. Her hold on him was firm, yet gentle, as she ran the towel over the long length of his penis in slow movements.

"Baby . . . you're killing me," Gideon groaned, his eyes still closed.

Tessa laughed. "If you think that's killing you, just wait . . ." she said and got on her knees.

She lifted his cock in her hand and licked the tiny eyelet in the center before sliding his dick deep into her throat.

"Baby . . ." She looked up and saw Gideon's eyes spring open as he placed shaking hands on either side of her face.

With his shaft in her mouth she smiled at him and grasped each side of his muscled butt cheeks. She slid her tongue underneath, along the thick vein that ran from the top of his balls to the knob of his cock, then hollowed her tongue to deep-throat him.

Within seconds his shaft grew, filling her mouth until she could no longer swallow his entire length easily. When the bulbous end bumped the back of her throat, Tessa opened her jaws, relaxing her throat muscles so that she could work more of him inside.

She moved one hand from his ass and used it to hold the base of his cock, while sliding her mouth up and down the length, licking his pretty, caramel-colored dick like it was her favorite lollipop, while the other hand eased from his hip to fondle his balls.

"Tessa, baby . . . I can't hold out much longer." He bit the words out in a gruff voice while he held her face and pumped into her mouth.

She felt his balls swell, becoming heavy with his cum, and knew he was seconds from coming. He moved as though to remove her from his mouth, but Tessa wasn't having it.

She held on, suckling and pulling on his cock, nursing him, until she felt him begin to twitch inside her mouth.

"Oh God, I'm coming!" he yelled, and thrust into her two times before releasing his hot seed deep into her mouth. Tessa held on to his hips as she milked him of every bit of his cum, relentless in her desire to drain him.

When she swallowed the last of his hot cum, she leaned back, allowing the water to wash over them both. With quivering arms, Gideon bent down and lifted her from her kneeling position and turned off the water.

"I can walk, you know . . . if you're not able to, uh, carry me," she laughed softly as he lifted her high in his arms and left the bathroom on shaky legs.

"The day I can't carry my woman out of the bathroom after marathon sex is the day I hang up my player's hat," he replied and plopped her in the middle of the bed. She bounced two times before his big body covered hers.

"Player? You know, Gideon, if you have to call yourself that, you really aren't one," Tessa smirked.

Her teasing, snickering laugh turned into gasping moans when he slanted his mouth over hers and sweetly assaulted her mouth, effectively swallowing her laughter.

When he reluctantly ended the kiss, he moved so that he lay beside her. He fingered the damp hair framing her forehead that had escaped the messy topknot on her head, a look of concern reflected in his dark gray eyes.

"You know, we didn't use protection, Tessa," he said.

For a minute, Tessa was confused, until she realized that while making love in the shower, he hadn't donned a condom. At the time, safe sex had been the farthest thing on her mind.

The thought of them producing a baby made her heart catch.

She bit her bottom lip, worriedly, searching his expression for how he felt about the possibility. Truth be told, even if they'd been more prepared for their lovemaking, she found that she didn't mind the thought that his unprotected seed had found a home.

But she didn't know how he felt.

"I'm pretty sure I'm safe. I just ended my period a few days ago," she replied, softly.

Her hands settled over her stomach, in an unconscious gesture. In fact, the thought of their lovemaking resulting in a baby filled her with a strange happiness.

In that moment she knew that without a doubt she loved Gideon. She also knew she needed to tell him about the baby.

He cupped her face. "I'm kind of sorry to hear that," he replied in answer to her telling him the timing wasn't right, and Tessa felt tears sting the back of her eyes.

God, she loved him.

When he pulled her close and captured her lips, she allowed the tears to fall.

He eased away from her.

Thumbing away the tears, his brows drew in a frown. "Hey, what's this?"

Instead of answering, she pulled his head back down to kiss him.

When the kiss finally ended he pulled her tight. "I can't help but think of all the time we had wasted. Time my father stole from us . . ." She stopped, tears clogging her throat, her anger and resentment resurfacing.

"He sat there and had the nerve to tell me it was all true. All of it. How when he found out I was pregnant, he knew he had to get rid of you. How when I lost the baby, he was glad . . ." She stopped, her throat clogging with unshed tears.

Gideon's hold on her tightened, the increase in his heartbeat told her he was as affected as she, yet he continued to stroke a hand over the back of her head in a soothing gesture.

She pulled back and looked up at him, tears washing her

reddened eyes. "I'm sorry I never told you about the baby. I didn't know how. I didn't want that to be the reason you said no to my father's offer. And then when I didn't hear from you. When I lost the baby . . ." she broke off and closed her eyes.

He pulled her back to him, running caressing hands over her back.

"Your father told me about the baby, Tessa, after you'd lost it. It was when I came back that last time. Had I known you were pregnant I wouldn't have ever left. No way in hell would I have left you," he said, and she heard the hoarseness of emotion in his voice.

"I came back and saw you. Your father made sure of that," he said and stopped.

"I'm sorry. I know. I didn't think you wanted me. I had just lost the baby a few weeks earlier. When Michael came by, it all came out. All the emotion. I was completely wrung out. He . . . he . . . consoled me," she finished, simply.

She felt his hold tighten for a fraction. She exhaled. "It never happened again. I told him you were the only one I loved."

They were silent for a long time, each lost in the pain of the past.

"I let my father control me for so many years. So many years I listened to his lies, half-truths. I'm so sorry, Gideon," she whispered.

"Baby, it wasn't just you. I'm to blame as well. I was older than you. I'd seen the world, been to places that should have hardened me more than they did. I shouldn't have left in the first place. Should have realized that all of a sudden he wasn't going to welcome me with open arms. Treat me like his son. I was a fool," he said, the anger deepening his voice. "But that's over."

Tessa lay her head on his chest and nodded her head. "I'm not going to allow him to control me anymore, Gideon. I'm done trying to please him. The only one I'm interested in pleasing is myself . . . and you," she said, boldly putting it out there.

She knew she should be afraid. Afraid that what she felt wasn't the same as what he felt for her. The longing, ache, and love she'd felt for him for seven years hadn't gone away. Instead it had grown.

"That is . . . if you want that as well," she stopped.

"Do you really have to ask that?" he asked, tracing a path down her face. He pulled her close and slanted his lips over hers, kissing her passionately. When the kiss ended she laid her head on his chest and listened to the steady, reassuring rhythm of his strong heart.

"So, what's going to happen to my dad?" she asked.

She felt his body tense. "He's decided to take a long hiatus from politics. He's also decided to move out of the country, indefinitely. He felt he was long overdue for a vacation."

Tessa knew her father's "decision" to move had strongly been motivated by Gideon. She toyed with the dark, silky hair covering his chest, biting her lower lip.

"Hmmm?" he murmured, and tilted her chin up so he could see her.

"What?" she asked.

"What are you thinking? You're playing with your lip."

Tessa laughed lightly. He knew her well. "About my father . . ."

He wrapped his arms around her waist, pulling her fully on top of his body. "What about him?"

"It hurts. You know?"

"I know, baby, I know. For what it's worth, I don't believe your father wanted you harmed. The ones he worked with were overzealous. For all his faults, he loves you."

He captured her face between his palms. "No one is ever going to hurt you again. And that means me, too. I love you, Tessa. And I hope you let me show you how much. I want a life with you. Do you want that?" No pretty words, just a simple declaration. His face was open, no mask to hide his feelings, no guard up.

"Yes . . ." She breathed the word, her heart filling with joy.

He lifted her body, angling her over his hard erection.

"I want to make a home with you. I want to go to sleep with you by my side, our bodies wrapped around each other." Her breath caught as he pressed into her, fully.

"I want to wake up with you in the morning, making love." He spread her so that her legs fell on either side of his lean hips.

"I want to make another baby with you." He allowed her to set the pace.

"I want to live the rest of my life with you."

Tessa's eyes fluttered closed as they made love.

As she rode him, an image flashed in her mind of the two of them on a beach somewhere. Laughing, a small child with wild black curls and dark brown eyes held one of her hands along with Gideon's as she swung between them.

GREAT BOOKS, GREAT SAVINGS!

When You Visit Our Website:
www.kensingtonbooks.com
You Can Save Money Off The Retail Price Of Any Book You Purchase!

- **All Your Favorite Kensington Authors**
- **New Releases & Timeless Classics**
- **Overnight Shipping Available**
- **eBooks Available For Many Titles**
- **All Major Credit Cards Accepted**

Visit Us Today To Start Saving!
www.kensingtonbooks.com

All Orders Are Subject To Availability.
Shipping and Handling Charges Apply.
Offers and Prices Subject To Change Without Notice